DEFENDED BY DEMONS

EVA CHASE

THE HEART OF A MONSTER

BOOK 3

CHAPTER ONE

Quinn

If you'd told me a month ago that I'd soon find myself on a road trip through Norway with a powerful demon as my only companion, I'd have suggested you needed your head checked. But here I was, sitting next to said demon while he drove our rental car through a landscape of mossy-looking hills and sparkling lakes. We hadn't passed any human habitation in half an hour.

I frowned at the journal I had open on my lap, full of loopy handwriting that'd faded with age. "We don't know for sure that the mention of *Alta* means the town up here. It could have been someone's name or who knows what else."

The sorcerer of decades past who'd recorded some of his thoughts on the worn pages hadn't been all that specific. He'd just mentioned "associates from the vicinity of Alta" and a few pages later commented on how the "established families" like those associates were more reliable than greener practitioners. But it was the only reference to anything that *could* have had to do with Norway that I'd found so far.

Rollick—who might have been a powerful demon but at the moment looked like technicolor made flesh with his human guise's movie-star good looks—made a derisive sound. "It fits with everything else we know: what the sorcerers said to you about the enclave up here, the little tidbits I've been able to dig up from that starting point. There are certainly a lot of places in this area where a clan of sorcerers with their little training center could hide themselves away."

He swept his hand over his fawn-brown hair, his dark blue gaze skimming over the beautiful but remote landscape. He did have a point. With all the hills and the more distant mountains rising from the earth, we could rarely see more than half a mile away in any direction, often less than that. And sorcerers with strong enough magic to be able to provoke the same talent in people who'd never had it before probably had major shadowkind at their command. Those supernatural beings could possess all sorts of talents for avoiding discovery.

Even though it was coming up on the evening, bright sunlight still washed over the terrain. The sorcerers I'd talked to briefly—before they'd been slaughtered by the particularly monstrous shadowkind beings we were hoping to stop—had mentioned the extremes of daylight in this part of the world as being a key feature of the enclave. During the winter months, there'd be little sunlight at all, which I guessed made for more opportunities to catch and enslave shadowkind.

I hoped the enclave was still active during the summer. The sorcerers had to do *something* the rest of the year, right? Otherwise we'd have come all the way out here—and done everything else we'd had to in order to get here—for nothing.

A sudden gloom swept over me. I stared at the vibrant greens and blues beyond the window and thought of how much Lance would have loved leaping and tumbling across those slopes with his acrobatic grace. In his dragon form with his jewel-toned scales, he'd have fit in with the scenery perfectly.

Had Crag ever gotten to fly over this gorgeous terrain and admire it from above, soaring on his gargoyle wings? Would Torrent have enjoyed taking a dip in those lakes, or would he and his tentacles have been more at home in the ocean we'd left behind after following a stretch of highway along the coast?

It'd only been yesterday when I'd last seen the three shadowkind men I'd fallen hard for. I'd gone longer without their presence just in the past week. But this time... this time it might be permanent.

A pang shot through my chest alongside a wobble of energy in my heart. I pressed my hand to my sternum instinctively. I'd used the magic *I* held, the sorcerer powers I'd gained thanks to my childhood heart transplant, to send my three lovers away. In a way, I'd briefly enslaved them. I'd forced them to act against their will.

I didn't know how long my control over them would last before the energies faded with distance and time, but even when they did fade—if they did, which I couldn't know for sure—there was no guarantee that the men I'd fallen for would want anything to do with me again. I'd betrayed them in the most horrible way any human could.

I shouldn't *want* them to come back to me. I'd sent them away specifically because of how much it was hurting them trying to fight my battles for me. But my entire abdomen ached with the sense of loss. A fresh burn of tears formed behind my eyes.

I'd felt so many things with them that I hadn't known I could feel, discovered new confidence, realized how much I was capable of. But I didn't know how to protect them other than by forcing them out of my life. They'd protected me so much in the past month. I'd owed them the same in return, even if they wouldn't see it that way.

Rollick's gaze flicked toward me as he took a particularly tight turn around a jutting stand of dark gray rocks. "Don't be regretting your choices, reluctant sorcerer. We've got to stay focused on the problems ahead of us rather than behind."

"I know," I said tightly.

He flashed his shiny white teeth, which I knew were veneers hiding the savagely sharp tips underneath. "Maybe I should be insulted that you couldn't be bothered to protect me too. You did them a favor, keeping them out of this mess, but apparently I'm fair game."

I couldn't help rolling my eyes at him despite the pain tangled up inside me. "*You* haven't given me a whole lot of reason to care about your well-being." Until a couple of days ago, Rollick had been essentially holding me captive, forcing me to develop my sorcerer talents despite the reluctance he'd noted. "Anyway, this is your battle too. You wanted to take this sorcerer-devouring duo on. Torrent, Crag, and Lance only got involved for my sake."

"I can't argue with any of that," Rollick said in his typically smooth, charming way, not that I was particularly in the mood to be charmed.

I stifled a sigh and sank lower in my seat. "How much farther is it to the village you think is an ideal jumping off point?" He'd identified a community smaller than the town of Alta that he'd decided was our best choice for a base of operations while we searched for the enclave.

"About ten more minutes." He kept the same mildly teasing lilt. "Are you that tired of my company already?"

"You're a wonderful conversational partner," I said with an edge of sarcasm. "I'm tired, period." We'd taken a flight from Salt Lake City to Oslo with a brief stopover in Amsterdam, leaving and arriving in the middle of the day as if night didn't exist thanks to the time zone jump, and then immediately hopped on a local flight up to Alta. At this point, I wasn't sure how long it'd been since I last properly slept, only that it'd definitely been too long. It was only the periodic spurts of adrenaline I got when I remembered our mission that kept me going.

The thought of that mission—and the full reasons behind it—brought my gaze back to the landscape. It might still be sunny out, but the tall, craggy hills were dappled with patches of shadow. Stands of trees cast broader swaths of darkness at their bases. I scanned the murk, my nerves jangling at a flicker of movement that turned out to be a branch bobbing in a gust of wind.

"Can you sense many shadowkind around?" I asked. I

wasn't sure how well the demon could pick up on their presence from inside the car while he was at least partly focused on keeping us on the road.

Rollick was perceptive enough to pick up on the worry underlying my question. "Just a few stray beings here and there, about what I'd expect in a place without much human presence. I don't see any sign at all that our enemies have marauded this far. Your heart is safe for the moment."

My mouth formed a tight grimace. Our main enemies were two very ancient shadowkind who were possibly even more powerful than Rollick—and who'd been killing sorcerers and eating their vital organs to take on some of the magic that would allow them to control their own kind in a way the monstrous beings usually couldn't. We didn't know what they were planning on using that power for now that they had it, but they'd also been very interested in getting their hands on me.

It'd appeared that the villainous duo was mostly active on the other side of the ocean right now, though. We were here in Norway to see if the sorcerers in the enclave—if we could find it; if it even existed—could teach me something that would allow me to get a greater handle on my own powers faster. Rollick thought it was possible that I might be the best chance of stopping these fiends now that they could brainwash their fellow shadowkind, since an actual sorcerer's powers would beat the bits and pieces of talent they'd absorbed from their violent meals.

Maybe I could also figure out how and why sorcery worked at all, and that would give us other ideas for bringing the fiends down.

I couldn't see the men I loved again until I'd eliminated

the threat. That was the condition I'd put in my command to them. As long as it held.

Nestled at the base of a low hill up ahead, a cluster of buildings came into view, most of them houses. A few darker buildings were interspersed between the white-washed walls, the roofs deep blue or red, all of them with a quaintly picturesque vibe that made me feel like I didn't belong here at all.

Rollick drove straight to one of the two-story houses on the outskirts of the village, which had a hand-painted sign proclaiming it the Daffodil Inn. It didn't look like it was big enough to host more than a handful of guests, but then, how many tourists came out this way anyway?

As it turned out, it was really more of a bed and breakfast. The grandmotherly owner bustled out to meet us, eagerly taking my backpack and fussing warmly about what a long trip we must have made. It was obvious from my first step inside that she lived on the first floor. She led us up a narrow staircase, opened one of only two doors at the top, and ushered us into a decent-sized bedroom. It held a queen-sized bed in a simple Scandinavian-style beech frame, a matching dresser and chair, and a door through which I could make out a shower stall.

Only one bed.

"Make yourself at home and let me know if you'd like anything to eat before you turn in for the night," our host said with a pat of my arm, and vanished, closing the door behind her.

I folded my arms over my chest and eyed Rollick. "You only got us one room. With one bed."

The demon spread his hands, his lips curving into a

slight smirk. "This town doesn't offer a whole lot of travel accommodations. I didn't figure it'd matter. It's not as if I *need* to sleep."

"I do," I muttered.

He tsked his tongue at me, still looking amused by my hesitation. "I won't even be here while you're doing that. You're very boring when you're asleep, you realize. I'll be off scouting around seeing if I can't determine exactly where this enclave is hidden away." He paused, and a sly gleam lit in his eyes. "Of course, we could share it if you'd really like to."

I made a face at him. "The only people I'd want to share it with can't be here."

I was trying to make a sharp retort, but my voice got rough with the last few words. I yanked my gaze away from him, not wanting to see him being amused by my sense of loss, but Rollick didn't push his provocative teasing any further than the little nudge he'd tested me with.

Maybe he realized just how much I wasn't in the mood for him to flex his seductive charms.

"What a shame that is. I'm sure you'd all have enjoyed that bed very much." He clapped his hands together. "Do you need anything to eat? Was the snack you picked up in Alta enough?"

He'd always been conscientious of my health, even when he was being a jerk about other things—I'd give him that. I rubbed my hand over my mouth, considering. I couldn't summon any interest at all in shoving more food into my knotted stomach. In an hour or so, it'd be time to take my second set of pills for the day to convince my body that my new heart belonged to me, and other than that, I didn't think I *needed* anything to survive until morning.

"I'm fine," I said. "I just need that sleep. Go do your scouting or whatever." I waved vaguely toward the door.

Rollick shot me another grin. "Pleasant dreams, my sweet sorcerer," he said, but he vanished into the shadows a moment later.

I sank down on the bed and nestled my head in the downy pillow without bothering to change my clothes. I barely wanted to move. And I couldn't fully change, not when the silver-and-iron beaded vest I wore under my shirt was the only thing ensuring that no other shadowkind, including our enemies, figured out where I'd gone.

Closing my eyes, I hugged myself. The squeeze of my own arms was a pale echo of the embrace any of my men would have offered.

How had my life ended up being so different from where I'd expected I'd be—where I'd wanted to be—just a month ago?

And what fresh hell was I going to find myself stumbling into next?

CHAPTER TWO

Torrent

It was always disorienting, being back in the shadow realm after a long time away. No color met my gaze, only a seemingly endless darkness, shifting between full blackness and dark grays with random currents. Nothing quite had a physical form—there was nothing exactly to touch or hold on to, although brushing too close to another being traveling through this space sent a prickle through my shadowy body. Only faint scents lingered in the wafting air, cool and almost mineral as if I were back in the cliffside cave I'd recently spent the night in.

How long had it been since I'd returned to what was technically my natural home? Years, definitely. Possibly more than a decade. Nearly all of my work for Rollick had required me to stay mortal side, and I had no interest in dropping in for a visit during my free time. Drifting through this dreary space and testing the quivers of energy that rippled through it was nowhere near as satisfying as a swim in the cool, vibrant depths of the ocean.

I'd have taken a swamp over this place.

As I prowled onward, I couldn't help thinking that as much as most mortal beings feared us when they met us, we shadowkind had to be meant for their realm. Why else were there so many rifts to give us access to the benefits of their vibrant world with all the variety of sensations it had to offer—portals only we could slip through, that the mortals had no awareness of at all? Why else did we all shift so easily into physical forms when we had the chance to?

We were born of this place, born out of the endless shifting gloom, but I couldn't believe it was all we were meant for. Whatever inexplicable powers called us into existence, they intended us to belong to the realm beyond the rifts as much as this one.

I just wished I'd understood how fully I could devote myself to that other world before I'd found myself forced back into this one. Maybe I could have convinced her— maybe I could have made her see...

I shook those thoughts aside and hurried onward, scuttling octopus-like with my now-ephemeral tentacles stroking through the darkness.

The others had to be around here somewhere. We'd all rushed toward the same rift, driven by the magic-laced command I could still feel humming through my body. But I hadn't been able to say or do anything other than give in to that command, and both of my companions could move faster than me through the shadows of the mortal world. I'd lost my sense of them before I'd even hurtled through the rift.

A faint tremor rippled through the miasma that gave me a vaguely familiar impression. Was that Lance's odd, erratic attitude rippling off of him? I propelled myself faster in the direction it seemed to have come from—and nearly collided with a hulking being nearly as big as I was and far sturdier.

I jerked to the side, and the other creature loomed, studying me with a menacing attention that weighed on me.

"Humph," she said in a voice that reverberated into me alongside the energies swirling through the shadows. "Cripple. Stay out of my way."

If I hadn't been so set on my goal, I might have felt more than the brief flash of shame that hit me before I shook it away. Why should I give a fuck what this monstrous stranger thought of me anyway? My limbs worked well enough to accomplish the most important things.

"My apologies," I said with just the slightest edge to my tone, and rushed on.

I passed a cluster of smaller beings scampering about in some kind of game of chase and a few higher shadowkind who were occupied with low rumbles of conversation. Then a hiss I recognized vibrated into my ears.

I dashed toward it, spotting a sinuous churning movement in the darkness up ahead in a shape that reminded me of the dragon shifter's physical form.

He was whipping between a couple of other shadowkind whose animosity was already thrumming off them. Then his energetic voice reached my ears, sounding more frenzied than buoyant at the moment.

"Don't you want to play a game? You think you're pretty tough, but can you dodge my claws? I won't go too hard on you."

"Get out of my way, nuisance," one of the shadowkind he was hassling growled, "or I'll—"

I sensed Lance moving to pounce and dove in with all the speed I could propel into my body. My tentacles swung out and lashed around the dragon shifter's body, shadowy essence colliding with shadowy essence. Where we touched, I could grip him well enough to yank him back toward me —just as he could have scratched up the beings he was antagonizing if I hadn't caught him.

Just as they could have pulverized him in retaliation.

We couldn't die here in the shadow realm. The atmosphere of the place sustained our life energy in a way the mortal world couldn't quite. But we could be battered to within an inch of death. Lance could have found himself pummeled to the point that he wouldn't have moved for months.

Of course, maybe that's what he'd been aiming for. He spun on me with another hiss and a swipe of a dragonish paw before he registered who I was. Then he froze, the guilt I'd sensed from him ever since our enemies had possessed his mind and forced him to fight us radiating off of him.

"I'll take care of him," I told the other beings, and dragged him farther away through the gloom.

"Torrent," Lance said in a mournful tone. "She sent us away. She put that magic into us and made us *go*." He squirmed out of my grasp with a violent twist, though still careful not to actually strike me with much force, and leapt wildly through the currents of shadow. "We can't go back. The sorcery has its claws in my head. I can't scratch it out. She wouldn't—I never thought she would—"

A sharp twinge ran through me, even more poignant than when I'd first found him picking fights and stirring up whatever trouble he could before I'd brought him on board under Rollick's authority. Then, Lance had been distraught and unstable after his imprisonment by mortals he'd hated. Now one he'd cared about deeply had stolen his free will using the same sort of power. I couldn't even imagine what was going on in his head right now.

"Hey," I said, not trying to restrain him again but tucking one tentacle around him to try to settle down his restless prowling. "It was only one command. She didn't fully enslave us. It'll wear off. We just have to give it time."

"How much time? It feels—it feels different than when this happened before. Both of them, with the other sorcerers and with the beasts who ate them. The magic is holding on so hard, like she knew how to squeeze every part of me into the shape she wanted..."

He thrashed to the side again, and I let him work out the wild energy he couldn't seem to contain.

I hated to admit it, but I knew what he meant. I'd never had sorcery worked on me before, but Quinn's command was still echoing through me as if it'd penetrated every particle of my existence.

She knew us. She understood us. That was why I'd fallen for her in so many ways... and I suspected it was also why she'd bent our wills so easily.

"It *has* to wear off," I said, as much for my own

reassurance as his. "Even shadowkind that are fully enslaved shake off the effects if the sorcerer leaves them to their own devices for too much time."

Lance made a strangled growl low in his throat. "And then what? She doesn't want us. She made us leave. She thinks I can't protect her enough, that I don't deserve to be with her."

I swallowed thickly. "I don't believe that's what she was thinking at all. She wanted to protect *us*. Because of how much we matter to her."

It was still difficult for me to wrap my head around that last part. Remembering the way she'd gazed at me as she'd told me she loved me brought a bittersweet ache into my chest that was laced with disbelief.

I'd known she'd cared about us a lot, that she felt a connection to us just as we did to her. Humans sometimes threw around those words far too lightly. But I'd been able to tell how much she meant them. How hard it'd been for her, knowing she was going to lose us, even if it was her own decision.

And she mustn't have fully understood how much *we* cared about her either. Otherwise I couldn't imagine she'd have banished us like this. I didn't care if the villains we were up against chopped off every limb on my body—I'd still rather be at her side, savoring every moment I could have with her.

This separation, the uncertainty about what danger she might be facing even now, hurt more than the mangling of my hand under Lance's fangs.

"We aren't the ones who need protecting," the dragon shifter was muttering, whipping his tail through the air with obvious agitation. "She's the soft one. The mortal one. Our Quinn." His next growl sounded mournful. "If those fiends get their maws on her..."

"She still has Rollick with her," I reminded him. "He might have wanted to use her, but he's been trying to use her *against* them. He's not going to hand her over to the enemy." I didn't trust our former employer all that much, but the demon stood a better chance of keeping Quinn away from harm than any other shadowkind I could think of other than the three of us.

Although we were only two right now.

I dragged in a breath and tugged at Lance with my tentacle again. He let out a huff, but he'd stopped thrashing around quite so much. The energy resonating off him had settled to a faintly frantic hum rather than a total cacophony of distress.

"We need to find Crag," I said. "He'll want to fix this as much as we do. Then we'll come up with a plan for how we can defeat those two brutes without being near Quinn, until we can get back to her. And for showing her that she doesn't need to worry about keeping us safe."

"Yes," Lance muttered. "The gargoyle. Where did the stony one go? He flies so fast."

"We'll find him," I said firmly. "We'll find him, and we'll set the rest of this situation right."

Or I didn't deserve the three words Quinn had offered me so emphatically.

CHAPTER THREE

Quinn

The road had just curved around the bank of a crystalline pond when Rollick said, "Stop the car there—right before that hill."

I coasted to a stop and jerked up the parking brake before glancing around. The hills loomed taller and pressed tighter together in this part of the Norwegian wilderness, another hour's drive down country lanes from the little village where we'd spent the past two days. Or, at least, I'd spent those two days there. Rollick had been gone for most of that time, sneaking around figuring out where the sorcerer enclave might be.

And he claimed to have succeeded. I lifted my chin toward the road ahead where it snaked around the nearest hill, shrouded in a pale mist. "It's over there?"

Rollick gave a casual shrug as if the answer wasn't all

that important to him, but the unusual intensity in his expression betrayed his actual investment. "If it's not there, then I don't think it's in this country at all. That mist is being generated by a shadowkind creature who has no reason to do it or to produce so much of it here other than because it's under command. I've identified several other beings lurking around in a loose ring with a circumference of about three miles. They're clearly guarding something, not roaming around the way a free creature might. I assume the enclave is located approximately at the center of that circle."

I sucked my lower lip under my teeth, my chest tightening as I absorbed his certainty. I knew what the next step was—and that it required me to go in alone.

I'd confronted a small community of sorcerers on my own back in the US, but I'd still had a couple of my shadowkind companions watching over me. And it'd been a much smaller and less formal community than what I had to assume this enclave consisted of. If sorcerers were genuinely *created* here... I couldn't imagine what I was going to find beyond that mist.

"I assume you didn't let any of the lurking shadowkind notice you were poking around," I said.

"I'm glad you have at least that much faith in my abilities," Rollick said dryly, but his smile was a bit tight. I doubted the demon was worried about my well-being beyond whether I'd still be able to help him with his plans, though.

I peered at the mist. "Do you have any idea what I'm going to be dealing with as far as terrain from here on?"

He shook his head. "I couldn't get a clear view, which is

obviously the intention. Just drive slowly and try to continue straight as much as you can. If you see any lanes smaller than this one, I'd give them a shot. Especially if you start to get the feeling that you definitely *shouldn't* go down them."

One of the shadowkind we'd dealt with before had cast some kind of supernatural vibe over a mountainside that'd discouraged intruders. "What if I can't get in at all?" I asked. Rollick had dispersed that repulsing energy last time, but he couldn't do the same here if he couldn't get close enough to find out it existed.

"Then we'll figure something else out," Rollick said breezily. "But they must allow *some* strangers to enter, or they'd have no one to train. Maybe your preexisting sorcerer powers will guarantee you admission. We'll just have to see."

"Right." I swallowed thickly. I didn't trust the demon beside me any farther than I could shove him, but a nervous wobble ran through my gut at the thought of continuing on without him. "You have to get out of the car now, I guess?"

He inclined his head and then fished around in his pocket before pulling out a simple gold pendant shaped like a dove in flight, dangling from a thin chain. I blinked at him as he held it out to me.

"It'd be a whole lot better for both of us if you get whatever information you can out of them and then leave without there being any trouble," he said. "Or if you can get yourself away from the enclave on your own even if there *is* trouble. But if the situation goes sideways and you're sure you're stuck, the pendant has a GPS signaler in it. Pull out the wing on your right, twist it ninety degrees, and fold it backwards. You shouldn't be able to activate it by accident, but it's a quick process if you need to do it."

I wrapped my fingers around the metal bird, simply holding it for a moment before moving to attach the chain around my neck. "And if I do activate it?"

"I'll get to you as quickly as I can." Rollick offered me a brighter grin. "I'm not letting you go in there completely defenseless, my sweet mortal. Not that I doubt your ability to hold your own if things don't get completely out of hand."

"Thanks," I muttered, but having the pendant nestled against my collarbone actually did reassure me a little.

"I realize it may take a while for you to fully infiltrate this 'enclave,'" the demon went on. "I'm not going to panic if you're busy with them for a few days. But if you can come up with an excuse to drive back into town and give me an update, I'll make a point of stopping by the bakery where we had breakfast this morning for an hour around noon every day."

I nodded. "What will you be doing the rest of the time?"

He made a flippant gesture with his hand. "A little of this and a little of that. Our enemies appear to have spent most of their time on this side of the Atlantic until recently. I intend to do some digging into their history while you investigate your fellow mortals. There's a rift not too far from here—I can use that to pop before this area and various other parts of the continent via the shadow realm."

"Sounds like a plan." I dragged in a breath and squared my shoulders, flexing my fingers against the steering wheel.

"Well, you'd better get going. It's about time to find out where all this sorcery stuff comes from."

To my surprise, Rollick appeared to hesitate for a moment, as if he hadn't expected me to dismiss him so quickly. As if he was as reluctant to leave me to my own devices as I was to be left. Then he flashed another smile and vanished into the shadows as if he'd never been beside me at all.

I gave him a few seconds to be sure he'd left the car and then released the brake. As the car rumbled on down the road and around the hill, the mist closed in around me. In less than a minute, I couldn't make out more than hazy impressions of green and gray farther than ten feet around me.

Keeping my breaths steady, I focused on the road ahead, watching for any changes to it or any oncoming side lanes. The road itself wasn't on any maps—we'd checked. No doubt the vast majority of wanderers who ventured this far off the beaten path would have turned back when faced with such apparently inclement weather conditions. Only those who knew there was something specific to find by coming this way would continue on.

Maybe that was why I didn't encounter any repulsive force. Or maybe Rollick had guessed right that my sorcerer talents would somehow grant me access despite other protections in place. I crept along at five miles an hour for several minutes without encountering any obstacles. Then I spotted a wooden post to my right, appearing out of the mist moments before I passed it.

I slowed even more, and it was a good thing I did, because otherwise I might have missed the lane next to the post completely. The road I was driving on was already dirt, but it was at least relatively clear. The path that veered off to the right had a vague impression of tire marks amid patches of grass and jutting stones. I had to angle the car carefully to make sure the tires didn't bump into any particularly threatening-looking rocks.

It wasn't long after I took the side-road, if it could even really be called a road, when I felt more than saw the terrain slant upward. It swung to the left and then to the right again, giving me the sense that I was weaving my way up one of those hillsides. Or this could be a full-out mountain now for all I could tell.

Then, without warning, the mist started to fade. One moment I was cloaked in it; the next I hit the brake, finding myself staring at a broad building looming out of the trees that covered the steep slope ahead of me.

Several rooms seemed to jut from between the trees, walled with smooth dark wood that looked regularly buffed. They gleamed in the now-piercing sunlight. A couple of the rooms had tall windows that stretched across most of the front, shaded by blinds; others had only small rectangular panes or none at all. Decks of the same dark wood wrapped around and even under the rooms on multiple levels, scattered with wooden lounge chairs and in one spot a long table.

Staring at the structure with my architecture-fanatic's perspective, I had the sense that there was a lot more to the construction than what was immediately visible, hidden by the trees or even delving right into the mountainside.

It wasn't the kind of building I'd imagined designing myself—I wanted to create something soaring and awe-provoking—but the way this place seemed to be fused with the natural landscape around it set off a flicker of admiration in me alongside my apprehension. Whoever *had* designed it had put a lot of thought into their creation.

The building materials and style appeared quite modern, but as I got out of the car, I noticed signs that this spot had been in use for many decades if not centuries. A path of square stone tiles led to the deck on the lowest floor, where only flat walls met my gaze other than a gap between two windowless rooms that was shrouded in shadow. The edges of the stone squares had become rounded with age, their centers dipping after being worn down by innumerable feet. And there was a large shed off to the side built out of logs rather than smooth boards, deeply weathered with patches of moss on its angled roof.

This far north and at this altitude, a chill wrapped around me even though the mist didn't creep after me. The breeze brought a pungent pine scent with it. While I had obvious evidence of civilization in front of me, the flavor of the place was distinctly feral.

A shiver passed over my skin, and I tucked my hands into the sleeves of my thin windbreaker, wishing I'd brought a warmer hoodie to wear under it. Avoiding a chill hadn't occurred to me when we'd left the August heat of the southwestern US.

I slung my backpack over my shoulders and headed up the path from where I'd parked, but before I'd made it more than a few steps, a man who looked around the same age as my dad emerged from the shadowy area on the deck.

He had slate-gray hair still flecked with some hints of auburn and an arched Roman nose that dominated his face.

His close-set eyes peered at me down that nose. I stopped in my tracks.

He said something in words I didn't know but that were presumably Norwegian, given where we were.

"I'm sorry, I only speak English," I said quickly.

He let out a soft huff and repeated himself, not exactly aggressive but definitely firm, with only a light accent. "Who are you, and what do you want here?"

"My—my name's Quinn," I said. When discussing our strategy, Rollick and I had decided that it was better for me to go with my real name so there was less chance that I'd slip up and reveal my deception in however long I had to stay among these people to learn their secrets. "Is this—I heard there was an enclave of sorcerers in this area. I came out here hoping to find you."

The man's lips pursed, but his shoulders relaxed at the same time. I got the immediate sense that I'd been recognized as one of his kind.

"You're looking to kindle the power in yourself?" he said.

A spark of excitement darted through my chest. Could they really do that, then? In that case, they had to know more about how this strange magic worked than any of the other sorcerers I'd talked to had.

"Not exactly," I admitted, clutching the straps of my backpack. "I have a little already. But I didn't have family to train me—they passed on before I was old enough to learn. I didn't even know I *had* any power until I started getting these strange feelings... Another sorcerer family directed me here saying that the people in the enclave might be able to teach me how to get control of and expand my skills."

I wasn't lying. I'd never really wanted to use the magic that turned shadowkind into slaves, but it didn't appear I had much choice. If I was going to use my sorcerer abilities to stop the fiends who'd been hunting me down for their malicious purposes, I'd need to be able to do a lot more than order around one little beast at a time, which was all I'd managed so far.

I simply wasn't going to mention that I had other goals I was hoping to achieve by coming here.

The man seemed to study me for a long moment—long enough that my skin started to itch. He raised his hand to his own face, motioning to his cheek. "You've been hurt."

My fingers twitched toward the fading bruise I knew lingered on my own cheek, where Crag had accidentally struck me with his rocky hand. There hadn't seemed to be any point in trying to conceal it when that deception would be easily uncovered too.

"A creature I wasn't strong enough to control," I said, which was kind of true.

The man hesitated again and then swiveled on his heel with a motion for me to follow him. "Come. Let's see where you're at."

I hurried after him, my sneakers thudding across the boards of the deck. As I approached the shadowy area, I spotted a set of double-doors set farther back from the protruding rooms we were walking between. A pine tree appeared to be growing right over the top of the doorway, its roots providing an extra frame.

As the man reached the doors, two more figures stirred —other members of the enclave who'd hung back while they'd observed me. They wore cloak-like jackets that fell to their knees with hoods that shadowed their faces. They flanked me as if to ensure I wouldn't run for it, as if they thought I might feel the need to make a hasty retreat. Uneasiness crept over my skin.

The man pushed one of the doors open, and I felt weirdly relieved to see bright light on the other side rather than some dank dungeon. These people lived here—even if they were isolated sorcerers, I shouldn't expect them to be skulking around in their own home like comic-book villains.

Ignoring my jittering nerves, I followed the man inside. This was what I'd come here for, after all.

I found myself in a long hallway with pale gray walls and light fixtures beaming at regular intervals down its length. Several doors were set along it—the man led me into the closest one on the left. The cloaked figures trailed after us inside.

We'd entered a small room with no windows and little furnishings—only a round, maroon rug that covered about half of the floor and a few metal boxes set along the far wall. As the door clicked shut behind me, I realized the boxes seemed familiar. They reminded me of the carrying cases Rollick had used to transport the shadowkind creatures he'd had me practice my powers on.

It seemed these served a similar purpose. The man wasted no time in walking over to one of the boxes and bending down to grasp the latch on the door.

"We'll want to know what we'd be starting with," he said. "Call this creature to you, as quickly as you can."

A sharper wobble radiated through my pulse, sending a tingling sensation all through my veins. I needed them to believe my story—I needed them to think it was worth spending time on helping me. I focused on the door of the box-like cage as the man swung it open.

Stark light flooded the inside, making the patch of shadow within it stand out starkly against the gleaming metal walls. My heart thumped faster. I imagined how the thing must feel, cooped up in that tight space, knowing people who wanted to manipulate it for their own ends were holding it captive. How it must long to be free again.

A twinge of sympathy formed in my gut. But I needed it to come to me. *Now.* Or I could end up just as screwed over.

And so many other shadowkind might suffer more.

The urgency of my resolve made the tingles of supernatural energy condense at the base of my throat. I opened my mouth, and the strange language I didn't understand spilled from my lips with an electric jolt. When I'd ordered my monstrous lovers away, the words had come out in English, but maybe I'd been able to use familiar words only because I'd known my targets so well. Every other time, my intention had translated into these foreign sounds.

At my command, the shadow leapt from the box, taking physical form as it darted toward me. It looked like a rat with spindly legs twice as long as they should be and several antenna-like whiskers poking from the top of its head. It dashed straight to my feet and then stopped there, quivering and looking up at me as if waiting for further instructions.

Someone made a soft sound that at first I took for consternation. When my gaze jerked up, one of the cloaked figures tugged back her hood as she stared at me. Her pointed features were framed by a cloud of salt-and-pepper hair. Her gaze was equally pointed, but her voice came out with a tone that was shocked rather than skeptical.

"What was your family's name?"

She had an accent too, but it sounded different from the man's. How many different countries had the sorcerers in this enclave come from?

"I don't know," I said. "I was adopted when I was really little—I just know that they died." It was kind of accurate —the heart that had brought my new powers with it had technically been adopted by me with its transplantation.

"You've never had any direct training, and you commanded the creature that quickly? How long did these other sorcerers guide you?"

I didn't know what the right answer would be, so I gave what was essentially the truth. "Not much. They offered me a few tips about how to focus and that sort of thing. I only found out about my powers about a month ago."

She blinked, her surprise echoing across her face. Then she schooled her expression into somberness as she swiveled toward the man who'd brought me in. She jerked her head toward the door.

"Wait here," she said to me, and all three of the enclave members stepped out of the room.

The shadowkind creature was still standing tensed on the floor in front of me. Taking pity on it, I let a little more of the wavery energy inside me bubble up from within and ordered it back to its box. At least it wouldn't have to worry that I was going to make it do something worse right now.

The sorcerers didn't return for several minutes. What

was taking so long? Were they arguing about whether I should stay at all? Had I handled this scenario wrong?

Finally, the man stepped back inside alone. His mouth was pressed into a flat line as if he wasn't happy about what he was going to tell me. I braced myself for a dismissal.

"You can stay," he said brusquely. "As long as you follow our rules and don't interfere with activities that don't involve you. We'll have some tasks for you, and if you seem dedicated enough, you may be chosen to participate in the rites that could awaken more power in you."

Bingo. I raised my eyebrows. "Rites?"

He frowned at me. "If you're chosen, then you'll hear more. If you're unhappy with the terms, you can leave."

I couldn't shake the feeling that he was hoping I'd take that option. Instead, I forced myself to offer him a sunny smile. "No, not at all, just curious. Thank you so much for giving me this opportunity. I promise I'll do my best."

CHAPTER FOUR

Quinn

Vera looked over the notes I'd written across several pieces of lined paper which I'd set on the table in front of her. She raked a slim hand through her cloud of salt-and-pepper hair and nodded thoughtfully to herself.

"You certainly applied yourself to the task," she murmured.

I'd spent most of the last two days in the large room around us, which had a gloomy vibe that was more what I'd have imagined for an enclave of sorcerers off in the mountains. It was the enclave's library: the walls were lined with built-in shelves packed with books, journals, scrolls, and loose notes gathered into folders. If there was a set system of organization, I hadn't been able to decipher it.

It wasn't totally gloomy though, despite the relatively dim lighting beyond the lamps positioned on each of the several birchwood tables. A large fireplace lined with stones crackled at one end of the room, casting some extra warmth and an appealing whiff of pine smoke into the space. The floor in front of it was clear of furniture, holding only a thick fur rug that I'd sometimes seen a small group of sorcerers hunker down on to hold hushed discussions in front of the hearth.

The enclave did seem to use the library quite a bit, with many of the sorcerers coming and going while I'd been completing the tasks I'd been assigned. I hadn't been able to get a clear read on how many lived in this place, as there hadn't been any mass gatherings during my time here.

Vera, who'd appointed herself my examiner or mentor or whatever exactly she was, had told me everyone operated fairly independently—that I could grab food from the kitchen area when I was hungry without worrying about specific mealtimes and make use of the laundry facilities if I needed them whenever they were free. From the number of different figures I'd seen wandering through the vast network of rooms, I guessed there were a few dozen sorcerers in residence at the moment.

So far, Vera's assignments had felt a lot like schoolwork—in a way that'd given me a pang of homesickness for my architecture courses back home. The two summer classes I was increasingly falling behind on, in particular. But there wasn't anything I could do about that other than throw myself into the work here in the hopes that eventually I'd find something that would let me get my old life back.

Two days ago, right after I'd arrived, Vera had set me

searching through the library's various volumes and documents to compile notes on the most established meditation strategies. When I'd finished that task yesterday, she'd gotten me gathering information on different types of identified shadowkind beings.

I'd actually learned a few things, but nothing I expected to help me conquer a duo of immense monsters with sorcerer powers of their own. Knowing the enclave had divided animal shifters into two distinct categories wasn't exactly earth-shattering information.

One benefit of the haphazard organizational system was that I'd encountered various items I wanted to come back to later. Like a journal written by a sorcerer who'd apparently specialized in enslaving particularly powerful shadowkind. And a book that sounded like it had strategies for dampening magical energies. But there were some questions I hadn't come across any answers to. Maybe now, while Vera was at least somewhat happy with my progress, would be an okay time to ask.

"It's fascinating," I said. "But I still find it hard to figure —how do we end up with the power to control these monsters at all? Why us and not everyone?"

Vera glanced up at me with a momentarily wary expression. "We put in the work—we made the sacrifices. Or those before us did. You don't understand because you had no one to teach you to honor those efforts."

I didn't think that was true, because none of the sorcerers I'd spoken to outside of the enclave, those who'd learned from their families, had seemed to have any clue where their powers had come from either. But arguing wasn't likely to get me very far.

"I want to understand—I'd be willing to make sacrifices too," I said.

She grunted and looked down at my notes again. "If you continue showing your dedication like this, perhaps you'll get there. We don't initiate newcomers without plenty of vetting."

I guessed that made sense, or they wouldn't have been able to keep this place or the powers they taught so secret. But if it was a year-long process, I really didn't have that kind of time.

I tamped down on my impatience, another question that had dogged me for as long as I'd known about my magic rising to the surface. "If there are ways of provoking the powers... are there also ways of removing them? No one could steal my potential from me, could they?"

It seemed wiser to frame it as something I was scared of rather than something I might hope for. Maybe my powers were the key to stopping the menace that might threaten everything I cared about, but they'd also made me a target in the first place. I couldn't help still wondering whether I might be able to get rid of them completely.

But Vera was already shaking her head with a wry smile. "Once it's in you, it's in you. No one can take your rightful inheritance away. Believe me, there've been a few I've thought should be shut down, but—" She shook her head again as if dismissing that thought. "That's why we're so careful about who we accept for the rites."

My heart sank even as I forced a sheepish smile in return. So much for that hope. If even the sorcerers here didn't believe there was a way, what were the chances I could find one elsewhere?

I'd heard about these "rites" multiple times since they'd first agreed to let me stay. I still didn't know anything more about them other than that they could apparently awaken sorcery in a person. But Vera and everyone else I'd overheard mention them had been incredibly tight-lipped on that subject.

Vera shuffled the papers into a neat bundle and handed them back to me. "You should hold on to these—you might want to look them over again to really absorb the information. The better you understand the creatures, the more adept you'll be at controlling them. But I think that's enough for today. You should get some dinner into you."

"I'll do that," I said, and then paused. There was one other subject I needed to broach with her, and I had no idea how she'd react. "Would it be a problem if I left the enclave for a little while tomorrow? I'm learning so much—I feel like I need to take a break so everything can get settled in my head before I stuff more in."

The wariness came back into Vera's eyes. "Where would you go?"

I made a casual wave toward the front of the building. "I figured I'd just take a little drive, maybe go back to the nearest village up the road and grab some lunch with a change of scenery. If that's not a problem. Obviously I wouldn't mention the enclave to anyone there. But if you have rules about everyone needing to stay in the enclave until they're finished their studies, I totally understand." I just had no idea how I was going to communicate with Rollick if that was the case.

To my relief, Vera's stance relaxed. She motioned for me to follow her out of the library. "It shouldn't be an issue.

It's not as if you know significantly more now than you did before you came here. But if you're gone too long, we may not welcome you back, so don't disappear on us."

"Of course not," I said quickly. "I figured it'd just be a few hours."

Would their rules be different once they did let me in on their more guarded secrets? Obviously plenty of sorcerers did leave the enclave, or they wouldn't be living all over the world.

There was still way too much I didn't know.

As we walked down the hall toward the kitchen, we passed two men I'd seen before—an elderly sorcerer with a short, pointed white beard and a young man who I didn't think was much older than me, whose shaggy wheat-blond hair always seemed to be falling into his eyes. This time, the younger man was mumbling to himself, his eyes eerily vacant. His skin looked almost as pale as his hair. As we strode by, his body twitched, though he gave no other sign he'd noticed our presence.

"Who's *that*?" I whispered to Vera. "And what's going on with him? Is he okay?"

Vera's next smile was tighter. "That's one of our two current trainees. He's almost ready for his rites—it takes a lot out of a person. You'll need to be prepared for the same if you want to expand your connection to the shadows."

"Definitely," I said automatically, but I had to force myself not to glance back at the sickly-looking guy. Just what did the sorcerers put their new initiates through?

When I left the enclave building the next morning, I half expected someone to yell out at me to stop. But Vera must have passed on word about my plans, or else the sorcerers here really didn't care all that much about people coming and going. I guessed they had a certain amount of security simply in the fact that if I *had* tried to tell any regular person what was going on here, they'd think I was insane.

The drive back to the village where Rollick and I had spent our first two nights was a little faster than the trip to the enclave because now I knew where I was going. I reached the bakery he'd mentioned around eleven thirty. Not seeing him inside, I popped into the village's one corner store to buy a few snacks out of the unfamiliar options on display and then went back to the bakery to buy a slice of what the owner haltingly translated as "spinach pie" for me to eat for lunch.

I'd just sat down at one of the three small tables at the front of the bakery when Rollick ambled inside with a ding of the bell over the door. He asked the owner for a puffy pastry that was stuffed with a creamy filling and dropped into the chair opposite mine, looking no different from how he had the last time I'd seen him, three days ago.

We couldn't talk all that openly here. He glanced me up and down and seemed to make a similar assessment of my state as I had with him. "You've survived."

"It's been all right," I said. "But I haven't found out much yet. They know a lot, but they're very cagey. I'm keeping my eyes out and doing my best to get into their good graces. We'll see." I took a bite of the cheesy pie and almost groaned at the richness of the flavors. "How's your searching been going?"

The demon shrugged. "I'm chasing down some theories —and becoming increasingly convinced of what I thought I saw at that mountain camp by the lake."

I raised my eyebrows. "And are you ever going to tell *me* what your theories are? You think you know what kind of... things we're dealing with, don't you?"

Rollick gave me one of his sly grins that always turned his movie-star looks twice as striking. "I think you've got enough on your plate without me adding that to the heap." His gaze slid away from me, his expression turning unusually pensive. "If I'm right, there's no way that enclave will have anything useful to tell us about our specific foes. They're one of a kind or close to it."

My stomach twisted, diminishing my enjoyment of the lunch. I swallowed hard. "That would make them pretty hard to beat, wouldn't it?"

"Let me worry about that." Rollick flashed me another smile, and a different sort of twinge ran through my gut.

He was all I really had here—the only ally, the only being remotely on my side. Before, I'd had my three monstrous lovers to count on. Protecting them and taking this on without them meant it was just the demon and me in this mess together against forces I could barely comprehend.

Maybe some of my uneasiness showed on my face, because Rollick's smile softened a little. He tapped my hand, not drawing out the touch long enough that I'd have felt the need to flinch away, playful but with a gentleness I wouldn't have expected.

"Look at how far we've come already, Quinn," he said. "You ferret out those mortal secrets as quickly as you possibly can, and between the two of us, we'll be unstoppable."

He sounded confident enough to settle my nerves a little. I sucked in a breath and brandished my fork again. "One thing's for sure: I'm not giving up."

The demon beamed back at me. "And that's exactly what I like so much about you."

The warmth of his expression came with an underlying flicker of fear. Because I still couldn't say for sure that being "liked" by Rollick put me in any less danger than if he'd hated me.

CHAPTER FIVE

Quinn

Vera appeared to have decided to give me the rest of the day off. When I returned to the enclave in the early afternoon, neither she nor any of the other sorcerers rushed over to give me a new assignment. So I drifted into the library to conduct some studying in line with my personal interests.

I'd set the records I wanted to return to on a specific shelf so that I could find them again in the vast chaos of the library. It didn't look like anyone had disturbed them. Probably no one could tell they'd ever been anywhere else, unless there was some bizarre system of organization to this place that was beyond my comprehension.

I skimmed through the journal accounts of the sorcerer

who'd made it his mission to attempt to enslave the most powerful shadowkind he could encounter, but found that it was full of a lot of self-aggrandizing with no real details about how he'd supposedly accomplished the feats. I kind of wondered if he'd even managed to pull off everything he claimed or if he just liked to pretend he had for an ego boost.

Some notes I'd set aside on tracking shadowkind were a little more useful, although mostly we'd been trying to avoid having our enemies track me rather than trying to track them. But you never knew when we might need to find them to enact a plan. Unfortunately most of the methods reported in the records hadn't worked. Dowsing, radio waves, and various other approaches the industrious sorcerers had experimented with hadn't shown any signs of being effective.

You must rely mainly on your sorcerer senses and the threads of commonality between you and the beasts, their finishing paragraphs instructed. Wonderful. Well, Crag was pretty good at picking up on the presence of other beings in the area and even identifying those he was already familiar with.

The thought passed through my mind in an instant and set off a fresh flare of loss. I closed my eyes for a second as I automatically choked up.

It was better that the gargoyle wasn't involved in anything to do with our powerful foes. That was the whole reason I'd sent him away. I just had to keep remembering that.

The last of my stash was the book on suppressing

magical energies. As I flipped through it, a tingle of excitement rippled over my skin.

This I could really use. It was mainly focused on strategies for dampening or shielding against the effects of shadowkind magic, but they included the basics like using silver and iron to repel their powers, which had also worked to stop the beings from picking up on *my* powers. I was still wearing my custom vest for that exact reason.

Maybe some of the other tactics mentioned in the book would give me new options for deflecting shadowkind attention. It'd sure be nice to be able to take a shower without having to wash around the vest, or to have an alternative method of protection if I needed to go somewhere that required the kind of clothes I couldn't hide the vest under. No one here at the enclave had noticed my unique undergarment so far since I could hide it under baggy sweaters and sweatshirts. The temperature in the building was tolerable but hardly cozy.

I glanced around, confirmed no one else was in the library, and then surreptitiously tucked the small leatherbound volume into my messenger bag, which I'd carried with me for exactly this reason. Now I'd be able to examine the book at my leisure, maybe even show it to Rollick to get his input on the contents. There were so many books haphazardly stuffed into the shelves around me that it seemed unlikely anyone would notice one missing anytime soon.

I browsed through the library again, but I'd already done some pretty thorough circuits during my earlier assignments. Nibbling at my lower lip, I slunk out into the hall. My sneakers rasped faintly over the dark wooden floor.

No one had told me I couldn't go exploring. Vera had simply instructed me to stay out of any rooms that were locked. What else might there be around here that could tell me more than the human inhabitants were willing to?

I wandered through the halls, passing the laundry room and a couple of what looked like meeting rooms, and then another larger room with smudged chalk marks on the floor but no other sign of magical practice. The chill in the air thickened enough that I shivered. I had the impression that I was walking deeper into the hillside the building was constructed into.

Turning a corner, I found myself facing a door that appeared to lead into a wing of the enclave I'd never ventured into before. Another sorcerer was just unlocking it with a twist of a key. I halted, holding perfectly still, as she tugged the door open and slipped past it without noticing me. Then I darted forward as quickly as I could move without making a racket.

I grabbed the door just before it clicked shut. There. It wasn't currently locked. I wasn't breaking any rules.

Ha. I'd still better not get caught, no matter how well I was obeying the letter of the law.

I eased the door open slowly to peek past it. Another long hallway lay beyond. The woman I'd seen entering was just disappearing through a doorway up ahead. I darted into the hallway, afraid someone would come up behind me and notice my transgression, and let the door close behind me.

Where to go from here? I padded carefully over the floor, which I realized was stone here rather than wood.

Another indication that I'd come right into the hillside. The walls were the same smooth, pale gray as the rest of the place, but I couldn't tell whether they were painted stone or the same material as the rest of the building.

It was definitely a feat of architecture. I wished I'd been in the right headspace to enjoy studying that aspect of the place.

I passed a couple of closed doors that I was too nervous to open in case someone was on the other side who'd accuse me of trespassing. Then a faint rattling sound reached my ears.

I followed the noise to a smaller side hallway that ended with a narrow doorway. This door was unlocked. Opening it, I stared into a room so brightly lit I had to blink several times before I could start making sense of its contents.

It was some kind of menagerie. Cages lined the walls, a few larger ones and many small ones stacked on top of each other, almost as haphazardly as the books in the library. Orderliness was obviously not something that went hand in hand with sorcery.

I could guess what I'd see inside the cages before I'd even squinted. Even more lights beamed from the tops of the cages, which were solid metal on all sides except the barred fronts. Those were held shut with latches and locks. Within the lights, blurs of shadows quivered and shuddered.

The enclave had its own shadowkind collection.

That wasn't surprising. Obviously most if not all of the sorcerers here were using their magic, which meant they'd all have at least one being enslaved. But Vera had indicated that most of those creatures were being put to work: guarding the enclave in various ways, hunting for food, luring fellow beings that the sorcerers wanted to trap closer to the building. These were simply being contained.

Maybe they hadn't been "harnessed" yet, if the sorcerers meant to at all. The assortment in front of me felt more like a set of collectables on display.

The thought made my stomach turn. I had no idea what creatures were trapped in these cages, but they were obviously miserable surrounded by all that toxic metal and pinned under the searing lights. Who knew if any of them had ever harmed another being? They might have been roaming around not much different from mortal animals before they'd been snatched up and shut away in here.

I walked closer to one of the larger cages. As I took in the details, my teeth set even more on edge.

The contraption, which came up to my shoulders in height, was obviously designed not just to hold the shadowy being inside it but also to hurt that creature if the sorcerers decided it was necessary. Maybe even to kill it.

Sharp blades that must have been silver, iron, or both poked from the walls on mechanisms that looked ready to propel them toward the creature hovering in the center of the space. A few crystals dangled from the top of the cage, the light beaming through them. Would they also move on command to concentrate the light even more painfully on the captive shadowkind?

My fingers itched to try to open the door and free it, even though I knew I couldn't break the padlock. I raised my hand, about to set it against the bars as if I could indicate to the prisoner that I sympathized with its plight, when the door squeaked open behind me.

I jerked back, my heart stuttering. God only knew what the sorcerers of the enclave would think if any of them saw me showing any kindness or concern to the beings they considered nothing but monsters.

I found myself staring at the pale, shaggy-haired guy I'd passed in the hall yesterday—the one Vera had told me was studying for his rites. He peered at me, looking briefly puzzled. "You're the new arrival, aren't you?" he asked with a mild British accent. "What are you doing in here?"

"I, um—" I groped for an easy explanation. If he was coming into this room, presumably the place was related to the rites in some way. "Just trying to get prepared," I finished with enough vagueness that it'd be hard for him to challenge me.

My answer must have made some kind of sense to him, because he hummed to himself. His gaze slid away from me as if he hadn't really wanted to be paying me all that much attention anyway.

He meandered farther into the room, focusing on the smaller cages along the back wall. "Have you picked one?" he asked.

Picked one? For what?

"Not yet," I hedged. "I figure it's a big decision. Better to take my time."

He nodded. "True. I've given it a lot of thought." He stroked the bars of one cage almost lovingly, with an avid gleam in his eyes that set my skin crawling. "I'm claiming this one, so take it off your list of possibilities."

"Oh, I hadn't even been considering that one," I assured him quickly, though I still wasn't sure what we were even talking about. The first shadowkind he'd enslave? That would seem to make the most sense. I was surprised that the sorcerers would simply hand one over rather than having him prove himself by capturing one from scratch with his new powers, but maybe the first "harnessing" was part of the rites.

"You'll be going through with it pretty soon, then?" I ventured.

An eerie smile curved the guy's lips. He stroked the cage again, gazing at the shadowy creature flickering within.

"Three more days," he said. "It's scheduled now. I can't wait."

Even as his tone sent another uneasy quiver through my nerves, I committed that number to memory.

"It's further off for me," I said, hoping I was keeping my tone appropriately casual. Like I was just shooting the breeze with a fellow initiate, not digging for info. "I'm not even sure where I'll be having my rite."

The guy's gaze flicked to me, and my pulse stuttered at the thought that there might be suspicion in his eyes. But he just chuckled in a slightly patronizing tone. "I think it's always done outside in the same spot. They lead us to the ceremony area. Wouldn't be fair to get an early look at it."

I made myself laugh in return. "Of course not. I can't help speculating, that's all. Lots to imagine. It'll be an intense experience, for sure."

He rubbed his hands together, his smile coming back. "I bet it's even more intense if you have a rite in the winter, when it'll actually be dark at night. But I wouldn't want to wait that long when I don't have to."

So the rites were held outside at night. This guy would be having his in just three days.

And I'd have to find some way of being there so I could find out exactly what it was he couldn't wait to experience.

CHAPTER SIX

Rollick

The trail I'd been following petered out along the outskirts of Berlin. The nature preserve I'd ended up in didn't hold much other than trees, grass, a murky stream, and a few low hills, but I was a lot surer of what I was looking for now and where I'd find it. Under the layer of vegetation and soil covering a slightly odd dip at the far edge of the park, I'd discovered a distinctive gouge in a buried stretch of rock.

I spent at least an hour swerving back and forth over the landscape in shadow form, extending all my senses toward the earth beneath me. There weren't any other markers of the being that'd spent a fair bit of time in this area decades ago. But it had hung around for at least long enough to dig into the local rocks.

I had to admit I didn't have any direct experience with

the being I believed I was tracking, but from what I understood through hearsay, it either fed off stone or rubbed the stuff into its body to build strength. Not totally unusual among shadowkind—I'd watched Crag munch on chunks of quartz crystals before for similar reasons. But the slabs this thing dug out of the earth were nearly as big as Crag himself.

And somehow I suspected the beast's temperament wasn't anywhere near as cooperative as the gargoyle's.

I left the park behind and wandered through the suburbs that bordered the reserve. In the wilder terrain, I hadn't encountered any beings likely to be able to report their observations, but higher shadowkind tended to gravitate toward human habitations if they could get away with co-existing there. Out of all mortal beings, humans were the ones who provided by far the greatest variety of entertainment and indulgences, after all.

I'd reached a commercial strip with a few small shops, still far from the bustling core of the city, when I caught a whiff of not-entirely-mortal feline. Ah ha.

It only took a minute to trace the scent to its source. The shifter was curled up in the shadows of a garden shed, lounging there for the day like an actual cat might have.

The being's presence tensed at my approach. From the intricacies of his scent, I could tell he was decently established—at least a century under his belt. Of course, that didn't mean he'd spent all that time in this area, but in my vast experience, shifters were a territorial bunch. Once they settled in someplace they liked, they weren't inclined to leave unless they were forced to.

No doubt he could tell that I wasn't any kind of being

he'd want to mess with just from whatever impressions of *me* he'd picked up already. I stayed in the shadows, propelling myself close enough that we were essentially face to face. If he'd tried to flee, I'd have pounced on him, but maybe he sensed that much. He stayed where he was, peering back at me, every nerve quivering through the atmosphere around us.

"I'd just like to have a quick chat," I said, flashing the shadowy equivalent of a smile. "I've got no beef with you. I only need information."

"Information about what?" the cat shifter asked in a voice with a hint of a lisp.

"How long have you been coming to this part of the mortal realm?"

The shifter let out a sound like a humph. "I saw the last king leave. Planes coming in. The big wall going up and down. I don't bother anyone. This is my little piece."

I held up my hands. "And I have no interest in taking it from you. I'm only hoping you can indulge my curiosity. There was a powerful being that came through here and maybe mucked around a bit probably toward the earlier parts of your time. Something ancient with ties to the earth. I doubt you'd have seen another one like it since, if you saw that one."

A shiver ran through the shadows from the cat shifter, and my spirits lifted. He knew what I was talking about.

"You don't want to mess with that one," he muttered, and I had the impression of him curling his tail around himself like a shield.

I didn't think I was going to have much choice, but there was no reason to share that observation with this stranger. I wouldn't have let him see me at all if my enemies didn't already know I was working against them. Quinn's little gambit had forced me into the center of the conflict, which meant there was no more point in trying to hide.

"I'd just like to know what he was doing here," I said. "Did he clash with any other beings in the area? Did he interact with the mortals at all?"

The shifter snorted. "He wanted to *crush* the mortals."

A chill prickled through me. I'd known the duo of ancient shadowkind was out to slaughter sorcerers for their power, but he made it sound like this one had wanted to destroy all humans. "What do you mean?"

"He started making the earth shake and crack. Buildings broke. A little bit here and there and then more. I think he was seeing what he could get away with. I didn't like it." The cat's tail twitched. "But the Highest must have found out he was getting too pushy. They sent some of their warriors, who drove him away. I don't know what they did with him, but he never came back here that I saw."

Wonderful. So we were dealing with a super-powerful being who'd added to his powers and also had at least used to be itching to wreak havoc throughout the mortal realm. Not that I'd assumed his other intentions were good, but they could definitely have been *better* than this.

I dipped my head. "Thank you. That's all I need to know. You can go back to your cat nap."

The shifter let out a wordless grumble, but I felt his attention on me as I slipped away. He didn't trust me to be any kinder than the fiend he'd just told me about.

As I drifted farther into the city, stewing in my thoughts, I let myself emerge into physical form in my human guise, keeping my usual veneers covering the pointed teeth I couldn't transform. The air had the usual chemical tang of city life, but it tasted fresher when I was breathing it into proper bodily lungs. The rhythm of my striding legs helped center my thoughts.

I'd seen signs of this one ancient shadowkind's presence in various spots across Europe and eastern Asia. This was the most recent spot, and the only one where I'd found a being who'd witnessed what he'd been up to. The other one, his partner, I hadn't found traces of in the same places, but then, I suspected theirs was a recent collaboration. The other's domain would be more difficult for me to explore and unlikely to contain many lingering traces.

A couple of tourists I passed stopped to raise their phones for a photo, and I glanced up to see what they found noteworthy. An immense tower jutted up in the near distance, slim with a spherical bulge partway up before tapering into an even thinner spire.

My sorcerer would have liked to see that, wouldn't she? It was along similar lines to her fanciful designs that she scrawled in her sketchbook. I found myself raising my own phone to snap a visual record myself.

I made it back to the little Norwegian village just a few minutes after noon. Quinn was already perched at one of the tables in the bakery, one foot tapping restlessly against a chair leg. Something had her more on edge than during our first rendezvous. Nervous energy radiated off every movement from the swipe of her pale hair back behind her ears to the pursing of her soft lips.

At least, I assumed they were soft from the look of them. She hadn't yet agreed to give me a chance to experience them for myself. Not for lack of interest, but out of the stubborn sense of loyalty she seemed to possess in spades. I still wasn't sure whether her defiance was ultimately going to turn out in my favor or against me.

But either way, it was impressive if sometimes irritating to watch.

The moment I stepped into the bakery, Quinn's spine jerked rigidly straight. Even now that we'd officially been working together for several days, she eyed me like I might pounce on her just as the cat shifter had been worried I would.

To be fair, I *had* pounced on her at least once in the past. But for good reason. And she'd kind of liked it, even if she didn't want to admit it.

I dropped into the seat across from her. She might have still been a little afraid of me, but she'd also generously bought me the same kind of pastry I'd picked up last time I was here. It had been pretty tasty. Such a mix of contradictions, this mortal woman.

Which was why I couldn't help speculating about how delicious she might be too. It really was too bad that we had to be stuck in a conflict that put her life, my livelihood, and who knew how much else on the line. Otherwise I could have focused on more enjoyable pursuits I'd eventually have persuaded her to join me in.

Well, plenty of time for that later.

"You managed to get away again," I observed. "They trust you that much."

Quinn shrugged. "I don't know how much it's trust. But I might get something really useful tonight." Her hands twined together on the table. She'd barely touched the slice of pie she'd bought. "One of the trainee sorcerers at the enclave is doing his 'rites' tonight. I'm planning on finding a way of watching and seeing what exactly it is they do to spark the magic in him."

I raised my eyebrows. "That will be a big step forward. Have you uncovered anything else that would bolster your own powers?"

She shook her head, her mouth twisting. "It's mostly been busy-work so far, making sure I'm dedicated to learning. They're being very secretive about the rites, so I'm guessing that's the key." She sighed and picked up her fork. "Have you gotten anywhere with your investigations yet?"

"I went out to Berlin yesterday," I said without thinking about it, and somehow both delighted in and regretted the glint of hopeful interest that lit in her eyes.

"It's one of my top ten cities I've wanted to visit," she said. "I mean, if I manage to fit in that kind of travel with the time I have..." Her hand dipped to the neckline of her shirt. Her sweater covered her entire chest, but I knew she was touching the spot where the top of her surgery scar was marked on the skin over her sternum. "Did you see the Upper West? We talked about it in one of my classes."

I felt abruptly ashamed that I didn't even know what she was talking about. "I took a picture of this one," I said, showing her the photo on my phone.

"Oh, the Television Tower. That's an amazing one too.

Did you know it's the tallest building in the whole country?"

I hadn't actually given it that much thought. "And here I thought you'd be one of those women who say size doesn't matter."

Quinn wrinkled her nose at me, but the eager flush that'd crossed her face at the overall topic of conversation made up for it. "It's an impressive feat of engineering. And I bet it's breathtaking to see up close."

"So you're all about looks, then."

She ignored my teasing tone. "It's not just *looks*. It's..." She paused, her bright blue eyes going momentarily distant as she searched for the right words. "There's something special about being able to make people feel something, having an impact on them. That's why so many people make art, right? To do it with a building—something that's functional but also art in its own way—something that's entwined in their lives and the city... Maybe it sounds silly, but I think that's just about the most amazing thing possible."

I was rarely lost for words, but in the first few moments after she stopped speaking, I had trouble deciding what to say in response. The passion in her words was obvious.

I hadn't really been fair to her. I *had* assumed that her interest in architecture was mostly about making pretty structures and achieving acclaim. The way she phrased it... her reasons for her pursuits weren't that different from my own reasons for setting up the hotels and other social venues I had over the years. Creating something that contributed to the larger community. Offering people something they might not be getting elsewhere.

Although in my case I was mainly concerned with inhuman sorts of "people."

"I hope I'll get to see what kind of functional art you offer up to the world someday," I said, keeping my tone languid but meaning it all the same.

"Yeah, well..." She swiped her hand across her mouth, her expression tightening again. "I'm trying not to think about that right now. Until it's more possible again."

The gloom that passed over her face spoke of the other things she was trying to talk about. The beings she'd have preferred were sitting across from her right now. Her fingers curled toward her palm as if she were imagining wrapping them around someone's hand, and my jaw clenched.

I'd nudged her toward sending those three mutinous lackeys of mine away. She'd cared about them, and I'd used her caring to my advantage. But when I saw the pain from missing them rise up behind her eyes like it had just now, some small part of me wasn't completely convinced I'd made the right call.

They'd been a distraction to her, and her to them. They'd also brightened her up in a way I hadn't figured out how to replicate. Was she really better off for *anyone's* purposes with that loss weighing on her?

I shoved those doubts away. She was mine, and sooner or later she'd figure out she wasn't badly off like that. I could be patient. The rest didn't matter.

Or it shouldn't anyway.

Quinn seemed to shake herself out of her melancholy. She focused on me again, though the sadness still lingered at the corners of her mouth. "Were you just sightseeing, or did you find out anything useful off in Germany?"

"I determined that one of our sorcerer-killers isn't a fan of any human, magical or not," I said. "Which doesn't bode well for this villainous duo's ultimate plans. I suspect he ended up going across the ocean because his habits were becoming too well-known over here."

"And have you figured out *what* he is?"

I dragged in a breath. Why should I keep avoiding the subject now that I was sure? It wasn't as if she'd fully understand my trepidation over the fact anyway, from her mortal perspective.

"I'm now completely sure that it's a behemoth," I said. "Or rather, *the* behemoth, because as far as I know, the shadow realm has only ever spit out one of those."

Quinn studied me. "And that's bad, I take it."

I gave her a thin smile. "It's only one of the most powerful beings ever to exist, outside of the absolute Highest beings that never leave the shadows—and now for some reason it's got a vendetta that's put both of us right in its path."

CHAPTER SEVEN

Quinn

I'd worn every piece of clothing I'd brought with me, and still I was shivering as I crouched in the dimness just beyond the enclave's sprawling house. The chill of the high altitude had deepened with the night, even though the sun didn't quite go all the way down at this time of year. It was past eleven o'clock now, but a hazy golden glow still gleamed at the edges of the sky. It felt more like mid-evening than the middle of the night.

It wasn't enough sun to warm things up. My face was prickling in the cool air. I tugged the collar of my windbreaker up over my mouth and let my warm breath flow over my cheeks with the exhale. At least it was dark enough that I shouldn't be easy to spot, but not so dark that I had to worry about tripping over things I couldn't see.

I could have waited tucked into my bed, listening for the sound of footsteps in the hall outside. But I'd been worried that I might drift off and miss the sounds of the rite beginning if I was more comfortable, and it would have been harder to sneak through the building itself if many of the sorcerers were bustling around.

Staking out a spot in the nearby wilderness had seemed like the best strategy. I just hoped they hurried up with the whole ceremony thing. I'd rather not witness it as an ice cube.

A distant rumble made me perk up. To my surprise, it sounded as if it was coming from off in the distance rather than from the building to my right. I squinted through the trees. The gleam of headlights came into view, and moments later a van pulled into the parking area under the lowest deck. I heard the thump of the doors but couldn't see what was going on down there from my perch.

Had they brought something special for the rite that had to be organized at the last minute? What would that be? It'd sounded like the novice sorcerer had already picked out his first shadowkind slave. I had no idea what else might be involved in the process.

Maybe this meant they were almost ready to begin.

I adjusted my position cautiously, stretching my legs. My backpack shifted against my shoulders. I didn't have much in it now that all my clothes were on me, but I hadn't felt comfortable leaving my pills, phone, or first aid kit inside the enclave while I embarked on this mission.

If anything went wrong, I might need to make a hasty run for it. There'd be no chance to duck back into my bedroom and collect my things.

Finally, the soft creak of the building's double doors reached my ears. A rustling of footsteps followed. I peered through the dim light and watched a cluster of robed figures crossing the deck to the packed earth path in front of it—and then veering to the right, farther away from me.

I wasn't sure if their course was to my advantage or not. I wasn't going to have to scramble to get out of their way, but I'd need to hoof it to make sure I kept track of them rather than losing them in the semi-night.

Setting my feet carefully the way I'd learned in my not-always-legal urban explorations, I clambered farther up on the forested hillside and circled around the top of the building, picking out the moving figures when they came into view. They'd come around the building and now were heading upward like I had, along a path I couldn't make out from my current position.

Good. Less distance for me to close.

I slowed down, slinking from tree to tree, my ears pricked for their footsteps. No one spoke. I poked my head out over a narrow but obvious path between the trees just as the last of the cluster vanished around a bend farther up the hillside.

I followed the direction of the path through the trees alongside it so I still had some shelter. It was slow-going, both to make sure I stayed unnoticed and because of the steepness of the slope. Within minutes, I was sweating despite the chill in the air. Give me a set of skyscraper stairs over a mountainside any day.

A flare of firelight up ahead warned me to slow down even more. I crept onward, eyeing the dancing flame of the torch someone had mounted on a post. Creeping to the side where its glow shouldn't reach me, I knelt down a few feet from the edge of what I could now see was a clearing.

The cleared area was a rare section of the mountainside that was nearly level, about twenty feet across and roughly round. Nine torches blazed at even intervals around the border. They gave off a pungent smoke with an acrid scent that tickled my nose even though I was keeping my distance.

The cluster of robed figures had stopped in the middle of the clearing. It was hard to count them because they kept moving around and they were all wearing matching cloaks, but I decided there were ten. One of them eased back his hood, and I recognized the new initiate. His face was even paler than before but set in a mask of determination. He held his chin high.

The other figures had started murmuring some kind of chant. The initiate closed his eyes and swayed with the rhythm of their words. The eerie melody made the hairs on the back of my neck rise. I didn't understand the words any more than I did the sorcerous commands that directed my magic, but they resonated with power.

One of the sorcerers handed a couple of two-pronged metal blades to the guy. Then all the surrounding figures drew back to stand beneath the torches, still chanting. With the space around the guy cleared, I could now see that one of those shadowkind carrier boxes sat on the ground near his feet.

Well, that was fairly self-explanatory. But what was he going to do with those weird knives? He was just standing there on his own now, still swaying, his lips now moving in unison with the chant, though I got the impression he wasn't actually making any sound.

Abruptly, the chanting fell away. Somehow its absence felt twice as unsettling as the racket they'd been making before.

The wind warbled through the branches overhead. The initiate raised his hands, each clutched around one of the double-pronged blades, toward the violet sky overhead. A shudder ran through his slim body.

He dropped to his knees in front of the carrier box and unlatched it. Then he thrust both of his hands, still gripping the blades, through the large opening in one violent movement.

I didn't understand what was happening until he drew his arms back out and straightened up. A wiry-haired, hissing creature was writhing in his grasp, skewered between the two weapons that had dug into its flesh. Its shadowy blood was wisping up from those puncture points.

A jolt of horror socked me in the gut. What was he going to do with the little beast? He'd speared it like it was a cob of corn he was about to dig into.

I had no idea how accurate that comparison would prove to be until a few moments later. The guy held up the flailing, bleeding creature and called out into the night, "Now I become one with the creatures I will rule. I will take their essence into me and make it my own."

With the last words, he rammed the blades in twice as deep, twisting them with the same movement. The shadowkind creature screeched, but its voice faltered, its struggles weakening.

The initiate pulled it right to his face and closed his mouth over one of the wounds.

My stomach lurched, nearly propelling my meager dinner up my throat. *He* was making some kind of dinner of the creature, sucking in the smoke that poured off its body in audible gulps, inhaling more with each heave of breath. He sounded like some kind of beast himself, tearing into its food after weeks of starvation.

As I watched, he mashed the increasingly limp body right up against his face as if he could absorb even more of the smoky blood right through his skin.

I couldn't help it—I doubled over and gagged as quietly as I could manage. Thankfully the savage noises the initiate was releasing and the lingering squeaks of the dying creature drowned out what I couldn't muffle with my hand over my mouth.

As my thoughts spun and more nausea bubbled up through my chest, it occurred to me that this awful "rite" made a sick kind of sense. The villainous shadowkind duo was taking the power of sorcery into themselves by consuming the most vital organs of the practitioners. Based on what I was seeing now, those sorcerers—or their relatives, somewhere far down the line—had activated their sorcery at least in part by consuming the shadowkind they exerted control over.

The cycle had come full circle in the most gruesome possible way.

I was so focused on the initiate in his horrible act and suppressing my reaction to it that I didn't notice the other figures appearing at the edge of the clearing until the guy glanced over at them. Two more robed figures had stepped into view, with a few other people I couldn't clearly see gathered with them, shoulders slumped, one of them small enough that it must have been a child.

The creature the guy had killed had all but disintegrated into his hands. Dark veins crawled across his face beneath his skin as if the shadowy blood had infected him with a disease. He turned his head, and I saw his eyes had gone totally black, even the whites consumed with darkness.

He tossed the scraps that remained of the creature away and lunged toward the newcomers as if he were an animal himself.

Which maybe was the point. The sorcerers along the edge of the clearing took up their chant again, their voices rising louder, and the newer arrivals shoved one of the hunched figures into the clearing.

It was a woman, not much older than me, wearing nothing but a white nightgown that fell to her knees. She stared at the guy charging toward her and let out a shriek.

My body tensed, a cry of warning snagged in my throat. It was too late anyway. As she stumbled away on her bare feet, he tackled her.

His fingernails dug into her skin; he clamped his teeth around her throat. There was a crack as a bone broke, and then a sickening tearing sound. The woman's scream cut off in a wet gurgle.

The guy raised his head and shook it, spraying blood from the chunk of throat caught in his mouth. He spat it out and snarled a few words I didn't recognize, but some part of me, maybe the sorcerer energies pumping through my own veins, thrummed with a growing sense of recognition even as I held back the urge to vomit.

He has taken the beast into him, and now he is one with it. He is letting the monstrous energies move through him to gain the deepest possible understanding of the fiends he'll bind to his will. To control monsters, you must become a monster.

That was the gist of what the chant said, I was abruptly sure. The sorcerers were urging him on, cheering for him to let loose this savagery and fully absorb the energies he'd consumed.

Because this was all they believed the shadowkind were. Monsters, wild beasts, interested in nothing more than senseless killing. How could they spend so much time around them and not realize there was so much more to the beings they enslaved?

And what had the sorcerers' human victims done to deserve being dragged into these awful rites? Even now, they were propelling a girl who couldn't have been older than nine or ten out from the trees.

My body tensed, my pulse pounding so loud it nearly drowned out the chant. The guy who was now barely a man whirled on the girl, bloody teeth bared. She spun with a sob and dashed toward the nearest sorcerer, but the robed woman flung her away.

Oh, God. How could they? How could any kind of magic possibly be worth acting like this?

The initiate was already bearing down on her. And while the sorcerers around me might have been willing to watch this scene with nothing but approval, *I* couldn't just stand by.

As the guy leapt at the girl, a cry of protest I couldn't restrain burst from my throat. My legs threw me forward without consulting the rest of me, with a desperate urge to wrench that poor kid away from her terrible fate.

The chanting stopped. One of the sorcerers sprang at me and caught my arm, just as the initiate smashed the little girl's skull into the rocky ground with a crunch of her skull. A sob of my own snagged in my throat, and I found every face around the clearing had turned toward me.

CHAPTER EIGHT

Quinn

"What are you doing here?" the man who'd grabbed me demanded in a raspy voice, his face shadowed by the hood of his cloak.

"You can't let him—" I protested automatically, straining to run at the initiate as he continued bashing the little girl's body, even though I could tell she was beyond saving now.

Before I could get my entire sentence out, the man who'd grabbed me smacked his hand over my mouth to cut off my words and dragged me back toward the trees. I squirmed against his grasp, but he held me too tightly. The others took up their chanting again as if I'd never intervened.

Another figure appeared beside us. I didn't recognize

her until I heard Vera's voice from beneath the hood, low and urgent. "That's the new one—the one I've been working with." She tugged her hood back enough that I could meet her eyes, hers cold and flinty. "How did you get out here? What do you think you're doing, Quinn?"

"Quietly!" the man ordered me in a harsh whisper as his hand loosened on my mouth. "You've already disturbed the rites enough."

As if I were anywhere close to being the most disturbing thing that'd happened out there in the clearing. A slightly hysterical laugh quavered up from my lungs through my constricted chest. I was afraid that if I let it out, I might puke again too.

"I heard you leaving, and I was curious about what was going on," I managed to murmur. "How can you— He's *killing* people."

But they already knew that. They'd brought those people to the enclave specifically for the guy to kill.

Where had his victims come from? How could the sorcerers possibly justify these murders to themselves?

They barely seemed to acknowledge how horrifying it was. "He's becoming one with the monsters," Vera said, confirming the impressions I'd gotten from their chant. "To be able to fully harness them, he must know them and their ways from the inside out. It's the *only* way to unlock the sorcerer power within. Your magic came from the same place, somewhere down your family line."

Not *my* family, I wanted to protest, but I didn't want to give away that much of my personal history—or the fact that I'd lied about the origins of my powers. More nausea flooded me. My heart was thudding so fast my body was trembling with the beat.

What were the sorcerers going to do with me now that I knew their secret? Now that they'd seen my reaction to it? Should I pretend I was accepting it after my initial shock to buy myself enough time to get away, or would they refuse to believe I'd changed my mind?

There was still another victim somewhere over amid the trees, waiting to be slaughtered. How could I stand back and let that happen?

All of those questions were rendered moot by the tramping of footsteps toward us and the rough clearing of a throat. A man I'd seen once or twice around the enclave was approaching us from lower down the slope, wearing a regular jacket and jeans instead of the ceremonial robes, his narrowed gaze fixed on me.

"I thought I might find her here when I saw her bedroom was empty," he said, shifting his focus to the sorcerers standing on either side of me. At his tone, the other man's grip on my arm tightened. "She's a spy."

My heart just about stopped. I opened my mouth, but no sound came out. I didn't know what he'd found out, what I needed to deny or explain.

"What are you talking about?" Vera demanded, her voice still hushed.

The new arrival lifted his chin toward me. "I followed her on her trip into the village like we discussed. She spoke with a man there, someone she was clearly familiar with. I stuck around after she left to see what he was up to. He was awfully shifty, but he couldn't completely evade me. I finally got close enough to tell it wasn't a man at all. It was one of *them*. She's working with the monsters."

Oh, shit. The bottom of my stomach dropped out. "I— what?" I stammered. I could still act like I hadn't realized, right? "The guy I talked to is just someone I met when I first got here. He seemed totally normal. He can't be one of those shadow things."

I couldn't tell whether I'd been convincing. Vera's lips pursed with a sour expression. She motioned to the man holding me, and he dragged me farther from the clearing, where the chanting and the sounds of a scuffle continued. Then she shook her head at me.

"It doesn't matter whether you knew or not. That *thing* will have known what it was doing. It was using you. Who knows what else it's up to?" Her gaze jerked to the man I'd had no idea had followed me to the village. "What did they talk about?"

"I couldn't get near enough to listen in," he said. "But they looked awfully chummy for two people who only just met."

I had the urge to protest the description of my relationship with Rollick as "chummy," but I didn't think that would do anything for my case. "We were just talking about our travels," I said hastily. "I didn't mention anything about the enclave, of course. This doesn't make any sense. He seemed like a totally normal—"

"We can't trust her," the newcomer snapped, cutting me off. "They've managed to infiltrate our ranks, whether because of her cluelessness or with her cooperation. Who knows how else the creatures have their claws in her? They might be maintaining a connection to her even now."

Vera's expression hardened even more, and my entire body went twice as cold as it'd been just from the chilly night air.

They were going to kill me. Maybe they'd even sacrifice me to their initiate alongside the other victims they'd tossed his way.

They saw me as being as much of an enemy as the shadowkind they despised, and eliminating me would be the only way to cut off the connection.

I reacted on instinct again, but this time it was all self-preservation. The techniques from my long-ago self-defense classes flashed through my mind, and I jerked my arm toward me with a twist of my elbow that broke the man's hold. Then I turned tail and ran as fast as my feet could take me.

I stumbled on the uneven terrain as I hurtled forward. The three sorcerers who'd been gathered around me sprang after me with restrained shouts and curses and the rustling of the underbrush. I swerved to head downhill, since that would give me more speed, but even as I careened onward, a sense of hopelessness closed around my heart.

The enclave lay downhill too—and it sounded like the man who'd spotted me with Rollick had already searched for me there. He'd have alerted the other sorcerers. They'd probably confiscated my car.

How the hell was I going to get back to any kind of safe place on foot? I wouldn't even be able to follow the roads without the sorcerers catching me. Assuming I could get far enough ahead of my current pursuers to even think about making the longer trek back to the nearest village.

I had my health essentials in my bag but no food and

only a single bottle of water. As soon as the enclave's residents had the chance, they'd send some of their shadowkind slaves to hunt for me too.

I swung to the side to dodge a stump, and the chain around my neck shifted. A spark of hope lit in my chest.

I had the necklace Rollick had given me. I couldn't think of a time I'd have needed it more. The last thing I wanted was for him to have to sweep in and rescue me somehow, but if I could at least get away from this bunch and hide out someplace where he could pick me up—

Even as I thought that, one of my pursuers gained enough ground to snatch at my backpack. I lurched forward instinctively at the feel of the tug, wrenching free, but my pulse stuttered. Getting away even for a moment was seeming less doable by the second.

A metallic click carried from behind me. "Give me a clear line of sight," one of the men barked, and I realized what the sound had been: the safety being released on a gun. He was going to shoot me.

In desperation, I leapt sideways and landed on a particularly steep patch of hillside. I ended up skidding down on my ass, just as a gunshot boomed overhead. The second my feet hit firmer ground, I was darting away again, my hand leaping to the necklace.

Screw dignity. I needed to get out of here alive, and I had to admit I couldn't do it alone.

I dragged out the bird pendant, tugged on the wing, and twisted it the way Rollick had said. Then I dashed on, the metal charm thumping against my sternum.

Would he even get here in time? The man had suggested that Rollick had stuck around in the village for a while after

I'd left, maybe because I'd told him about the rites tonight. He might have wanted to be nearby specifically for this reason. But he still had miles of territory to cover to reach me, and the regular shadowkind guards would be keeping watch along the edges of the sorcerers' domain.

But it could be that the demon had come as close as he could to the enclave's boundaries to wait. As I rushed on through the forest, one of my pursuers sucked in a startled breath. Then, between the thuds of my frantic feet, a distant shriek reached my ears.

I couldn't tell if it was angry or pained, but it sounded as though some creature off in the wilderness was not happy at all.

"Something's coming," Vera muttered to the men. They slowed as they took stock, and I pulled farther ahead, sliding down another steep portion of hillside. I fled to my right, through a denser stand of trees, and spotted a narrow crevice next to me in the rocky ground.

I didn't have time to think about it. I squeezed into the tight space that was barely a cave and pushed myself as far back into its darkness as I could get.

My legs were already wobbly from the exertion. I didn't know if I could outrun my pursuers for much longer, especially when one of them was taking literal shots at me, but maybe I could hide until help came.

Voices carried from the forest beyond, mumbled words in English and in the strange sorcery language I only vaguely understood. They were calling their "harnessed" shadowkind to them now. To fend off the intruder or to find me?

Maybe both.

I held perfectly still, keeping my breathing shallow. A thick mossy odor filled my nose. It was dark enough in the crevice that I didn't think anyone would be able to see me unless they leaned right into the opening, and then I wouldn't be much more than a vague shape. I could hope that my pursuers wouldn't notice the crevice at all.

Another cry rang through the air, this one a little nearer than the first I thought. It definitely wasn't a victorious sound. My fingers curled into my palms as I waited.

Footsteps trod closer outside. The voices had fallen silent. There was some rustling as hands pushed through bushes in their search for me. I swallowed thickly, still afraid to move so much as an inch.

A few shouts went up somewhere farther away. From the enclave building or the clearing for the rites? I couldn't tell. My pursuers murmured something to each other too low for me to make out. I waited and waited as they rasped through the vegetation around the crevice, willing them away with each second that passed by.

Abruptly, the sounds of movement stopped. Then I heard one phrase that turned my blood to ice.

"Over there."

Shit. They'd spotted the opening to my hiding spot. I closed my hands into tight fists, planning to fight them off as well as I could if they came at me. Although they'd probably just shoot me where I crouched. Should I burst out and make another run for it?

Before I could decide, a shadow cast extra darkness across the entrance to the cave. A figure was bending down to peer inside—

And then that figure was shoved to the side by another,

larger form I only saw as a blur. There was a bang of a gunshot and a strangled sound, followed by a crack of breaking bone. Then came a shout, a heavy thump, and the tearing of flesh. It made me think of the scene I'd just witnessed in the clearing, and my stomach heaved all over again.

A face appeared in the dim light beyond the crevice. Rollick gazed in at me, his human face flecked with what I had to assume was blood. His eyes shone darkly in the dusk.

"There you are," he said, somehow managing to make the remark sound jaunty despite the circumstances. "Come on out. I take it the rites didn't go all that wonderfully?"

A choked guffaw lodged in my throat. I pushed myself out of the crevice, scraping my shoulder against the rough stone surface, and found myself staring at the mangled bodies of two of the sorcerers who'd been pursuing me.

Vera must have left, possibly to warn the others of a potential attack or to summon more shadowkind to her side. The two men sprawled on the slanted earth, both of their necks sliced clean through, one with a gouge in his chest as if Rollick had punched straight through his ribs into his heart. Which maybe the demon had.

I drew in a breath and realized that I was shaking. But none of my horror was for the scene in front of me. Alongside my nausea came a surge of anger and defiance.

"They were killing people—a kid, even—for their awful rites," I said. "Then they tried to kill me. It's all—it's all some sick ceremony that isn't even *right*—"

I wasn't sure I was making much sense, but Rollick's gaze intensified. He grasped my arm, a brutal light flaring in his eyes. More shouts were carrying from across the forest in more than one direction.

"We can make them pay," the demon said, a hint of his monstrous nature coloring his voice in a husky note that promised vengeance. "I can tear more of them apart. You can call up the creatures they've been chaining to break free and turn on their masters. I know you could unleash all that fury on them if you give yourself over to the magic. Just say the word, and I'll be right there with you."

His words sent a shudder of yearning through me. Part of me did want to charge back to the clearing and rip the sorcerers to shreds for the horrible acts they'd carried out tonight and who knew how many times before.

But that kind of violence was exactly what had sickened me about them. I couldn't let my horror turn me into a person who was just as vicious.

"No," I said roughly. "Thank you, but— I think we should just get out of here. There's nothing else I can learn from them anyway."

Not even the sorcerers of the enclave seemed equipped to deal with shadowkind on the scale we were grappling with. And they were as monstrous as our other enemies.

"We'll deal with them," I added, my jaw clenching. "We won't let them keep doing this. But we're not going to slaughter them like the savages they think shadowkind are. Later, after we've handled the bigger problem, we'll come back."

Rollick considered me for just a few seconds and seemed to decide it wasn't worth a debate. He knelt down and shifted into his demonic form at the same time, his body expanding, his skin turning ruddy as his clothing vanished, his horns jutting up from over his angular features. As he held his hand out to me, his tufted tail lashed back and forth. "If you don't want the bloodshed, then we'd better run, or I'm not going to have much choice."

At his gesture, I stepped forward and let him heft me up so he could carry me piggyback-style. My arms wrapped around his neck, my knees bracing on either side of his expansive chest. His smoky scent flooded my lungs. As I secured my hold, he pushed off on his powerful legs, racing through the forest away from the enclave.

I closed my eyes against the rushing of the wind stirred by his swift pace. A lump clogged in the base of my throat.

The being I'd sworn never to trust had saved me. All I'd learned in the past week was that we were still on our own when it came to defeating the larger villains we were up against, with no more idea than before how to do that.

And the tremors of power rippling through my heart came from a source so horrifying I wished I could tear the borrowed organ right out of my chest.

CHAPTER NINE

Crag

A peculiar scent lingered along the shoreline in this part of the country the mortals called China. The notes of it had stuck in my memory after we'd barged into the mountain camp where our shadowkind enemies maintained a base of operations. It hadn't seemed like a smell that should be there, and it'd tugged at something deep in my memory.

I'd almost forgotten it in the chaos of the moment, but afterward—after Quinn had sent me away, when there wasn't much to think about other than mulling over the past couple of days and where I'd gone wrong—it'd risen back to the surface of my mind.

Quinn had ordered me to stay away. I couldn't have ignored that command if I'd tried—which I had. So I would help her whatever way I could. And the only way I could think of was by continuing to find out everything possible about the powerful beings that threatened her.

It'd taken me a long time to narrow down the smell. I hadn't been able to go back to the southwestern United States, at least not immediately after the mortal woman I cared for so much had cast me into the nearest rift. She must have still been nearby then. So I'd followed my instincts and shreds of memory across day after day until I'd ended up here.

No humans gathered on this lonely stretch of shoreline. It was a jumble of rocks and slimy seaweed that caught the froth of the hissing waves. Salt and all kinds of other ocean scents laced the air, but I could pick out that one specific odor clearly now.

What exactly was it? I allowed myself to emerge from the shadows, since there was no one around to see me here, and crouched down on the rocks. The smell wasn't coming from any of the bits of seaweed I raised to my nose, and it didn't seem specifically attached to the rocks, although I caught a slightly stronger whiff here and there. Hmm.

There was a flicker of bright green at the corner of my vision, and the next thing I knew, I was being bumped off my slightly precarious perch into the water. I spun as I fell, whipping out my wings, but I wasn't fast enough to stop myself from crashing into the shallows next to the shore.

I sprang back onto my feet in the waist-deep water, braced for a fight, and found myself staring back at Lance's grinning dragon face.

He shifted back into human-like form an instant later, nimbly leaping from one larger boulder to another with a rustle of his wild black curls. "Here you are. You wandered off far enough. It took us *days* to track you down."

Torrent wavered into being sitting on a rock beside him, his ever-present tentacles steadying his lean frame. He tipped his head to me, his rumpled dark red hair slanting across his pale forehead. "Sorry to take you by surprise. You know how the dragon is."

I did. But I found I didn't know what to say to either of them as I climbed out of the water, shaking it from my rocky limbs. I stayed in gargoyle form, both because it was more comfortable when I had the option and because I'd actually stand out less against the shoreline if anyone sailed at all within view of us. I'd look like one part of the scattered rocks.

"How did you find me?" I muttered. I wasn't sure I appreciated this interruption. I'd been in the middle of concentrating, and now my thoughts had scattered.

"I figured you'd be on the move," Torrent said in his typical coolly collected way. "You're trying to find something that'll help Quinn, aren't you? There aren't a whole lot of gargoyles roaming widely across the mortal realm. All we had to do was find one being who'd noticed you passing by and follow the trail from there."

I couldn't help scowling at him. We weren't exactly a squad anymore. He didn't have any official authority over me. "I was following a trail of my own. I don't know how useful it'll be."

"Oooh, the gargoyle is grouchy now," Lance declared, shooting a more human grin at me, his white teeth bright against his brown skin.

"I was in the middle of something," I informed him.

"What? We want to beat down the beasts who are after her too. We'll all tackle them together. And then we'll go back to Quinn and show her she doesn't need to worry about us. She doesn't get to tell us what to do. We protect *her*."

He said the last bit so firmly with a defiant jut of his chin that I might have chuckled if the sentiment hadn't jabbed right through my heart. The purposeful energy that'd buoyed me through the past several days deflated. My shoulders slumped despite my best efforts at keeping my inner turmoil in check.

Torrent, as usual, noticed everything. He leaned forward on his perch. "What's the matter? Have you come across anything that's made you more worried than we already were before?"

As if we hadn't been worried enough already. But that wasn't the reason for my reaction.

I debated telling him it was nothing, but I didn't think he'd believe it. And given that these two had hunted me down all across the mortal realm, I doubted he'd let the matter drop just because I tried to put him off.

"It was my fault," I said, low but even despite the pain that shuddered through my chest with the admission. "*I* pushed her away first. I made her feel like it was a problem for her to be around me. So she sent me even farther away —she sent all of us away. She thought *she* was the problem."

Torrent's sea-green eyes darkened with sympathy. "I think Quinn's concerns about us had to do with the way we *all* behaved after the battle in the sorcerers' valley." He looked down at his right hand, mangled to the point of barely being recognizable. Lance paused, following his gaze, and stiffened.

The dragon shifter had been the one who'd mangled that hand. He'd been in the grips of our enemies' stolen sorcery, so he hadn't *wanted* to attack us. But he had, and I'd seen before how guilty he felt about it.

And it was in trying to protect Quinn from him in his enraged state that I'd ended up hurting her. I'd smacked her across the face hard enough to make her cheek bleed. That had been an accident, no more purposeful than Lance's actions, but the thought of her bruised face still made me cringe inwardly.

"I was the one who made her feel unwelcome," I said, refusing to accept the out Torrent had offered me. I was the only one responsible for my own behavior. "Maybe she shouldn't *want* me back after the way I treated her. I damaged her body, and then I hurt her heart when I should have been there for her in every possible way."

Torrent's mouth twisted. "I don't think she would see it that way. But we don't need to harp on it right now. She can tell you herself when we're able to get back to her. Why don't you fill us in on why you've come out to the sea? This is more my domain than yours."

"I enjoy coastal terrain as well as higher elevations," I informed him, but I welcomed the chance to get back to actual work. Work that didn't require thinking about my past mistakes.

I turned back toward the water, giving myself a brief shake to remove the lingering droplets from my fall. "There's something here that was also in the mountain camp. Something that shouldn't have been there. I'm trying to figure out what it is."

Lance cocked his head. "What kind of thing?"

"That's what I'm trying to figure out. All I have is the scent..."

I prowled farther along the coastline, inhaling deeply. Lance and Torrent followed at a respectful distance, Torrent slipping into the shadows to travel more easily where his ruined legs wouldn't hold him back. My companions let me slip back into my zone of concentration.

That was better. I couldn't have explained the smell I was tracking anyway.

After several minutes of walking and pausing to lean closer to various spots on the ground, a sharper tendril of the odor reached my nose. I jerked around and spotted a scattering of bones in a notch between two of the rocks. As I bent to examine them, the scent grew even thicker, solidifying my certainty.

A jolt of memory passed through me—snatching a silvery body out of the water, digging my gargoyle teeth into its juicy flesh. A fish. It was a particular type of fish I'd found especially delicious and also enjoyable to catch.

Spinning, I caught a brief glimpse of a silvery body flashing amid the strands of seaweed farther from the shore. I'd only discovered them because I needed to do my hunting so far from human sight. They seemed to be particularly shy of people—I'd never noticed them when I'd lurked in mortal-made harbors.

But they were definitely an ocean fish. Why had I smelled them up in the mountains of Utah?

One of the shadowkind staying there must have brought them—for a snack or some other purpose? It would have had to be for one of the leaders, wouldn't it? I couldn't imagine them giving leave for their underlings—the ones supporting them of their free will and the ones they'd ensorcelled into helping them—to wander off to the ocean just to hunt down a particular delicacy to consume on their own.

Why hadn't the boss gone down to the ocean himself and simply had his meals there? Had it been difficult for him to make the trip? Had he enjoyed ordering his minions to do his bidding?

None of this made any particular sense to me. But I knew that this ocean was the same ocean as on the western side of the United States, the one by the beach of Rollick's hotel. It wouldn't have been *too* long an expedition from the mountain camp to reach the right waters if this sort of fish lived on both sides of the sea.

"One of the fiends from the camp was bringing fish from the ocean up to the lake," I said to my companions. "They couldn't have stayed alive there. I assume they were to eat. I don't know if the being that requested them *needs* them or not... but maybe we can assume it wouldn't go too far inland, if it prefers that meal so much?"

Torrent reappeared, picking up one of the bones I'd seen. "We have another piece of data to work with, anyway," he said. "Can you catch one of those fish for me now? Without killing it, if you can, since there's no need. I'd like to see exactly what it is so I'll recognize it in the future in living form as well as post-meal."

My renewed sense of purpose wrapped around me, lifting my spirits. Just for that moment, I could believe that

I might deserve the chance to earn back Quinn's trust after all. I was defending her in my own way, with every possible effort I could put toward keeping her safe, no matter how far from her I was.

"Give me a minute," I told Torrent, and launched myself over the ocean with a flap of my wings.

CHAPTER TEN

Quinn

For the past month, my life had kept getting more surreal, to the point that I was starting to expect that at any second I'd step through a doorway into an Escher painting. Like at the moment, I was somehow sitting on a smooth leather seat in the back of a fancy Cadillac, eating drive-through hamburgers for lunch with a millennia-old demon after fleeing for my life from a psychotic monster-enslaving cult.

It was hard to remember what it'd been like living a *normal* existence, without monsters or magic or death even more imminent than the possibility of a failing heart.

Rollick, through some supernatural ability he hadn't disclosed, managed to eat his entire hamburger and a carton of fries without getting a single drop of ketchup anywhere on his immaculate suit. I was still halfway through my burger because I was eating much more carefully, trying not to look like a slob, although I was starving. This was my first meal since he'd grabbed me from the forest near the enclave.

By the time we'd made it back to the car he'd stashed beyond their territory, I'd been so exhausted from the stress and the late night that he'd ordered me to sleep in the back while he drove us farther away. When I'd woken up to the morning sun beaming through the windows, he'd directed me to a motel room in whatever city we'd ended up in so I could shower and start to feel like a somewhat normal human being again. It wasn't until after we'd grabbed this quick meal and driven out to a secluded lane amid more hilly countryside that he'd allowed me to give my account of what I'd seen last night.

The hearty meatiness of the burger had fortified me, although my appetite was waning as I got to the most gruesome parts of the story. "They'd brought three people —I don't know where from. A woman around my age, a little girl, and I didn't see the third one because I couldn't help trying to intervene with the kid and they caught me then. The sorcerers sent them out into the clearing and the guy just tore into them like he was a rabid animal."

Rollick let out a soft huff, leaning against the door across from me in a casual pose that should have clashed with his formal clothing. "That's what they think shadowkind are—rabid animals. Monsters. It's not as if they're alone."

I grimaced and set aside the rest of my burger in its wrapper. "Most people don't even know you really *exist.* They're only going by stories and imagination. It's not their fault they don't know better. The sorcerers are interacting with actual shadowkind all the time. They should be able to see you're more than that."

"It wouldn't really be in their best interests to see anything worth respecting in us, though, would it?" The demon cocked an eyebrow. "That might put a damper on their enthusiasm for subjecting us to their whims."

I couldn't deny that he had a point. "It's still not right," I muttered, hugging myself. "Is it strange that those rites work at all? I thought you said that no shadowkind can manipulate other shadowkind. So how could something in them give humans that power?"

"I've heard of other ways a merging of human and shadowkind can create more than either was on its own," Rollick said. "That phoenix you met is an example. I'd guess that sorcerous power is generated by an interaction between the shadowkind qualities and whatever you mortals possess, transforming something inside you into an entirely new thing."

"A horrific thing. And then the shadowkind that kill those sorcerers are able to take that thing into themselves."

"So all available evidence suggests."

I sighed. "What do we do now?"

Rollick hummed to himself. "Well, I don't think we should stick around Norway now that they'll have their enslaved creatures on the hunt for us. I think I've found out all I can here about the beings we're up against. What matters more is what that villainous duo is getting up to right now."

"Back in the US. You think we should go home?"

He shrugged. "I think if we want to stop the menaces as soon as possible, we have to be where they are. And possibly the maniacal mortals here have given us some strategies for improving our chances of victory. You mentioned that the one who was mentoring you said that the rites could expand your powers just as they activate them for total novices, didn't you?"

At the recognition of where he might be going with that line of conversation, my spine stiffened. "She made it sound like that's the case. But what does it matter? I'm not going to murder and consume some innocent creature or run around attacking people just in case it gives a little more umph to my powers."

"I think we can assume that the attacking part isn't necessary," Rollick said with a chuckle. "Just their misinterpretation of what it takes to connect with the shadowkind experience on a visceral level. The absorbing of shadowkind essence might give your magic a boost that could tip the balance in the battles ahead, though."

I glowered at him, my stomach twisting. "I'm *not* killing some little beast the way they did. It was awful. And we don't even know for sure what effect it'll have on me. It didn't sound like the sorcerers usually did rites for people who already have the talent."

Rollick studied me with an intentness in his dark blue eyes that set me on guard. "To be clear, though, your main objection is to the slaughter of a random creature? If we happened to have some shadowkind essence on hand that you could drink in without any unwilling being suffering, you wouldn't object to giving it a go?"

"I—I don't know. I guess not." If it could make the difference between stopping more suffering, more murders, and whatever else our enemies had planned, then how could I say no? "But you don't have it bottled somewhere, do you? And if you're thinking you're going to wait until Torrent and the others can come back, if they even decide to come when they can, and convince them to—"

"Oh, I don't have any interest in waiting that long." Rollick grinned. "Especially when we already have everything we need."

Before I could process what he'd meant by that, he was already moving—launching himself forward across the seat as if he'd been braced to pounce the whole time rather than lounging there all nonchalantly. I barely had a chance to flinch before he was grabbing me by the waist and yanking me under him.

My head bumped into the soft padding of the seat, my breath jolting out of me. Rollick loomed over me, trapping most of my body in place with his powerful legs. His clothes were rippling away as his massive demonic form emerged. The heat of him washed over me, almost smothering.

Panic sliced through my chest. I whipped up my arms in an effort I already knew would be futile, smacking against his muscular torso to try to dislodge him. "Don't—what are you doing—get off—"

Rollick's veneers had already wisped away to reveal the jagged demonic teeth underneath. Without paying my protests the slightest attention, he brought his arm to his mouth and gouged open his own wrist all the way to the bone. Then he slammed the wound down over my lips, cutting off my voice.

Smoky blood poured out of him into me so fast it was congealing in my throat before I'd even managed to shove at his arm. Rollick snatched my wrists with his other hand and pinned them to my chest. When I tried to shut my mouth against the flow of his shadowy essence, he pushed his limb even farther between my lips where I couldn't dislodge it. It was either suck down the smoky substance or suffocate.

I dragged a ragged breath through my nose and sputtered and gagged, but the billows of essence seeped down my throat into my lungs and stomach. It prickled through my nerves with an electric tingling everywhere it touched. The shadowkind blood didn't actually taste smoky, I realized as I struggled against Rollick's hold. It was cool and misty and laced with flavors that made me think of an autumn forest at night.

My muscles strained, and the demon gave me a tight smile, his ruddy demonic face gazing down at me with a flicker of fire in his darkened eyes. "There's a hell of a lot more essence in me than some little beastie. And the sooner your powers are up to snuff, the sooner we can deal with the real brutes we're up against. You don't have to let your morals stir up doubts this way. I made the decision for you. It'll be over faster if you relax and let it happen."

Maybe he was right, but my body still wanted to resist. Tension coiled all through my muscles. I tried to wrestle my arms away from his grasp ineffectually.

But even as I squirmed with defiance, a different sensation was sweeping through me. With each gulp of Rollick's essence, the prickles in my nerves were softening into something almost giddy.

I wanted to... I wanted to run and rove and feel how fast my limbs could move. I wanted to stretch my body, lunge and leap. There was so much—so much I could do. Gravity didn't hold me back. I was strong, powerful, impervious. Nothing could keep me down.

Was this how the initiate had felt in the clearing as he'd absorbed so much of that creature's hazy blood? And then the sorcerers' chants and all the preparation he'd done had made him turn those urges into something viciously murderous. Or maybe he'd been a brutal soul all along.

I didn't feel any inclination toward violence, only power and freedom. But I was restrained still—fixed in place by the weight over me. I inhaled, drawing even more of the smoky torrent into my lungs, and a weird tremor of sensation rippled through my senses.

I was aware, suddenly, of the rise and fall of Rollick's breaths. Of the fragility he noticed in my mortal body and how carefully he was holding his own much beefier form to avoid hurting me. Of a flicker of admiration at the fight I'd put up even as he was annoyed that I couldn't just accept what he'd done.

It was his essence I was drinking in, and more of who he was coursed into me alongside it. It woke up a hunger to have even more of him than that. To take in all of the hauntingly impressive body I'd seen on full display weeks ago, to merge with him in every possible way.

I'd been attracted to Rollick before. It wasn't a totally unfamiliar sensation. But my uncertainties about his motives and my knowledge of the screwed-up things he definitely had done had made it easy to ignore those impulses. Now, my mind seemed to have detached from my body. It was floating away, worries and longings dispersing in opposite directions, my physical presence taking its own initiative.

My hips arched up. My cunt bumped against the bulge of what I knew was not just one but two cocks, one over top of the other. A fresh wave of need rushed through me, sweeping away more of my distant protests.

No, I yelled at myself from wherever that part of me was floating now, but even more of me called out, *Yes!*

My muscles loosened beneath Rollick, and he relaxed his grip on me, his own breath quickening with a flare of desire I felt with the flow of his essence. My hand slipped free and reached to trail down the planes of his naked chest. My hips lifted toward him again, beckoning, practically begging.

The demon let out a growl. He dipped his head, his wrist still clamped over my mouth, and buried his face against the crook of my neck. His hot breath washed over my skin, and a needy whimper reverberated out of me. Every inch of me was on fire with him pressing so close. I wrapped my arm around his shoulder to tug him even nearer.

"You want this now, do you?" Rollick murmured in a dark, velvety voice that shivered through every cell. "A little taste, and you realized how much you were missing out on. That's my sweet sorcerer. Let me hear you say it, Quinn."

He eased his wrist away, and my lips parted as if seeking to gulp down even more of the smoky blood he'd poured into me. My thoughts were jumbled, the giddying hunger scattering every other concern. The only sound that came out of me was a moan.

I slid my hands down Rollick's body again, but his form had gone still over me. I rocked upward impatiently as he gazed down at me with an impenetrable expression. His essence was still gushing through the enclosed space of the car from the wound he'd given himself, but he barely seemed bothered by it. I had the vague sense that I should have been wondering how much he could afford to lose, but that worry drifted away.

He was so close and yet not close enough.

"Quinn," Rollick said, softer than before, "tell me what you want."

Why was he making this so hard? "I—I—" I managed to get out, but the craving seemed to choke me. "Please," I mumbled desperately, the burning need driving my hips toward him again.

He wanted it too. The hunger thrummed through him loudly enough that I could taste it even without the direct stream of his blood filling my lungs. But a hint of hesitation had risen up alongside it. Something cool and unyielding. I didn't like it.

"This isn't you," he muttered. "You're drunk on the stuff." His head bowed, and for a second I thought he might kiss me, but his mouth never quite reached mine. Then he pushed himself off me.

In the first moment when his body pulled away from mine, I cried out at the loss of contact. But as the cooler air slipped in between us, my gaze slid to the window, and the other desires that had gripped me first raced back into my mind. I scrambled up onto my hands and knees and peered through the window at the landscape that called me to run riot through it.

"I don't think letting you loose like this would be a good idea," Rollick said from behind me, his voice carefully even. When I glanced back at him, he was back in humanesque form, wrapping a bandage around his wrist to stem the flow of smoky blood while he healed. One of my hands lifted to scratch at the window, more wildness coursing through me.

Rollick shook his head. "I'm not losing you that way either." He rummaged around and found the blanket he'd given me to sleep with, wrapping it around me. The weight of it dampened my restlessness just a little.

"Just stay here until you come down from it," he said. "I'm going to find us the nearest airport. And then we'll see whether I've accomplished anything other than making a total mess out of things."

CHAPTER ELEVEN

Quinn

The dirt lane through the misty fields ended at a stand of trees. Rollick parked his new car there and got out without a word. I followed on the passenger side, taking a deep breath of the late summer warmth.

It was funny how the scenery in front of us could look so similar to the terrain on the other side of the Atlantic but feel so different at the same time. Although I wasn't sure I was all that much safer now that I was back in my home country.

"Are you sure this is a good idea?" I asked Rollick, resting my hand on the sun-heated glass of the window. "I mean, the big bad duo that wants to capture me—or their minions, anyway—must have been here just a few days ago."

Rollick shrugged in his typical languid way. "That's exactly why we should check out the scene of the crime. They might have left some useful trace of their presence behind. I doubt there'll be anyone all that important still lurking around." He shot me a grin that was a little more subdued than I was used to, though that didn't stop his face from being as stunning as ever. "You've got me here to protect you, fair maiden."

All of his grins and smirks had been toned down ever since our encounter back in Norway two days ago when he'd forced his smoky blood down my throat—and I'd gone wild with it. Since I'd woken up from the essence-induced stupor, he hadn't referenced what'd happened, and all his other behavior toward me had remained unchanged. I'd kept my mouth shut about the whole thing because even thinking about talking about it made my cheeks flare so sharply I was afraid they'd literally ignite.

Like the time when I'd burst into tears in front of him, the demon seemed dedicated to pretending my momentary lapse in control had never happened. Which probably worked out in his favor at least as much as mine since it was his fault it'd happened in the first place.

"I think I'd like to be able to rely on myself too," I said, and jerked my chin toward the trunk. "You picked up all our stuff that you'd stashed away before we left, didn't you? The crossbow we got from the sorcerers in Arizona is still in there?"

Rollick arched his eyebrows, but he went around to open the trunk. "As you wish. You did seem to have gotten the hang of it when we stormed their camp. I doubt we'll encounter anywhere near as many beasties here."

"Better safe than sorry," I muttered.

He handed over the small weapon which was at least as much a gun as it was a crossbow and then stepped back so I could collect a handful of the slim silver-and-iron bolts that served as its arrows. Not much could stop a shadowkind creature in its tracks, but the combination of metals that were noxious to them did the trick well enough that even a powerful being like Rollick didn't want to handle objects that size.

I loaded three of the bolts into the crossbow and adjusted my grip, refamiliarizing myself with the weapon, which was about as long as my forearm. Its weight put a slight strain on my bicep, but I found it comforting all the same. "All right, let's go."

Rollick led the way along a foot path through the trees, and I was happy to let him go first. If we encountered any aggressive creatures, he was better equipped to fend them off than I was, crossbow or not.

At first the stretch of forest looked normal enough, but as we walked deeper, I spotted vicious gouges in the bark of the trunks up ahead. Near their roots, chunks of earth had been torn by what I had to imagine were thick claws. I braced myself for the sight we'd discover on the other side.

Word had gotten out through the shadowkind communities that another sorcerer family had been struck down while we'd been dealing with the enclave's sick rituals over in Norway. Rollick had heard about it within a few hours of our touching down back on American soil and decided it was as good a place as any to resume our stateside investigations.

I couldn't say I was super enthusiastic about the trip,

but when the alternative was probably searching out random shadowkind for me to test my possibly enhanced sorcery on, I wasn't going to complain.

Because of sorcerers' frequent preference for setting up their homes far from civilization, no one in the human community had discovered the murders yet. We came out into a wide glade that showed no sign of police presence. More claw marks had churned up bits of grass and wildflowers. A long single-story house with patches of moss on its stone walls stood at the far end of the open space, the door closed but the windows shattered.

Even from this far away, a rancid smell reached my nose. A shiver ran down my spine.

Rollick glanced over at me. "I'd say you can wait out here, but I'd rather not leave you on your own for reasons already discussed."

"I'll be fine," I said, clenching my jaw against the queasiness already stirring inside me.

He scanned our surroundings as we walked over to the door, his gait casual but his eyes alert. Apparently he didn't see any reason for worry, because he didn't hesitate. At the door, he made a gesture with his hand, and there was a snapping sound from within. He'd used his demonic magic to break the lock.

"You couldn't have just willed it to slide open?" I asked him.

"Breaking is simpler. I don't think the owners are in a condition to be concerned about their security any longer."

He had a point there. We stepped inside, the smell thickening enough that I tugged my shirt up over my face so I could get a little relief by breathing through the fabric.

This family appeared to have been made up of five people. We found an elderly-looking couple first, slumped and bloody in the kitchen. Then a younger man and woman in the dining room, where it looked as if they'd tried to use the table as a barricade. When we came around the flipped-over slab of wood, a smaller body was sprawled right at its base—a toddler so mangled I couldn't even tell if it'd been a boy or a girl.

My stomach heaved at the sight. I jerked down my shirt just in time to vomit my lunch onto the floorboards. Acid seared the back of my mouth.

I'd been horrified by what the sorcerers in the enclave had been doing to activate their powers, but some of the shadowkind *were* exactly the sort of monsters those people believed them to be. I guessed that unlike the little boy they'd stolen before, the villainous duo had decided this child was too young to be of any possible use to them.

Rollick didn't comment on my reaction. His mouth set in an expression of distaste that I could tell was aimed at the carnage rather than me. He turned away from the bodies, cocked his head, and knelt in the corner to examine a different spot on the hardwood floor that looked exactly the same as the rest of the boards to my eyes.

I gulped a little water from the bottle in my bag to wash out the sour flavor in my mouth, careful not to swallow so much that I'd set off my stomach again. "What are you looking at?" I asked a little hoarsely.

Rollick touched the boards and sniffed his fingers. "Water damage."

"And that's important?"

"It contributes to the larger picture."

He didn't seem inclined to say more yet, and I wasn't in the mood to badger him. I left the dining room behind to see what I might find in the rest of the house, farther from the awful spectacle.

I'd only made it two steps down the hall when a shadowy blur flung itself at me from a doorway up ahead.

A yelp jolted from my throat, but thankfully my reflexes kicked in even as my nerves jumped with surprise. I jerked up the crossbow and squeezed the trigger in one swift movement, throwing myself backward at the same time.

The silver-and-iron bolt hit the creature that'd sprung at me as it shifted into physical form, catching it square in the chest. With a pained snarl, it crumpled on the floor, smoke wafting up from the wound. The sight reminded me of the enclave's rites and made my stomach lurch all over again.

A different, distant sensation rippled through me: a flicker of consternation and fear. It arrived in tandem with Rollick rushing into the hall.

That'd been happening here and there since he'd fed me his filmy essence, the stuff that shadowkind considered blood. Just as I'd sensed his lust and hesitation in the car, I sometimes caught a whiff of his other emotions, maybe only when they were particularly strong. Which wasn't very often, but it was still a bit unnerving having an internal tie to the demon.

I wasn't sure whether he was aware of that consequence of his force-feeding. It hadn't seemed like a good time to bring it up yet. Being aware of his true emotions could turn out to be a good if small advantage to have in my back pocket.

He was definitely concerned about my current well-being. He stalked over and toed the slumped creature with his loafer. It cringed and groaned.

"Good shot," he said evenly. "We're not getting anything useful out of a lesser beast like this." Then he raised his foot and slammed it down on the thing's head, crushing its skull.

I dragged in a breath and loaded another bolt into the crossbow, not wanting to reach into the creature's disintegrating body to retrieve the one I'd shot. "See," I said, summoning more bravado than I felt. "I can look after myself."

Rollick shot me a look somewhere between amused and annoyed. "Not against every being that's been here. But I think anything larger than this is long gone."

I held my crossbow at the ready as we searched the rest of the house, Rollick never letting me get out of his sight. My heart thumped at a faster pace, but I couldn't say I enjoyed the tension that'd built up inside me. My thrill-seeker side was getting exhausted by all the close calls I'd had in the past month. Even it wouldn't have minded a break to just chill for a little while.

The place didn't hold anything else all that useful, especially now that I'd gotten a much more in-depth glimpse of the inner workings of sorcery at the enclave. I didn't lower the crossbow until we made it back to the car, and then I brought it into the front seat with me, feeling a little better having it within reach.

"Are you going to tell me what picture you've been putting together?" I asked as Rollick started the engine. "Didn't you already figure out we're dealing with a behemoth?" I had no idea just how bad that was, but the name alone and remembering the way Rollick had talked about it sent a fresh chill through my veins.

Rollick paused for a moment, and I caught another quaver of emotion from him: a deep uneasiness that I didn't like at all. He wasn't half as confident about our chances as he'd been acting.

"I've become increasingly sure that the other half of this dynamic deadly duo is a creature of the sea," he said.

"Like Torrent?"

The demon snorted. "If he were like Torrent, we wouldn't have anything to worry about. Torrent isn't the type to go around wreaking havoc. No, considering the powers at play and the company he's keeping—and a few details that've been adding up... I think our behemoth has allied himself with a leviathan. Possibly the only leviathan, since like the behemoth I've only ever heard of one."

A deeper chill washed over me. I resisted the urge to hug myself, not wanting Rollick to see how unnerved I was. "And we're taking on these two one-of-a-kind monsters on our own."

Rollick's mouth twisted for a second, the only outward sign of his discomfort. "I have some ideas about that. Don't worry yourself about it for now. I won't be putting anything in motion until we reach our next destination anyway."

I tipped my head back against the seat and closed my eyes, but I was too keyed up to have any hope of dozing, even though last night's sleep hadn't been all that restful. The pangs of emotion I'd gotten from the demon, especially his concern when he'd heard me being attacked, tugged at my mind. Suddenly the weight of all the things we hadn't talked about pressed in on me too heavily for me to keep my mouth shut.

"We haven't talked about what happened the other day. In the car. When you—"

"I remember," Rollick cut in, but he sounded more resigned than irritated by me bringing up the subject. "I didn't think you wanted to talk about it."

"I'm not sure *want* is the right word." I hesitated, staring at the road ahead. "I didn't want to react the way I did then either. Your shadowkind blood seemed to bring out these urges, and I couldn't get control of myself." My cheeks started to burn, but the worse sensation was the guilt clogging my throat.

I hadn't discussed exclusivity with the three men I'd fallen for. They hadn't minded that they were sharing my attentions with each other. And maybe, after the way I'd sent them off, they didn't even consider themselves my... boyfriends, or whatever I should call them. But it would still have felt like cheating to get it on with any other person —or being.

Rollick kept his voice light but steady with none of his usual sly teasing. "I know. I'm not sorry about feeding you my essence, because it could make a difference in the long run, and your only objections had nothing to do with the situation I created. But I am sorry that my actions had effects we weren't prepared for. I had no intention of messing with your mind or your inhibitions."

How could he have known? It wasn't as if he'd gone around feeding his essence to mortals on a regular basis. He sounded like he meant the partial apology, which was as much of an apology as I could imagine him ever offering.

Of course he wasn't sorry about the other part. I wasn't even sure I was angry at him about the rest, since maybe it would be better that he'd juiced up my powers—if he actually had. I'd known that might be the right call, and I'd been having trouble making it, so he'd done it for me.

"You've always said I'd decide to hook up with you eventually," I said, taking on a similarly breezy tone. "You didn't take me up on it while you had the chance."

Rollick let out a huff. "I don't think you being addled out of your mind counts as a real chance—or a real decision." He glanced over at me. Even seeing him just from the corner of my eye, I could feel the intensity of his gaze. "When—if—we go there, it'll be because all of you is on board, not just a burst of hormones you're too drunk to control. I have no trouble finding fully willing sexual partners. Even as a monster, I find those much more satisfying."

"Ah." My cheeks heated more, and I didn't know what else to say. I couldn't help noticing that he'd revised his "when" to an "if" despite his previous insistence that I'd eventually jump his bones. "Well... that's good to know."

The demon chuckled, and the tension in the car subsided. His smile turned sly again. "Maybe what I have in store for you next will make up a little for my miscalculation."

I raised my eyebrows at him. "That sounds ominous."

"Just wait and see."

It didn't take all that long to figure out where we were going once we got onto a major freeway with regular signs.

Rollick set a course toward Boston, and I sat up a little straighter as its downtown high rises came into view in the distance.

"Why Boston?" I asked, even as my pulse gave a giddy skip.

"You didn't get to come to Berlin with me, so I figured why not a different B city." Rollick tipped his head toward the cityscape. "From what I've seen, it's got one of the most interesting mixes of buildings in this country."

I doubted that was the only reason we were making the trip, but I wasn't going to complain. I could already pick out the Hancock amid the shorter buildings, its glossy sides reflecting the blue sky and tufts of clouds. And I'd love to see the stark modern design of the John F Kennedy Library up close after we'd talked about it in one of my college courses last year. I'd hoped to do a little road trip touring various cities around the country one summer, and Boston had been near the top of the list.

"Thank you," I said.

The demon shrugged. "You've been through a lot. You should get a chance to enjoy yourself a little along the way. Maybe your life's gotten off course, but that doesn't mean you're totally giving up what matters to you."

I supposed it mattered to *him* that I was relatively content so that I'd continue going along with his schemes. But I couldn't help saying, "It's not really the same, you know. It's not like all I wanted out of life was to look at cool buildings and admire them."

"Isn't that what those classes you've regretted missing are all about?"

"Yeah, but..." I gazed at the skyline we were approaching, and a knot formed in my chest. My voice dipped. "I wanted to make my own mark too. To add something to places like this. Like I told you before, great architecture isn't just about making something easy on the eyes. I wanted to create something that would keep inspiring people or at least making them feel something... after I'm gone. But I guess there isn't a whole lot of chance of that now."

Rollick frowned, an expression that sat oddly on his stunning face. Another waft of uneasiness tingled into me from him. "There's no reason to assume that."

I lifted my chin, stuffing down the pain that came with my growing sense of resignation. "I'm just trying to be realistic, seeing how things have gone so far. It was a long shot anyway, given my condition. I'm running out of time. But if I can save some people from *dying*, that matters a lot too. And I appreciate the chance to get to be inspired myself, even if I won't get to do a whole lot with that inspiration. So thank you."

The demon was silent for a long moment. Then he shot another grin at me. "Don't give up yet. That's not your style at all, is it? You still have your sketch pad. Consider me your professor for the week. I want to see two new designs by the time we're through here."

I rolled my eyes at him, though a flutter ran through my chest at the gesture. "Oh, first it's about me enjoying myself, and now you're assigning me homework?"

"Consider it my attempt at replicating the 'Quinn's real life' experience," Rollick said, and then sobered slightly. "It might not be such a long shot anyway, at least not any more than it already was. I've got my own plans while we're here."

Color me not at all surprised. "And what are those?"

He made a vague gesture with his hand. "There's a significant rift that leads to the shadow realm in one of the city parks. Big enough that one more being passing through shouldn't draw any attention. I'm going to go have a chat with the Highest."

My brow knit. "The Highest?" Something about the term sounded familiar—had he mentioned them before?

"The oldest and most powerful shadowkind," Rollick explained. "They're basically mountains in themselves, looming off in the deeper reaches of the realm. They themselves never venture mortal-side, but they've got a lot of lackeys at their beck and call, and they don't look kindly on any of us interfering with human society too aggressively. From what I heard, they've already cracked down on the behemoth once."

I perked up. "And you think they'd intervene again now?"

Rollick's mouth formed a tight smirk. "I believe our behemoth and leviathan have made more than enough trouble for the Highest to think it's worth stepping in. And if they send out the troops, all our trouble should soon be over."

CHAPTER TWELVE

Lance

We tumbled through the rift over a series of sprawling green hills that sent a crisp herbal smell into the air. I soared down through the shadows and twisted in a last-second flip to land in a patch of gloom at the edge of a boulder, enjoying the sensation of moving through the fresh mortal-realm air even in my invisible state.

I spun around to face Torrent and Crag as they descended the short drop from the rift after me. I had the vague sense that it was night in this area, but some sunlight still gleamed along the horizon.

"This is that Norway place?" I asked.

Torrent nodded, studying the landscape around us. "The country where Quinn thought the special group of sorcerers she heard about might be based. It's not that big a country. If we were able to come out here without her command pushing us back—"

I perked up with a burst of eager energy. "Her orders have worn off!"

Crag made one of his usual grim expressions. "Or she's left, so we're not so close to her that it's a problem. How long has it been since she planned to come here?"

Torrent hummed to himself. "I'm not sure. Let's find the nearest human habitation—there'll be some clue there."

I never paid much attention to the passing of days anyway, and it was particularly hard to keep track in the shadow realm, where there was no night and day, only that endless sort of twilight. It was good to be back. Good to think that maybe I could return to Quinn soon... even if the memory of her aiming that twisted power at me sent a shudder right down the center of my body.

But even as I tensed up inside, the ache of being without her pealed louder. I *needed* her, needed to be stroking her smooth skin and nuzzling her soft hair, needed to hear her gleeful laugh and the gentle voice she used when she was worried about me. I needed to make sure none of the beasties out there had gotten their claws into her in a much more vicious way than I ever would.

I needed to understand why she'd forced me to leave. How could she have turned that awful magic on me when she'd been so upset about how others had done the same thing? How could she think *I* needed protection, like Torrent said she must have believed?

I would get answers. I leapt after the others through the

swaths of darkness, doing my best to ignore the jitters passing through my nerves.

There were other sorcerers around here somewhere. Powerful ones, maybe ones who taught new sorcerers how to bend our wills and enslave us. The thought set my fangs gnashing and my ghostly claws digging into the earth, and at the same time it made me want to whirl around and dash as far as I could get from any of them.

No. Torrent had found me, and we'd found Crag, and we would stick together. Once we'd just worked together, but now we were something more than that. We were tied to one another by our feelings for Quinn, but our association went beyond that aspect too.

I liked them. I trusted them. They'd helped me when no other being would have, and I'd helped them when I could as well.

I'd also hurt them. My gaze slid to the impressions of Torrent's tentacles moving through the dusk, knowing that one of the tips was mangled beyond repair by my fangs and fiery breath, and a fresh surge of horror welled up inside me.

I shoved it away and pushed onward as if I could run away from that memory too.

Quinn hadn't blamed me. Torrent and Crag hadn't either. But how could I not blame myself? It'd been me, too weak to fight off the sorcery that'd slammed into my brain. Me who hadn't been prepared enough to fend it off. My fangs and claws that'd slashed at both of them.

I would have killed *Quinn* if they hadn't stopped me. If—

I stiffened up just as I started to fling myself at a shrub

we were passing with the urge to savage its brambles. To show I decided how I wielded my body now. I yanked myself away with gritted teeth, checking whether Torrent had noticed my lapse.

Going around destroying things and picking fights didn't help anything. I *knew* that, even if part of me still wanted to do it. My limbs itched with the uneasy restlessness.

"There's a cottage," Torrent said, veering to the right.

I trailed behind him and the gargoyle, burning off as much of the anxious energy as I could by taking unnecessary twists and turns to stretch my body. At one point I nearly crashed into a mortal animal that sensed me even through the shadows and hissed with a flash of pointed teeth. I snarled in return and was about to launch myself at it when the cuff of Crag's fist against my shoulder brought me back to the task at hand.

"Torrent's going in. Come on."

Chagrinned, I hustled after him to the wall of the cottage. It must have been night, because snores were carrying through the one window that was cracked ajar. Torrent had already vanished inside.

I circled the cottage, eyeing the weather-worn walls and the bed of flowers out front, but I'd only completed the circuit twice when Torrent emerged. He shook himself, flexing his tentacles. I could tell from his voice that he wasn't pleased.

"It's been more than a week. Plenty of time for her to have come and gone."

He paused, and I immediately filled in what he hadn't said with my mind. There'd been plenty of time for the sorcerers to have done something to Quinn that'd take her *out* of this world too.

"If she died, her magic would die too," I said, my lips drawing back with a growl. "When was the last time we felt it repel us?"

Crag drew his massive form taller as if to command our attention. "We can't make any assumptions from that. Hundreds of miles could be a fairly small distance compared to the entire mortal realm. It'd be easy for us not to have stumbled on that boundary."

"We need to be sure. We—"

"We will be sure," Torrent said in his firm but even way, so calm the growl faded in my throat. He rubbed his jaw thoughtfully. "If she came here and already saw the sorcerers or never found them at all and then left, she's most likely gone back to America, where she's most at ease. And where Rollick's most current resources are. That's where our enemies were making trouble. Once she finished with her investigations here, why wouldn't she return?"

That made sense. I spun around tightly enough that I could have snapped at my own tail with my jaws. "Then we go to America and see if we feel her magic pushing us away. Or should *we* track down these sorcerers first?"

Just asking the question made my skin bunch up beneath my scales. How many beings did that group have under their control? Would they try to grab our minds too? I wanted to snarl at myself for suggesting it, and to slash my frustration into the earth, and—

"We don't know where to start beyond getting to this country," Torrent said. "If Quinn didn't find them, then I doubt we could, and if she did, then she's already got it covered. I say we head to Jacksonville first and work from there."

He glanced at us as if checking for our approval rather than insisting on the course of action. Crag rumbled his agreement. I blinked at Torrent and then nodded too, although I'd have gone along with whatever he suggested.

Torrent always had good ideas. I'd have followed him to track down those sorcerers if he'd felt we needed to... but I couldn't promise what I might have done to them if they'd come within reach of my claws.

"Good. Let's go, then." Torrent turned back toward the rift we'd emerged through.

Thankfully, moving in our shadow forms didn't take up much energy. We traveled across the rolling landscape, leapt up to the rift, and then darted through the hazy plains of the shadow realm until Torrent found another rift he was satisfied with. When we sprang through that one, we found ourselves on a beach with salty ocean air wafting over us and the sun just setting beyond the buildings on the western horizon.

This was the city where we'd first watched Quinn. Where she'd clambered to the top of those tall buildings and looked so pleased as she gazed out over the city.

A pang hit me: the longing to have joined her properly for one of those expeditions, to have listened to her tell me what she loved about the view. And maybe to have offered some additional thrills near one of those precarious edges.

Then I registered that we had come out, and we were here, and nothing was deflecting us. But that didn't mean anything. She simply might not be here.

"If she's still with Rollick, they could have gone back to

his favorite city," I pointed out, lashing my tail. It was hard to say whether I'd rather she was with Rollick for the protection he could provide or far from him after the ways he'd manipulated her in the past.

Torrent gestured to the rift. "We'll check there next. She said we had to stay 'hundreds' of miles away, so two hundred at a minimum. We'll keep moving from city to city until we've covered every two-hundred-mile span or encountered the barrier of the spell."

And if we never encountered it? I bit back the question as a renewed wave of restlessness swept through my body. How would we find her then? She could be anywhere. She might not even be alive. But Torrent and Crag knew that as well as I did. What was the point in saying it?

The ache of longing inside me spread through my chest with each rift we slipped through. The place called Los Angeles offered nothing of interest. We emerged into desert and forest and flat plains of golden grass, small towns and soaring cities.

My spirits had sunk when we approached what must have been the twelfth or so rift—and my senses jarred on the threshold.

My eyes widened. I whipped my head around to look at the others. "I can't go through. She must be close—close to wherever that rift leads to." And wherever that was, she was alive.

"I feel it too," Crag said gruffly.

A smile crossed Torrent's face briefly before he became stern again. "This one opens out to just north of New York City. She's in the northeast, anyway."

But we still had no idea exactly where. Or what she was

doing there. Or if she was okay or simply hanging on to the barest thread of life after some major injury.

I pushed closer to the rift, unable to deny the impulse to tear my way through to her. The magic that'd clamped around my skull with Quinn's sorcery-laced voice clutched me harder, but I thought I felt a bit of a wobble through it that hadn't been there when I'd tried to double back to her before. I shoved myself even farther into the rift and caught just a glimpse of blue sky before my body forced me to recoil.

"It's getting weaker!" I rasped with uncontainable excitement. "The spell is wearing off." Hopefully that didn't mean there was something wrong with her. We'd expected the sorcery to dwindle over time on its own, after all.

Torrent's eyes glimmered with a trace of hope. "Then we'll stay nearby, figure out the exact boundaries we can't cross, and see what we can do to help her in the meantime. There are other rifts in this area." He paused. "Will you be okay, Lance? It might be... frustrating knowing she's there but not being able to reach her."

I understood why he was asking. The memory lingered in the back of my head of how I'd been careening around the shadow realm when he'd found me. Even now, my muscles were straining to fight the magic keeping me from Quinn with all I had.

But if I made a disturbance in the mortal realm, that could be bad for her and the three of us too. It could draw our enemies' interest. Or sorcerers' attention. Or who knew what else.

I closed my eyes and stretched my limbs one at a time,

exerting my will over each of them in turn. The need to see Quinn, to hear the answers only she could give me, still jangled inside me, but I would control it. If I couldn't command *myself*, how would I ever stop sorcerers from enslaving me again?

"I'll be good," I said, and flashed a fanged grin at Torrent. "Let's get back to our woman."

CHAPTER THIRTEEN

Quinn

"What are you up to now?"

Rollick's voice came with a tone of amusement mixed with mild exasperation, but it was so startling I flinched and dropped my multitool on the floor of the hotel room. I snatched it up before twisting around to glower at him.

"You could start with a hello. Or knocking on the door instead of appearing in the middle of the room out of nowhere."

The demon propped himself against the wall, more mirth sparking in his dark blue eyes. "But where would the fun be in that? It's important that I keep you on your toes, or you might get complacent."

I snorted. "I don't think there's any chance of that

happening." I motioned to the table I'd been sitting at, where I'd eaten a hasty breakfast about an hour ago while awaiting Rollick's return. "I noticed the table was pretty wobbly, so I figured I'd see if I could do anything about that. It looks like whoever assembled it tightened a couple of the screws too much and then couldn't tighten the others enough. I've balanced it out pretty well."

Rollick arched his eyebrows at me. "And that was the best way you could find to pass the time?"

"At least it's accomplishing something," I retorted, and straightened up for just long enough to flop onto the edge of the bed. "It's hard to just zone out and watch whatever's on TV with everything else going on, and you *still* haven't let me have my computer back or any internet access on my phone. And you did insist that I shouldn't leave the hotel room while you were gone." Not that I'd disagreed with that part.

"I'm simply protecting you from yourself," he reminded me with a grin.

And protecting my family and anyone else I might have been tempted to contact, which was the only reason I hadn't kept badgering him about my devices. What could I really have done online when I couldn't safely talk to my parents or professors?

The thought of how worried Mom and Dad must be getting after so long without even a brief text made my stomach knot up. I couldn't do anything about that, though, so I did my best to focus on the situation at hand. Our current plans might mean I *could* talk to them safely again before too long. "Did you manage to meet with the Highest like you wanted?

Are they going to help stop the shadowkind we're up against?"

Rollick pushed off the wall, looking abruptly more serious. "It took some time, but I made my appeal, and eventually persuaded them of the severity of the concern." He let out a huff. "The Highest don't have the greatest sense of anything outside their own vast hollow in the shadow realm where everyone caters to their whims. But they really don't like the idea of anyone riling up the mortal realm enough that there's a chance their leisure might be disturbed."

I perked up. "They're sending someone, then? Their warriors or whatever?"

He nodded. "Through my connections, I've been able to locate another of the villainous duo's camps—the one it appears they've moved to for the most part since we crashed their party in Utah. I might have promised I'd help ensure the fiends they need to talk to are actually *there* when the warriors arrive tonight... although it'll be much easier to give that help if you're willing to flex those possibly enhanced sorcerer powers of yours."

A weird tingle passed beneath my skin, both uneasy and excited at once. I liked my powers even less after seeing how they must have been provoked by whichever of my heart donor's ancestors had undergone the rites generations ago. Still, it was hard not to enjoy the idea of taking down the monsters that'd spent so much of the past month hunting me down, either to kill me or enslave me themselves.

"I could do that," I said. "What exactly are you thinking we'd try?"

Rollick motioned for me to gather my things. "Once

we get out there, if our behemoth and leviathan aren't already conveniently on hand, we'll hunt down a lackey or two of theirs and give them instructions. A panicked message to deliver to their overlords or something along that line."

I frowned as I grabbed my backpack. "Aren't their lackeys already controlled by *their* sorcery? Would I be able to override that?"

"I'm not sure," the demon admitted. "I haven't associated with sorcerers enough before you to find out the details of how their magic interacts. But we can try if necessary, and if it doesn't work, they do seem to have quite a few hangers-on who are in it of their own free will, just to suck up to a powerful leader."

"All right." I swung my bag over my shoulder. "What are we waiting for, then?"

By the end of the day, maybe this horrible situation would be over.

When Rollick indicated that we were getting close to the new camp, I started to understand how it might not have been all that hard for him to locate it once he'd seen their first base of operations. The Oregon mountain range we were driving up to after our flight across the country was a lot greener than the desert terrain in Utah, cloaked with trees lower down and other vegetation higher up, but the peaks were equally imposing. And we hadn't passed any human habitations in half an hour.

"They like the high elevations—because people are less

likely to just wander through?" I said. "And they stay far away from any major hubs of human activity in general."

Rollick smiled thinly. "Those appear to be two out of the three key factors. The other is water. The leviathan must prefer the sea, and while he can't easily ensure he's close to that, he doesn't want to stay anywhere he can't get decently wet at all. There's a lake nestled up there just like at their other camp."

"You're sure they've been here recently?"

"Remember that I can hop across the country in a matter of minutes using the rifts," he said. "I've already been here to observe with my own eyes. There's definitely more shadowkind activity happening than I'd expect if the base were just on standby. And other than their detours for sorcerer-murdering, the head honchos have mostly been rounding up troops and hassling the local shadowkind along the west coast. They probably figure you're still around somewhere. Or that *I* am, and they'd like to murder me too."

He didn't sound all that concerned about the possibility, but I knew his nonchalance was at least partly an act. A few tremors of apprehension had passed from him into me during the drive out here.

He parked amid a stand of trees. "We'd better walk from here. It'll go a lot faster if you let me give you a ride like we did when we were fleeing the sorcerers' enclave."

He made the suggestion equally casually as if it was no big deal, but when I shrugged and said, "Okay," a flash of his surprise hit me. He was so good at keeping it cool that not a single hint of the emotion showed on his face.

I wasn't sure how much I trusted the demon now, but I

believed that he wasn't going to take some kind of physical advantage of me while he had me in his grasp. If he'd wanted to do that, he'd had the perfect opportunity already. And I'd rather get this expedition over with as quickly as possible with a minimum of hiking.

As Rollick shifted into his demonic form, I secured my shoulder bag against my back, the crossbow tied to it with Velcro strips I'd constructed that should allow me to snap it off with a sharp jerk if I needed it quickly. The beads of my silver-and-iron vest slid between the two thin layers of fabric I wore around it, and I glanced over at Rollick, who'd hunched his massive frame down in a kneeling position.

"The metals I'm wearing won't bother you?" I asked.

He waved off my worry with a clawed hand. "With them covered up so they aren't directly touching me, it's just a minor irritation. I'd be much more irritated by having to match your much slower mortal pace going up the mountain."

He grinned to soften the criticism, and I made a face at him as I walked over. "We can't all be super-powerful demons with giant legs. Just be glad I'm taking you up on the piggyback ride."

Rollick chuckled. "Believe me, I am."

As much as I was trying to stay focused on the task at hand and not any other emotions that'd been stewing inside me, an ache spread through my chest with the heft of Rollick's hands fixing me in place where I could loop my arms over his shoulders and around his neck. Crag had carried me when we'd gone up the mountainside in Utah. Not like this, but cradled in his arms like an embrace...

although an embrace he'd only given because he felt the alternatives were worse.

He'd hesitated to hold me close for any other reason in those last couple of days before I'd sent him and my other two shadowkind men away. His fear of hurting me accidentally had been too painful.

I swallowed the lump that'd risen in my throat and closed my eyes, but as Rollick loped through the trees at a swift pace, the thoughts kept filling my head anyway. What were my three shadowkind men doing now? Had my magical command really held firm for this long? Or had it worn off, but they'd decided I was right—that they were better off staying away from me? Especially when I'd proven that I was willing to use my sorcery against them.

With each day that passed without their return, it seemed more and more likely I was never going to see them again. It would have been nice if I could convince myself that possibility was for the best for all of us. The warriors sent by the Highest would deal with our enemies, I could go back to my regular life pretending I had no magic at all, and everything would be almost the same as it had been.

Almost, other than the fact that I'd know about the world beyond the one I'd been aware of before. I'd remember what it was like to be wrapped up in the affection and passion of three men totally unlike any human guy I'd ever met. I'd wanted to believe I could find some kind of balance between normalcy and my relationship with them... but now the choice was out of my hands.

Rollick's taut muscles flexed with smooth efficiency beneath me. His breaths stayed even despite his quick pace.

It wasn't long before the trees dwindled and then disappeared completely, leaving a grassy landscape scattered with shrubs and rocks. He set me down carefully, peering around in the descending evening. "Now to find our prey. Stay close to me."

He shrank back into human-like form as he stalked forward, and I hustled along at his flank, pulling my crossbow into my hands. The slope we were on was still steep enough that I broke out in a sweat after several steps. The demon moved onward with unwavering focus. Then, without warning, he leapt forward and vanished into the shadows.

I froze in place, but I didn't have time to even start to panic. A moment later, he sprang into sight clutching a slim, pale-skinned being around the neck. The thing was vaguely humanoid, but with long sloth-like arms and a round face that intensified the animalistic impression. It stood only about three feet tall.

It'd gone limp in Rollick's grasp. He loosened his hold just enough that it would be able to speak. "Are you patrolling around here because your masters burned their orders into your brain, or because you think you'll get some kind of favors from them for your loyalty?"

"I don't know what you're talking about," the creature whimpered in a nasal voice. "I'm just looking out for myself like we all do."

Rollick snorted and clenched his fingers again, making the thing gag. He glanced toward me. "That sounds like a free mind to me. We won't need to strain your powers after all."

I squared my shoulders. My stomach was churning, but

I'd come too far to back down now. "What should I have it tell the head honchos?"

The demon hummed to himself. "Let's stick with what's almost the truth—that the sorcerer Quinn has come to negotiate with them for her life. She'll be waiting by the lake. But she needs to talk to both of them before she'll come to any agreement."

I inhaled deeply and fixed my gaze on the sloth-like figure. Just thinking about using my powers sent the energy prickling through my limbs. A warbling sensation flooded my chest, more intense than I ever remembered it before. For a second, I lost my breath completely, and I hadn't even really started.

Oh, Rollick's essence had given my powers some kind of boost. I could already taste it in the electricity crackling up my throat onto my tongue.

I knew the creature in front of me even if I'd never encountered a being like it before. I could picture the conflicting desires tangled inside it—to roam wildly, to indulge its basic hungers, to ensure it allied itself with the right sorts of beings, to curry favor it might need later. It was wary of me now and frightened of Rollick but still confused. In the back of my mind, I could see how it would scurry across the terrain at my command.

The magic seared through my mouth and over my tongue. My lips parted, the language of sorcery spilling from my lips as I focused on the message I meant to convey.

You will go to the powerful shadowkind you serve. The two that give the final orders. You'll tell them that Quinn the sorcerer has come to their camp here to negotiate for her life. She's waiting by the lake. She will only speak with them if they both come. Go to them and deliver that message as quickly as you can.

Before, the casting of sorcery had left me drained. This time, as Rollick released the creature and it darted off exactly as I'd imagined, a fresh wave of energy surged through me. I was exhilarated rather than exhausted.

I could have commanded a hundred more beings like I had that one, I was suddenly sure.

Rollick was eyeing me. "Nicely done, sweet sorcerer."

I tamped down on my giddiness and met his gaze. "What happens if they get to the camp and find out I'm not there before the Highest's warriors get there?"

He offered a wry smile. "Not a problem. They're already here, waiting."

My head jerked around. "What? Where?"

"Closer to the camp, but they're aware we've arrived—and that we have no beef with them." He paused. "We could leave now and get you farther away where you'll be safer... or we could watch this villainous duo fall like they deserve."

The first option was probably the smart one, but the high of my casting and the thought of how much torment these monsters had put me through renewed my boldness. "I want to see them go down."

Rollick's smile widened. "Then come with me."

He led me along a winding path to a small outcropping of rock that looked down over a vast dip between a few different mountain peaks. Just as he'd said, there was a lake up here, at least a mile distant beyond my current perch, its waters turned black in the dimming light. We wouldn't be all that close to the battle.

"Will we definitely be able to see anything?" I couldn't help asking, hunkering down on the gritty stone. The wind whipped over us, chilly at this altitude. I reached to twine my hair into a hasty braid. "I mean, they might just fight in the shadows, right? And it's getting dark besides that."

Rollick sank down next to me with his legs sprawled out. "It's difficult to make as much of an impact as our shadowy selves. I expect the violence will be perfectly corporeal. And beings this powerful will bring out the special effects. You'll get your fill."

I glanced over at him, the angles of his striking face deepened by the falling dusk, and couldn't stop myself from thinking of the violence these fiends had dealt out toward him. Because of other choices I'd made.

"I'm sorry about your hotel," I said abruptly.

Rollick's gaze flicked to me. "What?"

I braced my hands against the cool rock, looking down at the rough surface. "It's my fault—that they realized you'd had me staying there. I set things up so there'd be a fight, and because of that you had to shut the hotel down."

The demon had obviously figured that out a long time ago. I didn't catch any hint of surprise over the revelation. He simply shrugged. "I'll go back when I can, or I'll set up a new one. It won't be the first time. I'm surprised you have any regrets—or is it only because your plan didn't work out the way you'd hoped?"

I grimaced. "I know the hotel was important to you. For good reasons—or reasons I understand, anyway. I don't hate you. I just—it was the only way I could see to get out of the situation. You'd already shown that you'd use every tactic you could to control me in your own way. I didn't know what else you might be capable of."

"Well, I'm glad I've risen above the level of outright hatred," Rollick said with a laugh. "And I don't suppose I can really blame you for thinking the worst of me when by your standards I had behaved pretty badly. But I don't think I've done too terrible a job of looking after you since then, have I?"

"No," I admitted. "You haven't."

The past several days when it'd just been the two of us had gone a lot less horribly than I'd been prepared for. Rollick had been a pretty decent traveling companion, and I'd been able to count on him when I'd needed someone to have my back. I still didn't really know how much he was doing this for his own selfish interests, but I was at least sure he didn't want to gain glory or security at my expense.

So no, I didn't hate him. I might even have liked him a little, right now as a companionable silence settled over us. It didn't really matter since after the night was over, I'd probably never see him again either, but at least I'd cleared the air.

Whatever came next, it had to be better than what'd come before... didn't it?

CHAPTER FOURTEEN

Rollick

From what my former employees had reported, Quinn was more used to clambering around on rooftops than mountainsides. That didn't stop her from looking perfectly comfortable perched on the ledge with a hundred-foot drop below its lip, her feet braced against the stone surface just a few steps away from a fatal fall.

There was a stillness to her that I hadn't often seen in mortals. I hadn't gotten much chance to notice or appreciate it while she'd technically been my prisoner back in L.A.—she'd been too restless in captivity, like any being would be when caged. But even then I'd gradually realized she wasn't a typical human in many other ways.

She really was lovely, poised there in the dwindling light with wisps of her pale hair floating free from the hurried braid she'd pulled the strands into. Not just in a way that called to my cock, but that made me think it really was a shame no one had tried to capture her form with paint or pencil to commit it to posterity.

Which then made me think of the dreams of her own that she'd talked about more than once now. The monuments she'd wanted to build for the rest of humankind to revel in after she was gone.

I knew that wish wasn't any kind of self-aggrandizement on her part. Most human buildings didn't come etched with the name of their architect. She didn't even care about being remembered for herself, only about leaving some kind of impact—and a positive one—on the world. A meaningful trace of her existence that would give people something more than they'd had before.

How many mortals would worry about something like that when they only had a handful of years left? She could have been making as many happy memories as possible with family and friends, squeezing all the joy and pleasure she could out of the small amount of time her illness had left her with—like most humans focused on even with their full lifespan—but this was what gave her the most pleasure: making a difference. Contributing something.

It wasn't as if I didn't understand. Probably it niggled at me precisely because of how well I *did* understand, despite our situations being so very different.

"What do you think they're even after?" she said, stirring me out of my thoughts. Her gaze was fixed in the direction of the camp.

"Our sorcerer-killing duo?" I paused, but I'd given that question a lot of thought over the past few weeks, and even now being fairly sure of what kind of beings we were dealing with, I had to admit I didn't have much clue about their end goal. "They want to be able to manipulate other shadowkind, obviously. And from what I heard during my travels through Europe, the behemoth has some animosity toward humans."

"So, what, they want to convince other shadowkind to make more trouble for us or something?" Quinn frowned. "Would they really need to go to all this trouble just for that goal?"

"No, probably not. And it'd be a stupid plan anyway, for exactly the reason they're about to pay for their actions now. As soon as they started messing with mortals in any significant way, their days were numbered. They only got away with it for this long because it's been sorcerers and I can't think of any of us who quite *mind* seeing them lose their lives."

The Highest themselves hadn't exactly reverberated with rage when I'd mentioned the duo's most popular current pastime. Their vast, dark shapes had simply glowered at me from within the depths of the cavernous space in which they passed their own time. But when I'd pointed out how careless the fiends and their followers were being in their kills, leaving the bodies for mortal law enforcement to find, clearly savaged in unusual ways, they'd stirred with a little more consternation.

It'd taken a fair bit more talking, emphasizing that the two ancient miscreants were taking on the powers we all hated for themselves and using them against our own kind, before one of them had said in her fathomless voice, "This cannot continue." Then it'd only been a matter of arranging the logistics.

Quinn rubbed her mouth, still gazing pensively at the darkening landscape ahead of us. "Yeah, I guess that's understandable."

It wasn't just stillness, I realized, watching her. There was an air of sadness to her that I hadn't quite recognized in the past. A sense of loss. Over what she'd already sacrificed or what she expected she'd have to next?

Maybe a little of both.

Her phone buzzed softly in her messenger bag. Her body moved with automatic swiftness, her arm reaching to unzip one of the pockets and retrieve her pill case, her other hand grabbing her water bottle. She popped her evening pills into her mouth and swallowed them with a single gulp of water as if it were nothing.

I knew what a lie that was. If it'd been nothing, she wouldn't have worried so much about the alarms and taking them at the exact same time. They were the only thing ensuring she kept whatever little time she did still have.

How could I say I understood her dreams and fears when I really didn't have any idea what it was like to see the end of your life approaching like headlights speeding toward you on a freeway? My own potential death rarely even crossed my mind.

My stomach twisted with an unfamiliar sense of discomfort. Before I could dwell on it, Quinn looked over at me. "Why would they want to mess things up for humans anyway? No matter what the sorcerers think, that's clearly not a standard attitude among shadowkind. Torrent and Lance and Crag didn't see mortals that way. *You* don't."

"I don't," I agreed. "But I don't think it's any great mystery. There are humans who go on killing sprees, aren't there? Animals that have a particularly aggressive streak. It happens in all species, so why not in shadowkind too? Most of us just want to continue our lives and make what we can out of them, and there are some who specifically want to make suffering for others."

"And unfortunately when you get a psychotic higher shadowkind or two, they can do a heck of a lot more damage than a serial killer or a rabid bear," Quinn muttered.

"Well, that's why the Highest exert some kind of rulership over the rest of us. So those of us who want to just live our lives can continue doing so in peace."

"Or even building something to help each other, like you have."

There was a wistfulness in Quinn's voice that twisted me up even more. But before I could put my finger on exactly why I was unsettled, a flare of light on one of the slopes below us caught my eyes.

"There," I murmured, touching her arm and pointing. Another glowing spurt and another burst into being along the inner mountainside to our right, close to the ridge. Not all that near the lake. My lips tightened into a caustic smirk. "Our enemies must have been poking around on the outskirts of the camp seeing what was up rather than heading right in. The Highest's warriors decided it was time to step in."

Quinn leaned forward, squinting at the distant slope.

Enough light now dotted the landscape there for us to make out a wide ring of figures, large and humanoid but with wings and horns and other appendages that made it clear they were much more than any mortal. Several other figures stood in the middle of the ring, but I could tell most were cringing lackeys. Only two stood tall, one even blockier-looking than Crag and the other towering but sinewy. That was all I could make out from a distance.

"What are they doing?" Quinn whispered. "They're barely moving."

"The warriors will interrogate them first." I lifted my chin toward them, relief starting to spread through my chest. It was almost over. "They'll want to be sure they've got the right delinquents and to give them a chance to come back to the shadow realm and face their judgment willingly. Somehow I don't think these two are going to take that option."

And I was looking forward to watching the Highest's warriors crush them.

I'd hardly finished speaking when a few of the warriors leapt forward. Someone over there was bellowing loud enough that a hint of the sound reached my ears even across that huge distance, though I couldn't pick apart any words. They charged at their captives, swords and claws slashing.

The beings I'd taken for lackeys fell left and right with plumes of essence. Two of the warriors slammed the bulky being I assumed was the behemoth into the ground. A few more sprang at the leviathan.

I almost looked away, thinking the fight was basically over. But just before I did, another distant yell rippled through the broad valley between the mountains.

One of the warriors who'd pinned down the behemoth turned and stabbed his sword into the neck of his colleague next to him.

My gut lurched. I was on my feet before I'd realized I was going to move.

No. They couldn't—with just some sorcerer organs in their gullets—I'd *specifically* told the Highest to send the most powerful underlings they had working for them. How many actual sorcerers could have commanded a shadowkind that potent?

But somehow this duo had managed it, maybe working in tandem. The one warrior crumpled with the fatal injury, and the one possessed by sorcery hurtled toward those pinning the leviathan. The behemoth heaved himself upward at the same moment and charged into the fray too.

"What—what's happening?" Quinn asked, a waver running through her words. "You were sure whoever the Highest sent would be able to deal with—"

"I know what I said," I cut in roughly. My heart was thudding faster than I could ever remember. If these fiends could manage to cut down a whole squad of the Highest's top soldiers...

They were managing it. Even as denial clanged through me, the two beings who'd once been at the warriors' mercy were carving up their opponents with the help of one—no, now *two* dupes who'd fallen under their sorcerous spell. Other shadowy bodies were racing in from the camp to help them as they turned the tide. Another of the warriors fell, and another—

Quinn dashed to the edge of the ledge and crouched down there, sliding her legs over the lip. A different sort of panic jolted through me. I leapt after her. "What in the realms are you doing now?"

Her face had totally blanched, her eyes wide in the dimness. "I have to—they're not going to make it on their own. The warriors. But maybe if I can get to them—I can try to use *my* sorcery on the others, force them to stop..."

She was absolutely insane. She was also already easing her way over the edge, about to slide down the nearly sheer slope to the slightly more even ground farther down.

I lunged forward and caught her arms before she could get that far. Quinn squirmed against me with a hiss of protest. "I have to—there isn't much time—"

"There isn't *any* time," I snarled at her, somehow furious and anguished all at once. "It'd take you at least half an hour just to clamber your way over there. They'll have fallen ages before then. All that'll happen is those beasts will carve you open too—or worse."

"This was our only real chance—they'll be distracted— let me *go*. I have to try. I know I can't cast any magic at them from this far away, but if I got a little closer, maybe..."

Every particle of my being rejected that thought. I could already see them bashing open her fragile body, shattering the skull that held all those hopes and dreams.

She had such big aspirations, and she was willing to throw them away on a one-in-a-million chance. While I stood here with my millennia behind me, already knowing there was no point.

This woman deserved more than that. She deserved so much more than she'd gotten, so much more than I'd offered her since she'd come into my grasp. But I could do this one thing for her.

The resolve swept through me so abruptly and fully that it blanked every other thought from my mind. I released my demon form as I hauled Quinn up from the ledge, ignoring her protests and the smack of her limbs. Setting my hand on her forehead, I willed a rush of demonic magic into her mind to knock her into unconsciousness.

She went slack in my arms. I bit back my horror at the feel of her gone so limp and eased her over my shoulder. Then, casting one last glance at the carnage the victory I'd tried to orchestrate had turned into, I spun on my heel and stalked off to descend the mountain.

CHAPTER FIFTEEN

Quinn

I woke up with the sense of a cry lodged in my throat. When I opened my mouth, a sound more like a squawk tumbled out of it. I shoved myself upright on the leather seat, my pulse racing, getting my bearings.

I was sitting in the passenger seat of Rollick's car, wearing the same clothes I'd had on for our trip up the mountain in Oregon. My messenger bag lay at my feet. The driver's seat appeared to be empty. The car was parked on a city street, the buildings around me draped in the darkness of night.

Knuckles rapped against the window next to me. As I flinched, Rollick opened the door from the outside. He was holding my backpack, slightly unzipped. I made out the corner of my laptop through the gap.

I stared up at him, blinking against the glow of the

streetlamp beyond him. The warm air that wafted over me smelled strangely familiar.

"What's going on?" I demanded, and memories rushed back to me. "You took me away! I could have—I was going to try—"

"It wouldn't have done any good," Rollick said, calmly but firmly. He motioned for me to get out of the car. "Come on now."

I eased gingerly out of the car onto the sidewalk and peered around me. Even in the darkness, my surroundings looked kind of familiar too. It was a residential street lined with two-story houses.

Wait. That one on the corner with the arched windows —I *knew* that place. It was just down the street from...

From my parents' house.

My gaze jerked to Rollick's face. I kept my voice low, thinking of the sleeping people in all the houses around us that we wouldn't want to wake up and notice us. "We're back in Jacksonville. What the hell are we doing here?"

The demon let out a huff of breath. "It shouldn't take too much explaining. If you're going to insist on it now, let's get more out of view."

He ushered me into the playground where I'd spent so many hours of my early childhood. As we walked past the swing set, I glanced around at the equipment with a sudden burn of tears behind my eyes.

What sick game was he playing at now? I'd thought we were past emotional manipulations.

I spun toward Rollick. "What the fuck are we doing here? What's *wrong* with you? I—"

He caught me by the shoulders, his expression so

strangely intense that the words died in my throat. A smack of anguish hit me, like the turmoil of emotions I'd felt from him as we watched his plan fall apart... earlier this night? Last night? When the villainous duo of ancient monsters had overcome the warriors sent by the rulers of the shadow realm.

A chill of my own rippled through my limbs in the wake of the demon's anguish. Had something even worse happened since then?

I opened my mouth, but before I could say anything else, Rollick broke the momentary silence.

"I'm trying to fix this," he said raggedly. "I'm trying to put this one thing back the way it should have been."

I blinked at him, totally bewildered. "What are you talking about?"

"You—" He sucked in a breath, an almost frantic light dancing in his eyes in the darkness. "You weren't supposed to be a part of this. These aren't your powers. It wasn't your heart. You wanted to do so much with the little bit of time you have, and this conflict has stolen it from you. You belong *here*. You should get the chance to do as much as you can with your life, however long you can extend it."

My brain couldn't quite compute what he was saying. "You... want me to go back to my regular life? My parents— my classes—but the behemoth and the leviathan are still out there, aren't they?"

"It doesn't matter," Rollick insisted. "You can let me deal with them. I've already had thousands of years more than you're going to get. I should be the one taking that burden. I should have from the start, but I was too caught up—" He cut himself off with a growl. "I was selfish. I'm ashamed of that, but I'm trying to make it right. Let me do that."

I was still having trouble wrapping my head around this switch of attitude. "Won't they come after me? Isn't that why I've been on the run from the beginning anyway?"

He tipped his head toward my torso. "You've got your special vest now. You'll want to keep that on for the time being. I'm going to look into other options... I might be able to have some shirts constructed for you that simply have silver thread woven through them to enough effect that they'd effectively shield you, so it isn't quite so awkward." His mouth set in a grim smile. "And whatever I do next, I'll make sure the bastards are too distracted to even think about you."

"What the heck *are* you going to do?" I demanded. "I thought you said those warriors were the toughest shadowkind out there."

"They probably weren't the smartest. I have resources I haven't called on yet—a lot of them. I'll figure something out."

"This doesn't make any sense. *You* pulled me into this situation."

Rollick closed his eyes with a pained expression that echoed the emotions radiating off him. "I know. I realize I'm changing my tune. And maybe you still can't trust that I mean what I say." He fell silent for long enough that my nerves started to twitch. His fingers squeezed my shoulders gently. Then he met my eyes again.

"I didn't get into this business for myself, you know. At first, I was a lot like Torrent used to be, though lighter on the chemical indulgences. I enjoyed all humanity had to offer, and I could exude enough charm and authority to get pretty much whatever I wanted. But I was still getting my footing, and a demon who'd been around the block a few more times than me with similar inclinations took me under his wing."

I raised my eyebrows. "So, the two of you ran around partying like kings?"

"Something like that," Rollick said. "But as we roved around, I got to know other beings who couldn't enjoy themselves the same way. They had something about them that wouldn't allow them to move among mortals quite as easily... which is the situation most shadowkind are in, really. And it occurred to me that I could build the sort of place where the indulgences would freely come to them rather than them seeking out the fun they wanted and failing. Which did work out to my benefit as well."

"And your friend's," I suggested.

"My lover's," Rollick corrected without missing a beat. "For as long as he was that. He thought my venture was a waste of time. He stuck around for a little while and then he took off, and I haven't seen him since then. Which probably means some dire fate came for him, or our paths would have crossed by now."

For just a moment, he looked pensive, but I guessed that relationship was far enough in the past not to bother him all that much, because he focused his attention on me again.

"He wasn't totally wrong. I was too soft. I welcomed the beings who came to take advantage of my services and supported them as much as I could, and in return plenty of them took advantage of *me*. Mortals I should have protected died under my roof. So I stopped coddling anyone. I cultivated the persona I wear easily now—unpredictable and detached so my fellow shadowkind never feel totally sure of me or how I'll react, harsh enough that they fear crossing the line and so that when I am kind it's mercy rather than weakness. That's who I need to be."

He spoke so emphatically that my stomach knotted. "Why are you telling me all this?"

"Because I need you to understand. I didn't start out like this. I know how to care. I know how to stick out my neck for those in need. I've just... gotten out of the habit. But I decided to harden myself, so I can decide to allow a little softness when the moment is right. This matters. That vicious duo making their plans that can't be good for anyone—taking them down matters. And *you* matter."

Rollick lifted one of his hands to touch my cheek, and my heart stuttered. "If you see through what you want to do, you'll have accomplished more in the few years that might be all you have left than I've achieved in centuries. I'm not going to take that chance away from you any more than I already have. You deserve this life more than anyone. Let me give it back to you. *Take it.*"

I stared at him, his words sinking in. A strange heat had flooded my body at the touch of his fingers. I wanted to laugh and cry at the same time. But as much as my thoughts were spinning, it didn't take long before one clear fact surfaced in my mind.

"I can't."

Rollick bared his teeth. "What do you mean, you can't? I brought you back here. I'm giving you your things back. You have everything you need."

I reached up and set my hand over his, swallowing thickly. I *could* take his offer, couldn't I? I could walk back into my parents' house, resolve their worries, slip back into the life I'd left behind as if I'd never been torn away from it. Throw myself into achieving the goals that it'd wrenched at me to set aside.

Closing my eyes, I pictured myself slipping down the stairs from my bedroom in the morning, surprising my parents at breakfast, feeling the squeeze of their relieved hugs. Opening up my computer and digging into the latest assignments. Taking a moment to relax in the backyard with the sweet scents from Dad's garden wafting over me.

I let the image of that life settle over me... and my answer remained the same. The pang of homesickness that resonated through my chest couldn't change what I knew to be true.

"No, I don't have everything I need," I said quietly. "I need to know that people are going to be okay—not just the people I know, but people all around the world. I need to do everything I can to make sure those monsters don't hurt any more of them. Maybe some action I take will make the difference between other lives being lost or not. Maybe the whole world will go to hell if every person who could pitch in doesn't."

"After what we saw last night, I doubt even your boosted sorcerer powers could work on those menaces," Rollick said.

"That's not the only way I've pitched in. I haven't been completely useless."

"Of course you haven't. But, Quinn... it's not your responsibility."

I made a face at him. "It's not yours either. And I..." The truth of what I was going to say swelled in my chest. "I care about *you* getting through this mess okay too, all right? I would feel like a jerk to walk away and leave you to handle it on your own. This is my world more than it's yours. I know that it matters to you, and it matters to me too, so I can't back down any more than you will."

It was Rollick's turn to stare at me. His jaw worked. He exhaled in a rush. "You're really not going to change your mind, are you?"

The corner of my mouth quirked upward. "I think you already know how stubborn I can be."

"Yes, I'm very familiar with that particular quality of yours."

His hand swiveled so his fingers could twine with mine, his knuckles still resting against my cheek. His head bowed toward me. My heart skipped a beat with the sudden thought that he might be going to kiss me—and the awareness that I wasn't sure I'd want to stop him.

But then he stepped away, tugging at me through our joined hands. "All right, stubborn sorcerer. I can't *force* you to live a normal life, no matter how much I might want to. So we'd better figure out where we go from here."

CHAPTER SIXTEEN

Quinn

I bit into the Thai chicken wrap, taking a moment just to appreciate the crunch of the crisp lettuce, the tangy sauce filling my mouth, and the fresh breeze that brought a refreshing coolness over us in the glade where we'd stopped to eat our takeout lunches.

An elm tree offered a swath of shade over the sole bench that seemed to be left over from when this spot might have been a more happening park of some sort. At the moment, it didn't look like much more than a weedy field a short drive off the main road.

I chewed through a few mouthfuls, took a gulp of my water, and glanced over at Rollick, who appeared to be very pleased with the Caesar salad wrap he'd opted for. He licked a fleck of dressing off his thumb, and my gaze focused a little too long on the sculpted perfection of his mouth.

Jerking my eyes away, I brought my thoughts back to more important matters. Like what the hell I was going to do now that I'd doubled down on my commitment to this quest. It was still kind of hard to believe the demon next to me had offered me a free ticket out of this mess. But I'd been able to feel how much he meant everything he'd said.

He'd always been a strange mix of callous and considerate with me. I'd assumed the considerate parts were solely to advance his own agenda. Had that changed during the time we'd spent together, or had I always been a little too hard on him?

I guessed the answer to that question wasn't really important now, only how we moved forward.

"You said you don't think I could be powerful enough to use my sorcery on the head honchos," I said. "But you didn't think they'd be able to manipulate the warriors that the Highest sent either. We should test out my magic. Because if I *can* control the villainous duo, then all we have to do is find them and our problems are solved."

Rollick gave an amused hum. "Forgive me for not believing the solution could be that simple. But I agree that we should evaluate your newly enhanced powers. You seemed to work the magic faster than I remember from before when we sent off that lackey the other day."

I nodded. "It felt easier... like I was more sure of what to do, even though it's still instinctive. I had the feeling I could do a lot more than just that."

My companion grinned with his shiny veneers on full display. "You already had the benefit of a powerful lineage, and then you got a particularly strong demon's essence on top of it. I'm assuming most sorcerer families make do with lesser beings. That should give you some kind of leg up."

A surge of conviction gripped me. "Then maybe I *will* be able to work my magic on those two. I could try with you—you're at least almost as powerful as one of them, right?"

"I'd like to think we'd be on a similar playing field," Rollick said. "But it'd hardly be a fair test. You know me a lot better than you know them—at this point, you know more about what matters to me than just about anyone. It seems like having a personal understanding gives your powers a lot more punch. You might be able to turn me into your puppet, but it wouldn't prove anything about going up against those menaces."

I narrowed my eyes at him. "Are you just trying to get out of becoming a test subject? You didn't have any problem offering up *other* beings for that purpose."

He spread his hands, putting on an innocent expression. "Feel free to make me your slave if you can manage it. I'd be curious to see what you decide to do with me for as long as you can hold on to the control. But it's obvious that a deeper understanding makes it easier for you to command someone. How else could you have managed to keep my three mutinists away for so long otherwise? You hadn't gotten a power boost back then, and they were no slouches as far as shadowkind go."

He was right, but the reminder of how I'd sent the three men away—and the fact that they hadn't come back yet— put a damper on my enthusiasm. My throat constricted.

I forced down the last of my wrap, staring off across the field toward the sedan. "Maybe it has worn off. Maybe they just haven't wanted to come back in case I'd manipulate them again."

Rollick snorted. "I think it's more likely that they decided to start a rock-n-roll band and are currently touring New Zealand than what you just said. The only thing I can imagine that *could* keep those three from sticking close to you is magical compulsion."

He sounded so confident that I wanted to believe he was right, but the ache of loss didn't subside. I clenched my jaw. "I knew what I was doing. I knew it was kind of an awful thing to do to them. The most important thing is that they're safe."

"Quinn." Rollick let out a huff and turned toward me. He tucked his hand beneath my jaw, resting his fingers lightly on the underside of my chin to draw my gaze to his. "I saw how they were with you. I know you well enough by now to comprehend how you earned their devotion. There isn't anything in either realm that I can imagine keeping them away from you other than you yourself."

"You can't know for sure," I had to say.

"Well, if it isn't the case, then at least you have me for company, even if I'm not a very good substitute."

My eyebrows rose of their own accord. "Humbleness— not something I thought I'd ever see from you."

A sly smile curved Rollick's lips. "I have all sorts of dimensions you've yet to uncover."

A quiver that wasn't entirely unpleasant raced over my skin from where he was still touching my chin. The memory of the moment when I'd thought he might kiss me this morning flitted through my head, and my cheeks flushed with a mix of desire and shame.

I didn't want to be thinking like that. Why couldn't my brain get the memo?

I was tensing to pull back and wishing it didn't require as much effort as I was finding it did when three forms burst from the shadows amid the trees.

I startled and jerked around. Next to me, Rollick stiffened, but only until he'd recognized the figures facing us.

There was no more than an instant when Torrent, Lance, and Crag stood there a few feet from us, perfectly familiar other than the hint of uncertainty crossing all their expressions. I gaped at them, losing my breath. My lips parted, my heart leaping and stuttering at the same time, and then Lance was launching himself at me.

Angling his claws carefully away from my body as he always did, he caught me in his arms with no sign of concern about my vest, lifted me up, and spun me around with his face buried in my hair.

"We're back. The magic's gone. And you're okay." He paused and twisted around to press his hand over my mouth, gently but insistently. "No more magic-y words. You don't tell us what to do like that again. All right, baby girl?"

He stared me down, his violet eyes flaring beneath the tumble of his wild black curls. Tears welled up behind my own eyes.

He was here. They were all here, and it felt as if I could finally properly breathe again for the first time since they'd left. But at the same time, the terror that had gripped me before at the danger they'd already put themselves through and almost definitely would again wound around me. I couldn't move.

Lance nuzzled my temple and then resumed his hold on my gaze, his hand still fixed over my mouth to prevent any speech. "You have to say it. I'm not letting you go until you say you won't do that ever again. Promise us."

Even after everything, he trusted me to tell the truth—trusted that I wouldn't lie just to get free and then use my sorcery after all. As that fact sank in, my resistance melted. How could I deny that kind of devotion? How could I tell him that my worries for him mattered more than his dedication to me?

The tears behind my eyes overflowed. I grabbed him in a hug just as tight as the one he'd initially wrapped me up in and nodded emphatically.

Lance withdrew his hand, but only far enough to swipe at my tears as he drew back to look at me. His forehead furrowed. "Are you sad?"

"Not that you're back," I choked out. "That I made you leave at all. I didn't *want* to, I just—I didn't want to see you get hurt more than you already had been, because of me. It's my fault you're mixed up in this situation, and—"

Lance's growl cut me off. "Not your fault," he insisted. "None of the hurt had anything to do with you. You didn't ask for the beasties and whoever else to attack you. You didn't make them use their tricksy magic. *You* make me nothing but happy. Except when you forced me to go away. That's the only thing you ever did that hurt me."

I blinked hard, but the tears kept coming. "I'm sorry. I didn't know what else to do."

"You keep us with you, and you let us protect you from the vicious beings out there, and everything will be good."

I didn't think it was quite that simple, but then Lance pulled me into a kiss with all the eager passion he exuded so easily, and I couldn't bring myself to argue.

He was back. All three of the men I loved were back. Maybe the other two wouldn't forgive me quite as quickly, but they'd come, which had to mean they didn't hate me.

Lance drew out the kiss with a pleased thrum in the base of his throat and then eased back to stroke his knuckles down the side of my face. He cocked his head. "What were you talking about with Rollick when we got here? He was touching your face too."

Even though I'd been about to *stop* Rollick from touching me in that moment, guilt hitched in my chest. But the demon spoke up swiftly and smoothly before I had to figure out what to say.

"We were actually discussing the three of you—whether you would come back once our reluctant sorcerer's magic wore off. She wasn't sure. And she was quite despondent about it."

Lance beamed down at me, apparently more than satisfied with that answer, and I soaked up his brightness. Then I glanced past him to the two men who'd arrived with him.

Crag strode over, his stony jaw looking starker than ever against his bronze skin. He hesitated just before he reached me, and my gut clenched, but then he propelled himself the last short distance to tug me from the dragon shifter's arms. He enfolded me in his brawny embrace, holding me closer than he'd dared in the last day when we'd been together, and I let myself sink into his broad chest.

"*I'm* sorry, Softness," he muttered in his usual gruff tone. "I pushed you away first. I didn't mean to make you feel—I was so worried—but it was the same as you told me. It was the fault of those villains, not either of us. I won't let them tear us apart again."

My eyes started to burn again. "Good. You never need to protect me from *you*."

"As long as you remember that the sentiment goes both ways, Ms. Fix It," Torrent said, his tone as dry and even as ever.

I turned in Crag's arms, not forcing him to relinquish me when he seemed determined to keep hugging me, and met the tentacled man's sea-green gaze. He didn't rush in to embrace me, but then, my relationship with Torrent had always been a little more complicated. I couldn't tell whether he was being careful of my potentially awkward feelings or his own.

"How long did the spell last?" I asked. "How did you find me?"

"It only just wore off," Lance announced triumphantly. "We came straight to you the moment we could."

Torrent inclined his head. "We'd determined the general area you had to be in by keeping track of where your magic repelled us as that boundary shifted with your movements. And we spread out to get a sense of the larger reach of that magic, knowing you'd be in the middle of its circle. So we knew which direction to head in as soon as its effects dissipated. And once we were close to Rollick, Crag could pick up on his presence."

"Speaking of picking up on my presence..." Rollick brushed his hands together and motioned toward the car. "I think we've lingered in this spot for long enough, especially since our enemies now have even more reason to want to hunt me down than they did before. But I have a property not too far from here where we can regroup. As long as you weren't planning on ousting me from the group next. In the past, I think we've accomplished a lot more working together than going our separate ways."

A twinge shot through me at the thought of sending the demon off now, but Torrent gave him a small but amicable smile. "I think we can manage to cooperate for a little longer in the interests of keeping Quinn safe."

CHAPTER SEVENTEEN

Torrent

I peered through the tall window on the Mediterranean-style house into its inner courtyard, where Quinn had stretched out on a lounge chair by the pool. Her toned but slim torso was unencumbered by the layer of metal beads that had weighed it down for so much of the past month. It lifted a weight in my own chest seeing how relaxed she looked without that burden, but a twang of anxiety reverberated through my nerves at the same time.

"Are you sure the protections around this place are enough to ensure her powers aren't noticed?" I asked Rollick, who was sprawled on the modern sofa perpendicular to the window. "In that cabin in the swamp—"

"I'm well aware of what happened in the swamp,"

Rollick interrupted, "seeing as that incident was the start of my plans derailing. I hired some mortals to add to the silver and iron deposits around a few of my properties as soon as Quinn came to the hotel. I wasn't so naïve as to think I could count on remaining there as long as I'd have liked to."

I had felt the unnerving prickle of the metals' effects as we'd cruised up the winding drive to this sprawling estate in the Texas badlands. And we were far enough away from anyplace we'd clashed with our main opponents that it was unlikely they were searching for us too thoroughly anywhere nearby. But hearing Rollick confirm the property's security measures soothed the worst of my worries.

He'd been confident about his hotel, and no shadowkind had detected Quinn's presence there... until we'd purposefully tipped our enemies off to her location. Rollick wasn't the type to cut corners when it came to things he cared about.

And from the atmosphere I'd sensed between him and our mortal since our return, I was starting to suspect his caring had expanded in dimension. It didn't seem anything overt had actually *happened* between them, but it was clear he no longer viewed her as simply a tool.

I didn't know whether to see that change as more comforting or unsettling.

"Sit down," he added, tipping his head toward the chair across from him. "Rest those legs—there's no shame in it. She isn't going to vanish the second you take your eyes off her."

I grimaced at him, but I sat as he'd requested. We did

have business to discuss. "You said there's something specific you think I can help with. What exactly is that?"

Rollick exhaled in a slow sigh that told me he wasn't happy about what he was about to say. "I believe one of the fiends we're dealing with is a—or *the*—leviathan."

Whatever I might have anticipated him saying, I hadn't expected that revelation. I stared at him for a beat in case this was some bizarre prelude to a joke, but he showed no sign of taking back the statement.

"What the fuck would a leviathan want with a bunch of human sorcery?" I asked. "Wouldn't he have better things to do?"

"Wouldn't it be nice if that were the case?" the demon muttered. "Who knows what goes through the mind of a being that ancient? Maybe he's simply gotten bored. It's not as if anyone's heard much about him or any being like him in ages, so he can't have been occupying himself all that thrillingly. But that's where you come in."

"With the thrills?"

Rollick chuckled. "Preferably not so much thrills, more with the hearing about him. The ocean is your domain. I want you to cruise around through the seven seas calling on whatever other watery shadowkind you come across and see whether anyone knows anything about what might have motivated our serpentine foe."

The request did make a certain amount of sense. All the same, I couldn't stop myself from saying, "So I just got back, and you're sending me off again on a mission of unknown length."

"You're allowed to say no," Rollick replied languidly, although the slight tensing of his fingers as he picked up his glass of expensive gin showed he wasn't quite so relaxed about it. "I think it's become very obvious that I no longer have much of any control over what you do or where you go. But it will be for her benefit." He glanced toward the window.

The sunlight was gleaming off Quinn's pale hair, but that wasn't what caught my attention most. It was the strange, almost wistful expression that crossed the demon's face. I found myself bold enough to say, "And *you* seem nearly as concerned about that now as about everything else that's at stake."

Rollick's penetrating gaze flicked to me. He smiled again, looking only amused rather than offended. "I don't think I need to tell you that she's a rather impressive example of her kind."

He hadn't even tried to deny his interest. I bit back the urge to shout out that she was mine, that he could make no claim on her—because what would the point be? If he'd been going to, he'd had every chance while the rest of us were gone. Maybe he *had*, and she'd rejected him. Although she hadn't exactly looked uncomfortable in that moment as we'd emerged from the shadows when he'd been sitting so close to her.

They'd spent a lot of time together just the two of them in the past several days. That was a recipe for either killing each other or developing some sort of closer rapport. And they definitely hadn't killed each other.

I willed my teeth not to grit and kept my voice even. "She is. You were the one who wanted her to tap into her sorcery to begin with. Now I can't help wondering if you encouraged her using it on us."

Rollick's smile tightened just slightly. "If I nudged her in that direction, it was only bolstering feelings she already had. I wasn't the one who put the idea in her head—she came up with it all on her own. And if it makes you feel any better, afterward I realized the emotional toll on her wasn't really worth the benefit of not having to argue with the three of you over our plans."

I folded my arms over my chest. "So you're not worried that we'll run off with her again?"

"You know what?" Rollick said with a wave of his hand. "Feel free to, if you can convince her. I tried to drop her off at her family's home, to hand her old life back to her, and she wouldn't take it." His attention slid back to the woman by the pool. "Much too stubborn for her own good. This shouldn't have been her battle to begin with."

The admission struck me momentarily speechless. He'd have let Quinn go? He'd already attempted to? After all the lengths he'd gone to in order to get his hands on her...

The prickles of apprehension and jealousy faded, and for a second I felt almost ashamed. It made sense that I'd been wary of his intentions. They hadn't always worked in her favor. But I'd misjudged just how much of an effect she'd had on him while we'd been gone.

"I think we'll just be lucky if she doesn't feel the need to send us away again so she can take on the entire battle herself," I said, more honestly than I wished I was being, and stood up. "I'll go scout out word about the leviathan. But we've only just gotten back. I need to talk with her first."

Rollick got to his feet too with a brisk gesture toward the courtyard. "Talk to her, do whatever you like with her.

I've got my own business to attend to. It seems I need to raise an army." He made a face. "Just remember that the faster we get these menaces dealt with, the safer she'll be."

If we could deal with them, I thought but didn't say. I'd heard his account of what had happened with the Highest's warriors, and I wasn't sure I liked our odds.

But that didn't mean I was going to give up. I'd only just found real joy in this world; I wasn't going to let any monsters, no matter how ancient, steal it from me again.

And I'd better make sure the source of my joy knew it too.

As Rollick ambled off to see to his army-building, I opened the door to the courtyard and stepped out into the desert warmth. It would have been easier to simply leap through the shadows, but I forced myself to walk over with the support of my tentacles, ignoring the twinges of pain in my lower legs.

Quinn straightened up at my approach, setting aside the small, leatherbound book she'd started paging through. Concern flashed across her pretty face. I sank onto the chair next to her before she felt the need to express her worries about my physical limitations out loud and tipped my head toward the book on the side table. "Getting some reading in?"

She looked at it and wrinkled her nose. "I got that from the sorcerer enclave. It's a record of different strategies for warding off supernatural powers. I thought it might have something useful for keeping our enemies from sensing me, but so far nothing sounds as effective as my vest has been." She frowned. "I wish it had some method that would work to protect all of you from sorcery, but the approaches all seem to involve things that would be uncomfortable for shadowkind in general."

"A quick fix would be a bit much to ask for, I guess," I said. "But we'll get it figured out one way or another."

She glanced toward the room I'd come out of. "Is it time to get going again? Have you all been making plans without me?"

I offered a wry grin. "Not plans for you. I'm going to go information-seeking. Since I'm the most comfortable of us in the water, Rollick thinks—and I agree—that I'm the best one to learn more about the leviathan's intentions."

"You're leaving?" She couldn't quite smooth the disappointment from her voice, which made me feel both gratified and guilty. "For how long?"

"I'm not sure yet. But I didn't want to go without talking to you first. We haven't had much of a chance." After Lance and Crag had glommed all over her this morning, I hadn't known what to say. I didn't know how to crack open the walls around the churning emotions inside me without too much spilling out.

But maybe there wasn't such a thing as too much. This woman had told me she loved me. She'd sacrificed her own happiness and security to try to protect me. If I hadn't already known I didn't need to hide myself from her, that should have convinced me.

Even now, she was hanging her head. "If you're angry, I'd understand. It was a shitty thing to do, even if I was trying to look out for you. I—"

"Quinn," I broke in, scooting to the edge of the chair so I could lift my good hand to her cheek. "I'm not angry. I wish that you hadn't felt the need to do it, but I know it came from a place of caring. I just don't want you to ever feel like you should have gone farther or that you've made a mistake by letting us come back."

Her gaze slid to my other hand, the ruined one resting on my knee. It didn't ache as much as it used to. I could close the thumb and the remaining fingers in a sort of pincer grip, which seemed somehow appropriate. A little crab appendage to add to my overall sea-creature theme.

Quinn obviously couldn't see any humor in it. Her voice came out rough. "You've lost the most out of anyone. I hate that."

"I can't say it's my most favorite thing in the world either, but—" I tugged her face up so she'd meet my eyes. "I don't mind. You have to understand that. It's a tiny trade-off compared to everything I'm getting in return."

"How can you say that? You're about to go off nosing around after some uber-powerful, murderous monster, and—"

"I don't care." I cupped her jaw, willing her to understand how much I meant this. "The whole time, I'll be thinking about how I can come back to you. About what I've already had with you. And that makes it more than worth it. You told me that you love me, and I don't know what it would even mean for me to say it in return. But Quinn, you have no idea how empty my life was before. I used to fill it with drugs and parties, and then I filled it with carrying out jobs for Rollick, but none of that stopped me from feeling alone."

"You had Lance and Crag," she said, her voice dipping low.

"In a way. They were more colleagues than friends. I

had to keep up an air of authority. I wasn't sure, if I let that waver, if they'd still respect me given my other weaknesses."

Quinn's eyes flashed. "There's nothing *weak* about you."

I smiled at her. "And you're the only person who could say that who I'd believe. Because you've seen every part of me, you recognize my difficulties, you've heard about who I've been, and you don't shy away from any of it."

"There's nothing to shy away from," she said with the stubbornness Rollick had commented on. He had been right about that.

"Not when I'm with you," I said. "You see me, and you embrace all of it—and when I'm with you, I know I can be the man you see. I still have a place in this world. I'm more than just an outcast. And I have more of a purpose than I ever did before. You gave me all of that. So losing part of a hand *really* isn't that big a deal. You're worth it. And I am too."

For a second, she looked as if she might cry. Then she leaned forward to wrap her arms around me and bury her face in my shoulder. I slung one of my tentacles around my waist to tug her closer, and she let out a ragged sigh.

"You are," she said. "You were before you met me too."

"Maybe so. But it didn't feel like there was anywhere near as much of a point before I met you."

She pulled back to look into my eyes again. "There is one part of you I haven't seen. You've never shown me your full shadowkind form. I'd like... I'd like to totally know you. If you don't mind."

Even with all the faith I had in her, doubt jabbed through my chest for an instant before I nodded. It seemed only fair. And maybe I wanted her to have that piece of me too before I had to leave again.

The pool gave off a faint oceanic tang, laced with salt rather than chlorine, which I was grateful for. It'd feel better on my skin. I stepped to the edge and dipped my feet in, not bothering to remove my clothes. They'd vanish as I transformed anyway.

With Quinn watching from her chair, I sank into the water. As it flowed over my head, I released the human guise I'd always worn with her even when I brought all of my tentacles out.

My body expanded, torso and head ballooning, tentacles widening and stretching. In a matter of seconds, I filled most of the pool. The cool water rushed over my pliant flesh with a welcoming sensation, but I turned my eyes toward the surface of the water with tension wound through my innards.

What if this had been a mistake—one step too far?

CHAPTER EIGHTEEN

Quinn

As Torrent's pale skin and auburn hair vanished amid a vast maroon body that expanded through the water, my breath caught in my throat. I got up, walking to the edge of the pool so I could see all of him properly.

I'd had a general sense of what he must look like in his most natural form from having seen his tentacles, but it hadn't really prepared me for the reality. The tentacles themselves had expanded to twice the length and width I was used to, and the body they attached to now was no more human than Lance's reptilian dragon form. Even *less* human, with twice as many limbs and no clear facial features other than the large eyes set low on either side of Torrent's immense, rounded head.

He was, in essence, a giant octopus. Large enough that

he had to curve his tentacles to allow them to fit in the rectangular space, his head alone longer than I was tall. To accommodate him, the salty pool water sloshed over the lip of the walls onto the slate tiles.

Most people probably would have been terrified. But I'd spent most of my life pushing myself to my limits, turning the things that scared me into an adventure. As alien as Torrent's appearance was, there was also something sublime about it, like a vast mystery waiting to be unraveled. A secret I'd never quite get to the bottom of.

I'd taken my shoes off in the summer heat, and the water streaked over my feet, cooling my skin. After everything he'd said to me, an impulse gripped me to show him that I accepted him this way too, that our connection meant just as much to me as it did to him.

Normally I avoided pools like all stagnant water, but Rollick had specifically mentioned that he'd had this one replenished with clean water for our arrival, by whatever means the demon had at his disposal. Without hesitation, I pulled off my tee and shorts and darted around the corner of the pool to the steps in just my panties and bra. Unlike Torrent, I couldn't dry off my entire outfit with a quick trip into the shadows.

I waded down into the water until my feet reached the floor and the salt-laced liquid reached my chin. My hair floated out around my face like flaxen seaweed. I'd placed myself carefully in an open space between two of Torrent's tentacles. Now I reached out and rested my hand on one.

It might have been larger, but the soft yet firm skin felt the same as it always had. Torrent eased closer, the end of that tentacle wrapping loosely around my waist. As he moved into the shallower end of the pool, the top of his head protruded from the water. I stepped forward to meet him, my heart skipping a beat as I touched the spot at the base of his head between those two fathomless eyes.

He was even more awe-inspiring up close. "You're amazing," I told him, stroking the velvety slope of flesh. I had no idea how well he could hear me in his current state, but I had to say it anyway. "Totally amazing."

Another tentacle coiled around my calf, its tip trailing in a teasing line up my inner leg toward my thigh. I'd barely had time to consider whether the heat that abruptly flooded me was reasonable or deeply weird when Torrent surged toward me.

He shifted as he came, with a warble of the water. The next thing I knew his human body was pinning me to the side of the pool, his human head bowing over mine as droplets streamed from his drenched hair. Four of his tentacles held me in place with the kiss of their suckers. He clutched the side of my neck and slammed his mouth into mine.

The salt of the water lingered on his lips, and his human skin was slick when I wrapped my arms around his shoulders. I kissed him back hard, all of me aching for the ultimate closeness that I'd gone without for days.

His warped hand came to rest on my side. The other and the ends of his tentacles caressed my curves as he devoured my mouth. The hooks of my bra released, and the water washed over my breasts. Suckers plucked at one nipple while his palms and then his thumb swiveled over the other, sending jolts of pleasure through my chest.

My hips rose instinctively, my thighs splaying around

his hips. He'd reappeared without bothering with clothes, and the head of his rigid erection slid against my sex through my panties so perfectly that I gasped into his mouth.

He pulled back just far enough to mutter words, his lips grazing mine with each movement. "I will always come back. There's no pain that could be greater than this joy. You are... everything."

His voice rasped, and then he was claiming my mouth again at the same moment as he wrenched at my panties. The fabric split, and his cock plunged into me.

He swallowed my pleased cry and rammed even deeper. I arched into him and groped at his shoulders, desperate to feel all of him, to solidify our connection in the most fundamental possible way.

It felt like it'd been forever since we'd come together like this. My body melted into his, bliss surging with every thrust, impossibly fast. I rocked with him, clung to him, gasped my eagerness into his ear.

The flood of pleasure stole my breath. A tentacle slid between us to pluck at my clit, and sparks of pure delight seared through my pussy. It only took a few moments of that monstrous, marvelous touch before I was shivering and shuddering my release against him.

Torrent groaned and bucked faster. I felt his own climax in the tremor that rippled through his muscles, pressed so tightly against mine.

As he caught my mouth again, our bodies sagging together against the side of the pool, a shadow fell over us.

"Hmm," Lance said in a teasing tone. "Getting up to so

much fun already, and not inviting the rest of us. That's not very... what's the word humans use?"

"Sportsmanlike?" Crag suggested in a rumble from a little farther away.

I tipped my head back to peer up at them. Lance had crouched down at the edge of the pool over us—he reached to brush the tips of his claws over my hair. Crag loomed just a couple of steps behind him, his stance relaxed but his eyes smoldering.

I was still trembling with the force of my collision with Torrent, but more giddiness rushed through me at the desire in my other men's expressions. I lifted a hand toward Lance. "There's no reason you can't join in now."

He grinned wide and might have leapt into the water right then if Torrent hadn't cleared his throat. "Maybe we should take this to a more private venue. I actually found a little something in the guest bedroom that I'd like to try out with our woman if she's up for it... I just got a little caught up in the moment." He pressed a kiss to my temple as if in apology.

I laughed. "Feel free to get caught up whenever you're in the mood. But now I'm curious. What are we trying out?"

His pale eyes glinted with promise. "You'll see." He scooped me up in his arms with an extra boost from one tentacle and lifted me into the edge of the pool. "Can I count on the two of you to get her to the bedroom?"

Lance nuzzled my damp shoulder. "As fast as we can."

"I'll take care of that." Crag bent down to gather me in his arms the way I was used to.

I tucked my head against his brawny chest, weirdly

turned on and yet also comforted by his embrace. "I'm getting your shirt all wet."

"It'll be gone soon!" Lance announced gleefully, and bounced ahead of us into the house.

Crag squeezed me a little tighter as he carried me after the dragon shifter. "You're as lovely like this as you are every other way, Softness." He paused, and a smile touched his usually somber lips. "And he isn't wrong."

Torrent vanished, trailing alongside us through the shadows where he could move more easily. Crag strode down the hall with its cream-colored walls and pale birch flooring and into the airy bedroom Rollick had assigned to me "in case you're in the mood to sleep before we leave again." I didn't suppose he'd be all that surprised by us making other uses of the king-sized bed.

Crag lowered me onto the fluffy duvet and climbed up next to me, lowering his head to seek out my mouth. As I kissed him, reveling in the tenderness he could offer even with his rocky jaw, Lance leapt up at my other side. The dragon shifter lapped his ridged tongue up the side of my neck and flicked the tips of his claws over my breast to send a rush of giddy quivers over my skin.

A bittersweet ache spread through my chest like melting wax. This was where I was meant to be. This was who I was meant to be with. I'd denied myself and these men what felt right to all of us for too long. But this interlude, right now, was even more of a homecoming than the moment when they'd appeared before me this morning.

Another presence knelt by my legs, and I knew Torrent had rejoined us. He trailed his fingers along my leg and let one of his tentacles nibble my toes with its suckers.

"Mine," Lance murmured with typical possessiveness. He eased down my body, swiping his claws back and forth with just enough pressure to leave me tingling, slicking his tongue along the same path. He teased them right over my clit and jerked them back when I couldn't stop my hips from bucking up to meet him.

"Needy girl." He nudged my knee to the side and bent his head between my legs as I gasped against Crag's mouth. "I'll take care of you good."

At the first swipe of his tongue over my pussy, I moaned. Crag swallowed the sound and lowered one of his massive hands to massage my breast. His calloused fingers worked over my nipple with a friction totally different from but just as thrilling as Lance's claws.

Torrent eased around to attend to my other breast with a tentacle. Watching over me, he reached to tug open the drawer on the bedside table. I was too occupied with my other lovers to see what he retrieved.

Lance plunged his tongue right inside me and then started pumping into me with his knuckles while he sucked on my clit. At my growl of need, he chuckled with a wash of hot breath over my sex. "I'll give you what you're craving, baby girl. I need it too."

He moved up my body in one smooth motion, his clothes disappearing somewhere along the way. As he nipped the edge of my jaw, he speared me with his cock, sliding all the way to the hilt in one go.

I arched to meet him, and he clutched my hip with the slightest prick of his claws. I pulled away from Crag to catch the dragon shifter's mouth.

As Lance's tongue delved between my lips, Crag

crouched down to suckle the breast he'd been fondling. My men seemed determined to leave no part of me unattended.

My body thrummed with pleasure, every nerve alight. We'd only come together all three of us once before, and I'd forgotten just how exhilarating an experience it was. Lance's cock swelled inside me into its bulbous dragon form, stretching me and rubbing against the perfect spot inside with every stroke, and I started to tremble with delight. I bucked with his thrusts, matching his rhythm as well as I could, tipping my head to kiss Torrent and then meet Crag's mouth again.

Lance kept up his ferocious pace and trailed his claws down my side at the same time. The quiver of bliss they woke up twined with the pleasure swelling from my core. My head jerked back against the pillow, and I clenched around him as I came. Sparks danced behind my eyes.

The dragon shifter let out a strangled sound as he careened after me. He bowed over my body, panting and grinning with satisfaction. I ran my fingers down the side of his face, but I still had one more lover I hadn't fully reunited with yet.

As Lance withdrew, I pushed myself upright and turned toward Crag. He drew back far enough to take in my expression.

I nudged him into a sitting position. "Clothes off. Now."

He smiled with a hint of a flush beneath the bronze of his cheeks. "How do you want me, Softness? The man or the gargoyle?"

I let out an impatient sound. "I love both of them. Which feels better to you?"

He paused and then admitted, "I like it better when I know I'm not at all pretending."

"Then give me the gargoyle."

He blinked into the shadows and back again, a foot taller and nearly as much broader on his return. His wings arched from his back. The bed's frame creaked but held under the weight of his flexible stone body.

I clambered onto his lap and stroked my hands over the solid planes that felt rock-hard yet as warm as regular flesh. When I reached past his shoulders to trail my fingers along the tops of his wings, he made a sound somewhere between a growl and a purr of encouragement.

One part of him was *particularly* hard, stiffly erect in anticipation. I slid my cunt along it, licking my lips and closing my eyes as the friction brought a fresh surge of giddiness.

Torrent and Lance had warmed me up, but Crag's gargoyle cock was by far the biggest I'd ever taken. We'd managed it before, though.

He slipped one hand between us to prepare me, sliding between my folds carefully and then with more confidence. With each sweep of his fingers, he stretched me wider. A little moan escaped me. I swayed with the movements of his hand, kissing his rough-edged jaw, his cheek, his mouth again until he was groaning too.

"Now," I mumbled when I couldn't stand the wait any longer. "I need you now."

A rumble reverberated from deep in the gargoyle's chest. He withdrew his hand, and I positioned myself over him. I eased down a couple of inches, and then a couple more, a sigh escaping both of us in unison. I was so perfectly, incredibly full.

Another hand glided down my back to my ass. Torrent leaned in to kiss my shoulder. "This is the perfect position for my experiment." He glanced at Crag. "If you don't mind me collaborating."

Crag gave me a look that was both fond and hot enough to turn my blood scorching. "If it makes our woman even happier, I'm all for it."

I sank a little deeper, taking even more of Crag into me, and paused to absorb the heady sensation. Then I peeked at Torrent from the corner of my eyes. "What's this secret?"

His smile was sly. "Not really a secret. We've discussed it before. And Rollick seems to keep his guestrooms well-stocked." He held up a bottle of lube. His caressing hand dipped between my cheeks to my back entrance, and a jolt of unexpected pleasure raced through my body. "We could find out how you enjoy being taken from two directions at the same time. We'll go slowly with it—I'll use a tentacle so I have even more control."

The thought of one of those lithe appendages stimulating me there turned my breath ragged in an instant. "Okay. Yes. Please."

Lance chuckled. "So eager, baby girl. I want to watch this. And hear every sound you make."

I did make a lot of sounds as I slid up and down on Crag's cock while he palmed one breast and then the other and Torrent slicked gel-drenched fingers over my other entrance. When the tentacled man hooked one finger inside me, I whimpered. It turned out I *could* feel even more full, and that feeling was glorious.

He worked another finger inside me, careful but firm, pulsing in and out. "How are you liking that, Quinn?"

"Good," I mumbled before another moan escaped me. "So good."

His fingers vanished, but only for a second before one of his tentacles replaced them, nudging at my now pliant entrance. It slid into me and began to thrust in and out in an echo of my rhythm over Crag's cock.

I cried out at the rush of pleasure radiating all through my torso. Crag caught my cheek and yanked my mouth to his. We kissed wildly, and I bucked faster, and both men picked up their pace to match me. It was a whirlwind of blissful pressure and friction and then—

I came apart with a cry that must have rung through the whole house. My body sagged between the two men, quaking with the aftershock of my final orgasm. Crag roared at the same moment, spilling himself inside me as he caught me against his chest. He hugged me to him as if he never meant to release me from his hold.

Torrent propped himself against the headboard next to us, outright smirking now. "It seems like that was a successful experiment."

I laughed breathlessly. "Yes. Very."

Lance sprawled out at my other side, totally comfortable leaning against the gargoyle's bulk as he stroked my arm. "So lovely. So sweet. Our special mortal."

"So lucky, to have the three of you," I said with a wave of emotion.

Torrent leaned forward to tuck a few stray strands of my hair behind my ear. He studied my face with a sudden intensity. "Have you had any interest in getting even luckier?"

His voice came out soft with its usual evenness, but something about the words made my pulse jump. I raised my head to peer at him. "What do you mean?"

"I mean," he said, and hesitated as if grappling with the words, "I've gotten the impression you and Rollick have made your peace with each other over the past little while. Maybe even become somewhat fond of each other?"

Guilt tugged at my gut. "We haven't done anything," I said quickly. "I didn't *want* to do anything."

Torrent's gaze was knowing. "Because you thought you'd be betraying us, or because you honestly weren't interested?"

There was no judgment in his tone. Still, my shoulders slumped. I didn't want to lie to him—to all of them.

"He has a certain appeal. He always did. And now I trust him... more than I did before, anyway. I understand why he did what he did. But I have the three of you. I don't need anyone else. You're more than enough."

Lance hummed to himself, his violet eyes sparkling in his golden face. "But is there such a thing as being *too* happy? I think the more we can give our woman, the better."

I blinked at him. "*You'd* be okay with him being a part of this relationship? He used you too—all three of you."

Lance shrugged. "He did what he thought was the best thing without worrying too much about anyone else. That's what shadowkind do. None of us got hurt. And he did protect you. He's trying to protect you every way he can. That means he's all right now."

Crag nodded slowly, watching me with a thoughtful expression. "If you wanted him, Softness, I wouldn't resent you or him for it. He's tackling this problem alongside us, as one of us. I can't say we're somehow more deserving."

"It's not about *deserving*," I protested.

Torrent slung a gentle tentacle around my shoulders. "When it comes to whether we can accept it or not, it is. But I only brought it up because, after talking to him, I realized *you* might deserve what he can offer too. I think whatever he would bring to the table, it'd be honestly, not a game. But all that matters is whether you really do want it. I don't think any of us would object to getting to keep you all to ourselves either."

"I don't know," I said, my emotions whirling.

"Lots of time to decide," Lance said. "I don't think the tricksy boss is going anywhere."

Torrent nodded. "No. I didn't mean to put you on the spot. I just thought we should be clear that the option is there, if you wanted to go down that path. I wouldn't like to see you tearing yourself up because you wanted something you thought would upset us."

All at once, I choked up. Still braced over Crag, I pulled the tentacled man into a hug. "Thank you," I said.

I didn't know what I was going to do with the information he'd just presented, but at least it dissolved the guilt that'd lodged deep inside me. We could figure the rest out when we needed to.

For now, we had two of the most ancient shadowkind in existence to bring down, and we still didn't know for sure what their endgame even was.

CHAPTER NINETEEN

Quinn

Even though we'd only been here for a matter of hours and Torrent often stuck to the shadows wherever we were, the house felt quieter after he left. At least for the half hour or so before Rollick prowled into the kitchen where I was eating a pot of yogurt I'd found in the fridge.

"They have to be doing it on purpose," he was muttering. "Of all the fucking cities in the entire world..."

His angry tone made me immediately tense up, even as a flicker of heat raced through me at the memory of the conversation I'd just had with my lovers... about the potential of this man becoming my lover too. But any consideration along those lines went out the window when I took in his furrowed brow. There was obviously something more important going on.

Rollick didn't often let any emotions show through his cool confidence. He wasn't upset enough for me to have picked up on it through that weird one-way bond we now had, so maybe the situation wasn't that bad, but he was definitely irritated.

I set down my spoon, bracing myself. "What happened?"

Rollick swiped his hand over his face and composed it into a more typical nonchalant expression. "Oh, just that the bastards have decided to target the one city I particularly like around here. They're menacing mortals all over L.A."

A chill washed over me, deeper than the cool currents from the air conditioning system. "What? What are they doing to people?"

"Mostly just spooking them from the shadows, from what I'm hearing from my contacts back ho—back there. But a few humans have been outright attacked by their minions."

He'd almost called the city *home*, I thought. Did it bother him to think of any mortal place that fondly? Even if he wasn't willing to say it out loud, he clearly felt particularly protective of the place. And the thought of the kinds of shadowkind beasts I'd been attacked by threatening the entire city made my stomach knot, even though I'd only spent ten days there.

Lance leapt into being out of the patch of darkness by the doorway and clicked his claws against the counter near me. "They're hassling mortals openly? Isn't that against the rules?"

Rollick grimaced. "Slaughtering them openly is against the theoretical rules too, but that hasn't stopped this bunch. I don't understand their game plan, though. Terrorizing a city full of non-sorcerers hardly connects to their other activities."

I folded my arms over my chest, hugging myself. "Could they be looking for me there—or trying to provoke me into showing myself? They know I was staying in the city before."

"I think they'd be more likely to pick your hometown for that," Rollick pointed out. "It could be intended to rankle *me*, in which case, bravo, they're succeeding. But it's too random right now. It has to add up to a larger picture."

"Maybe they're just cuckoo," Lance suggested, making a spinning gesture next to his ear that he must have picked up from his mortal observations.

The demon sighed. "As much as I'd like to believe we're merely dealing with a couple of ancient beings gone ferally unhinged, they've handled themselves very efficiently so far. I don't think we can count on that."

Crag strode into the room then, back from the patrol-slash-hunt he'd gone off on after our interlude in the bedroom. He frowned at Rollick. "Who's unhinged? What are the villains up to now? I didn't spot any concerning activity near the house."

"No one much comes near this part of the country," Rollick informed him. "That's why we're here. They're toying with the mortals in Los Angeles for purposes unknown."

"What are we going to do about it?" I asked, drawing my spine straighter. "I mean, we're not going to let them get away with it, right? If they're attacking people—innocent people, not just sorcerers now— Have you been able to get many of your contacts or whoever ready to push back against the behemoth and the leviathan in general?"

"I'm working on it." Rollick rubbed his jaw, his gaze going momentarily distant. "It'll take some doing, you know, considering I didn't develop my connections with the idea of building an army in mind. And most shadowkind aren't inclined to stick their necks out unless it's necessary to save their own hide. I'm having to start slow —planting the idea that their hides are actually at stake. I don't think they're ready to rush into battle just yet."

My spirits sank. "Then what can we do? What about Sorsha and the shadowkind she hangs out with? She said we should go to her if we need more help against our enemies. She's pretty powerful, isn't she?"

The demon gave me a baleful look. "How much do you know about the shadowkind who calls herself 'Sorsha' and her history?"

I paused, abruptly uncertain. Did Rollick know some reason to distrust her? I'd never gotten any bad vibes from her... but then, I wasn't all that experienced at judging shadowkind intentions.

"She's a phoenix, right?" I ventured. "She can conjure fire. I thought... she saved a whole bunch of people a while back. She said something like that when we first met her, and Torrent knew what she was talking about."

"Well, that's essentially true. From what I understand, she's some kind of hybrid: a nearly impossible mix of shadowkind and human origin that makes her powers particularly potent—and unstable. I've heard from beings who were there during the final showdown she was involved in, and they say she nearly burned down the entire continent before her friends managed to calm her down. The Highest believed she might destroy both this world and ours."

I blinked at him. "Oh. Um, she didn't mention that part."

Rollick smiled thinly. "I wouldn't either, if it were me. But I'd rather not count on allies whose main fighting skill is razing everything around them to the ground. Personally, I'd prefer if Los Angeles was at least mostly still standing when we're done dealing with these pricks."

I could see his point. But still... "Are you saying we're just going to hang out here and let them harass people until you can convince the other shadowkind you know to actually help, then?"

"No," he said. "I'm going back to L.A. to see if I can't decipher their motives. You should be safe enough here with—"

"No," I broke in, raising my chin. "You're not leaving me here to just sit around and relax either. The fiends are attacking humans—my people. I can help. You need to question the creatures carrying out the attacks—I can use my sorcery to compel them to answer, right? I don't mind wearing the vest, and no one should notice I've arrived in the city while I have it on."

Rollick fixed me with a steady, penetrating stare. I gazed right back at him. If he figured he could glower me into submission, he obviously didn't know me as well as he thought he did.

I didn't even have to make the stand alone. Lance bobbed his head and tucked his arm around me. "I want to tackle the beasties too. We'll keep Quinn safe wherever we are. Right, stony one?"

He glanced over at Crag, who hummed low in his chest. "Yes. We should all find out what we can. They're escalating the threat. We don't know how much time we have until they do something worse."

"There," I said to Rollick. "We're all agreed—well, except for you. Three to one. We can leave a note for Torrent for when he gets back to let him know where we've gone. Or maybe you have other ways of sending him a message."

Rollick exhaled with a sound of exasperation, and then, to my surprise, he grinned at me. "I shouldn't have expected anything less. Come along then, sweet sorcerer. We've got quite a trek ahead of us."

When Crag nudged me from the doze I'd fallen into in the back seat, the city ahead of us was nothing but gleaming lights amid the darkness of night. We'd flown into California on a small private jet that was apparently in Rollick's arsenal, but he hadn't wanted to land too close to L.A. itself in case our enemies were keeping a close eye on more blatant comings and goings.

I straightened up and rubbed my eyes. At my awakening, Lance blinked back into physical form in the passenger seat. He kicked out his legs, eyeing the oncoming buildings avidly. "Now we teach some beasties a lesson."

"We take a cautious approach," Rollick reminded him in a dry tone from behind the wheel. "We're not in a position to go head-to-head with the dastardly duo just yet."

"Do we have any idea where to start once we get into the city?" I asked.

"I'll touch base with my contacts when we're there."

That only took a few more minutes. Rollick pulled over to the side of the road and got out his phone. As he skimmed through his messages and placed a couple of calls, Crag tugged me closer to him with his arm around my shoulders. He seemed determined to show he wouldn't shy away from me anymore, and I couldn't say I minded. I leaned my head against his solid chest and let myself relax just for a moment.

It *was* only a moment, because then Rollick let out a sound of consternation. "They're really getting bold. Look at this."

He passed his phone back to me with no hesitation or warnings not to exploit the opportunity. I might have reveled in the trust he'd shown if my eyes hadn't widened at the sight of the news video he'd brought up on the screen. The headline said, *WILD DOG ATTACKS RAMPANT.*

"What the heck?" I muttered to myself, and hit play.

The reporter in the video feed talked in an urgent voice about the rash of brutal assaults across Los Angeles, which appeared to be the work of feral animals—they were assuming packs of stray dogs. One shot of a victim showed deep gouges across his face, neck, and chest. I winced at the sight.

"Six attacks already tonight," I said as the video finished, my gut churning. "What are the shadowkind thinking? What are they getting out of this?"

"I don't know," Rollick said. "They're really skirting the line of exposure. Some of those victims must know it wasn't dogs, but whatever they've reported, the human authorities will find it impossible to believe."

Lance growled. "The beasties should know better."

"Maybe they do," I pointed out. "They might be under a spell, not doing it because they want to." But we didn't know yet whether my sorcery might be able to break our enemies' hold on their enslaved minions. "If we could find the beings who are carrying out the attacks and question one of them—if any of them *can* talk—"

"Already one step ahead of you." Rollick started the engine. "Three of tonight's attacks and one of yesterday's two were in the same general neighborhood. It must be a favorite stalking ground for at least a couple of these creatures. And if they can't tell us anything, we'll see if they can lead us to someone better informed."

He drove into a part of the city much less posh and shiny than the neighborhood around his hotel. Low-rise brick and concrete apartment buildings stood amid a few smaller homes with scruffy lawns and the occasional corner store. Some of the streetlamps were broken, leaving the sidewalks cast in intermittent pools of light.

Not many people were out at this late hour. Most of the activity seemed to be centered around a few bars on the outskirts of the residential area, their windows still glowing and occasional shouts and barks of laughter carrying from within. Rollick parked down the street from them and motioned for us to get out.

I hefted the crossbow I'd left at my feet, fully loaded, and unzipped the pocket on my messenger bag where I was keeping a stash of extra bolts so I could grab them quickly if I needed to reload. Once I was out of the car, I held the weapon down by my thigh where it wasn't too obviously visible in the darkness.

"We'll patrol in the shadows," Rollick said. "Quinn, you amble around and keep a close eye on any pedestrians who could become targets."

"*She* could become a target," Lance pointed out.

The demon shot him an amused glance. "I think she's proven she can handle herself. At least for long enough to give one of us the chance to jump in there as need be."

His confidence in me didn't stop my nerves from jittering. I might be able to handle a shadowkind creature on the attack, but that didn't mean I enjoyed the thought of it.

Taking a deep breath, I set off down the street. The men vanished into the shadows, but I took comfort from knowing they were nearby. I walked past the bars, circled the block, and was just coming back into view when a man and a woman came out through one of the doorways.

I meandered along behind the couple for a short distance until they got into a car. No beasts showed themselves.

A guy who looked like he was probably homeless shuffled by. I trailed him for a few blocks without any interference. He hunkered down on a bench by a bus stop, and I watched from the other end of the street for several minutes until it seemed better to search for other potential targets. Who knew what criteria the creatures on the hunt were using?

After doubling back, a murmured voice reached my ears

as I neared the bars. A woman strode my way from the direction I'd been heading, swaying a little on her feet, her phone pressed to her ear. I pulled back against the building I'd been passing, and she walked on by without showing any sign that she'd noticed me. I waited until she'd almost reached the next corner, then pushed myself forward to follow her.

She lowered her phone—and a clump of shadow burst from a nearby alley to hurtle toward her.

A yelp of warning broke from my throat. I dashed forward, raising my crossbow and registering that it was *two* creatures leaping at her, not just one. But I couldn't risk hitting her with one of the bolts.

I sprang to the side, bumping into a parked car, and fired at the smaller beast that'd landed on her shoulders as it solidified. It tumbled off with a squeal. The woman was shrieking and flailing out her limbs at the larger creature, which looked like a cross between a wolf and a sheepdog. It shoved at her from behind as if trying to knock her down.

I aimed at its head as it snapped its fangs, but it was moving too quickly for me to get in a good shot while avoiding its intended victim. My fired bolt hit it in the shoulder instead. It stumbled to the side, and the woman took off with a sob. She left her heels behind on the sidewalk, her bare feet pattering frantically across the concrete.

As I spun toward the wolf-thing, which was heaving itself back to its feet while smoke streamed from its shoulder wound, my three men materialized around it. Crag caught it by the shoulders, digging his thumb into the wound. "Shift," he demanded.

Before my eyes, the being shed its shaggy, course fur and canine shape, swinging upright into a man with rumpled hair and eerie yellow eyes. The wound from the bolt didn't disappear. He hissed through his teeth as Crag gripped him harder.

Rollick stepped over beside me to look the shadowkind in the face. "Why are you hunting the mortals like this? Is it your idea, or did your masters force you?"

The wolf shifter simply growled at him. A quiver of my power raced through my nerves. I drew myself up as tall as I could and willed the energy from my heart to sizzle through my whole chest, into my lungs, and up my throat.

The words that spilled from my tongue weren't any I'd have recognized, but I understood the compulsion behind them. *Answer our questions.*

But the command seemed to smack against a barrier, the energy tremoring apart between us instead of taking hold in the being's mind. I'd never felt that sensation before.

"He must already have sorcery on him," I said. "It's blocking mine. But I might be able to break through."

I inhaled deeply to try again, and the man squirmed in Crag's grasp, panic flashing across his face where before he'd only looked defiant.

"My masters will it, so it is so," he snarled. "And they'll destroy all of you too."

Lance leapt in. "Be careful. The one I caught before—"

He was too late. The wolf-man jerked his head—and managed to smash it into the brick side of the building next to us so hard his skull caved in. Horror congealed in my stomach as his body crumpled.

That hadn't been an action I could imagine any creature, mortal or shadowkind, managing on its own. There must have been a suicide command implanted in the spell his masters had cast on him.

Rollick muttered a curse and motioned for Crag to release the body that was now gushing smoky blood. "Well, now we know for sure that some of the beings responsible aren't acting of their own accord. We'll have to restrain the next one more carefully. If we can find a next one." He glanced grimly down the street. "Back to the patrol."

CHAPTER TWENTY

Crag

After an entire night of stalking the city streets and failing to capture another being capable of speech, Quinn slept through most of the day. She only woke up in the apartment Rollick had brought us to when the sky beyond the narrow window was starting to darken with the next evening.

She came into the small living room with her messenger bag. I suspected it was nearly time for her next dose of pills. The sight of the surgery scar poking from the neckline of her top made something inside me clench up.

The new heart had saved her life when she was a child, but it might also have doomed her to a worse fate at the hands of these fiends we were facing off against.

Rollick had returned to the apartment just minutes ago and was pouring himself a sour-smelling drink in the kitchen area. Quinn flopped into the chair next to the window and glanced between me and him. "Any progress?"

"Lance is out having another prowl," Rollick said. "But we haven't turned up anything substantial. It's very clear the vicious duo are in the area, but I haven't managed to pin down where they're hiding out. If we knew where they were sending their minions from, that'd make catching those minions easier."

Quinn pinched the bridge of her nose. "There aren't any convenient mountain lakes nearby that they'd be using?"

Rollick guffawed. "Believe me, that was the first thing I considered. Maybe they realized after two invasions in a row that they'd become too predictable." He wrinkled his nose at his drink. "I often appreciate a challenge, but I wish these particular opponents weren't quite so on the ball."

Their comments about the mountain lakes stirred a memory in my head. After we'd gotten so focused on what was happening on this side of the ocean, I'd almost forgotten the evidence I'd come across when Torrent and Lance had found me in China.

"I noticed something at the first camp by the lake," I said, hesitating. Maybe it wouldn't be meaningful at all. But I should let the others decide how useful the information was. "There were traces of fish—a specific kind of fish I recognized after I did some more searching afterward. It's a fish from the ocean that must have been brought up into the mountains specially. I'm guessing one of the bosses— probably the leviathan, since he's the watery one—must like them a lot."

Rollick's eyes gleamed with an eager light that gratified

me. "Good work! You should have mentioned that before. Do you know exactly what this fish is?"

I frowned. "I don't know what the humans call them. But I could tell from a picture. They're silver and about this big." I spread my hands in front of me. "They like waters near the coast where there aren't many people around. I first encountered them along the Asian side of this ocean, but I'm guessing they're on the American side too."

"It doesn't seem likely that the leviathan would be importing his fish from a distant continent," Quinn agreed, and knit her brow. "Unless they were taking them through a rift or something."

"Let's see what we can find." Rollick was already tapping on his phone. "Fairly small, silver, Pacific ocean, coastal... There we go." He held the device up with the screen facing me, a grid of photographs showing across its glossy surface. "Do any of these look right?"

I spotted the right one immediately, with a flash of memory of its tender flesh in my mouth. "It's that one," I said, pointing.

Rollick grinned. "*Very* good. That's just the sort of thing we need. I can send some people along the coast and other secluded areas within a reasonable distance from the city and see if they can't track down a trail of fish bones that'll point us in the right direction."

He brought the phone to his ear and breezed out of the room as he started talking to the person on the other end. A smile crossed my lips. My searching when I'd been forced to leave Quinn had been worthwhile after all. Maybe it would get us closer to ending the threat that loomed over her.

I looked at her where she was perched on the armchair. "Are you hungry? I brought back some food."

Quinn made a face. "Not really. Not yet. I'll eat later. I feel like my stomach is too full of worries to have room for anything else."

I couldn't quite picture that sensation, seeing as I never really felt hungry the same way mortals did, but it made a certain kind of sense. I didn't like seeing her plagued by those worries. Hoping to offer some kind of reassurance, I walked over to rest my hand on her shoulder—but just as I reached for her, a scream split the air from outside.

Quinn leapt to her feet, fear flashing across her face. "Someone else is being attacked. Shit. Where's my crossbow?"

She dashed into the bedroom and sprinted out a moment later clutching the weapon. I could have leapt right through the shadows outside the window, but I wasn't leaving her to rush down into the possible fray alone. I'd already pushed the door open. As she darted past me, I melded with the patches of gloom to follow her where no mortals would see my face with its clearly inhuman jaw.

The apartment was only the second floor of a building with a storefront below, the shop now closed for the night. Quinn raced down the single flight of stairs with thudding feet and burst out into the thickening dusk. Her head whipped around as she tried to locate the source of the scream. "Where did it come from?"

A yelp from around the corner gave us a clue. Quinn ran over, and I hurtled alongside her through the shadows.

Foot traffic was already diminishing in this part of the city, but there were still a decent number of people around.

A small crowd had gathered around the mouth of an alley. Quinn rushed over to them, tucking her crossbow close to her body to avoid notice, and bobbed up on her toes to peer at the scene.

I slipped right through the clustered feet and halted. A young man's body was sprawled in the mouth of the alley, his eyes staring sightlessly, blood saturating his shirt from where his throat and chest had been torn open.

It wasn't like the sorcerer attacks. None of his organs had been taken, only mangled by vicious claws. I couldn't sense the creature that'd done it—it must have carved him up with a few brutal strokes and then fled.

Rollick came up beside me through the shadows. I sensed his grimace. "That's not promising. They're escalating from injuring to murdering. I'll tell my people on the hunt that they'd better move *fast*."

I shifted my attention back to Quinn. She'd eased back from the crowd, her mouth tight, her knuckles whitening where she was gripping the crossbow. My heart lurched for her, but I couldn't easily comfort her with all these mortal witnesses around.

Her gaze darted around the darkening street. Then she turned and marched swiftly back to the apartment.

I decided it was safe enough to emerge in the stairwell, since it didn't lead to anything other than Rollick's apartment. I leapt into physical being on the steps ahead of her, and Quinn kept moving forward, right into my arms.

I hugged her tightly as she let out a choked sound. She pressed her face against my chest. Her voice came out muffled.

"We weren't fast enough. He wouldn't have had any

idea what the thing that attacked him even was. Why are they killing random people who never did anything to them?"

I didn't have any answers for her. My throat constricted. I held her close, abruptly aware again of the strength in my arms, the grip that could turn crushing if I let it.

I was like the thing that had killed that man. It would be so easy for me to hurt her—I'd done it before without intending to. How could I—

Closing my eyes, I shoved those thoughts away. They were what had wrenched us apart in the first place. I would never harm her like that. I'd protected her so many times. I had to focus on what I'd accomplished and not the rare mistakes.

Or I might lose her in a totally different way.

"I don't know," I said, trying to keep my voice from sounding too gruff. "They want to cause pain—they're more monstrous than most of us."

"I wish I knew how to stop them."

"We'll find a way. They can't get away with this forever." I let my determination color my tone. I wasn't going to *let* them get away with it, no matter what it took.

"They might hurt you too," she said.

They probably would. I didn't say that out loud. "Then I'll be hurt, and I'll recover, like I have many times before. You know I'm made of tough stuff."

But saying that didn't feel like enough. She'd spent the last few weeks running from catastrophe to catastrophe—and I'd contributed to those disasters. If I could just take her away from all the horrors for a little while, remind her of all the goodness that was still left, give her a glimpse of the peaceful future I wanted so badly to share with her...

An idea sparked in my head. I scooped her right off the steps and carried her upward.

"Where are we going?" Quinn mumbled.

"You've asked before what I love about being in the mortal realm. I'm going to show you one of the things around here that I love most."

She lifted her head. "What? Crag, don't you think we should—"

"I think right now you need to get away from all the awfulness we can't tackle yet," I interrupted. "I'm not taking no for an answer."

Quinn raised an eyebrow at me. "When did you get so bossy?"

I glanced down at her. "When I saw what happens when I let our problems tear us apart instead of bringing us together."

A hint of tears shimmered in her eyes. She leaned forward and wrapped her arms around my neck without any further protest. A faint prickle of discomfort spread through my skin at the sense of the metal vest beneath her shirt, but her embrace gave me more pleasure than that minor irritation could ever dislodge.

I'd noticed when we'd arrived at the apartment that there was a set of maintenance steps leading up to a small landing above the level of Rollick's apartment. After popping into the apartment so Quinn could leave the crossbow there, I busted the lock on the maintenance door open and stepped out into the warm night air at the edge of the roof.

Streetlamps still glowed below us and artificial light streaked the wisps of cloud and smog overhead, but it was dark enough that I didn't hesitate. I let loose my gargoyle form, my wings unfurling from my back, and pushed off toward the sky.

I didn't throw caution completely to the wind. I shot straight upward with swift flaps until I was sure no one would be able to make me out against the deep indigo of the sky. Only then did I turn and soar toward the spot I wanted to show the woman I—

The woman I loved.

The realization hit me so hard my wings stuttered in mid-flap. Quinn tensed in my arms with obvious concern, and I picked up my rhythm again even as my mind reeled.

She'd told me that she loved me when she'd said the same to the others, right before she sent us away. I hadn't really thought about the exact nature of my feelings toward her, because they had nothing to do with thinking, they simply were, as if they'd always been a part of me. But that was the word for it, wasn't it—this all-encompassing desire to see her safe and happy? Love.

And somehow she felt the same incredible emotion toward me.

I'd flown out over the ocean. I swiveled around and kept my wings sweeping up and down to bring us in a slow circle, adjusting Quinn's position in my grasp so she could take in the view with me.

"You asked me before where I like to fly, what sights I've enjoyed taking in," I said. "While I was working with Rollick mostly in this area of the world, I often came out here at night to enjoy the view. And do a little night fishing, but we'll skip that part while you're with me."

"Maybe another time," Quinn teased, but awe wound through her words. "It's beautiful. That's the highway?"

"Yes." A glowing golden line wove along the coast, undulating with the curves of the green-dotted hills. Starker lights glided along it as cars cruised by. The glow mingled with the moonlight to catch on the foam of the waves below, bringing out hints of lavender and turquoise against the blackness of the night.

It was amazing how humans had taken a landscape that was already striking by daylight and used their inventions to transform it into something eerily gorgeous after sunset.

"No matter what the fiends do, this view will be here," I said. "Mortals will survive and bring their light. And even if we can't do it perfectly, we are helping to protect that light. Together."

"Together," Quinn murmured, looping her arm around my bicep and squeezing. "Even if we get hurt."

"Even if we hurt each other accidentally." I kissed the back of her head. "I love you, Quinn."

She craned her neck to meet my eyes, a smile lighting her face so it shone as stunningly as the landscape before us. "I love you too. Thank you for this. I think I needed it. I—"

Her gaze slipped past me for a second, and her forehead furrowed. "What's that?"

I spun in the air just in time to see the starry sky before us ripple as if it were a pond someone had thrown a pebble into. My body tensed.

"That's a rift," I said. "And someone's messing with it."

CHAPTER TWENTY-ONE

Quinn

"And what makes you so sure this rift is important?" Rollick asked as he turned the wheel to follow the curve of the road.

I spoke up for the gargoyle. "Crag could sense that there was a lot of shadowkind activity near it—a bunch of them, and at least one particularly powerful one. It's got to be the sorcerer-killers, right?"

Not just sorcerer-killers now, I corrected myself silently. Human-killers in general. I restrained a shudder at the memory of the savaged man we'd seen on the street earlier this night.

"More tricks from the big beasts," Lance muttered in the back seat, clicking his claws together restlessly.

"We might be able to learn more about their plans," Crag says. "I could go ahead and—"

Rollick shook his head, peering down the road through the glow of the lights along the highway. "We all stay together until we find the spot. I want to get some idea what we're dealing with before we decide on a strategy."

I squinted at the sky, still black and dotted with stars. I couldn't make anything out, but then, I hadn't seen anything other than a brief, vague distortion when I'd first spotted the rift. It'd vanished before my gaze right afterward, even though Crag had still been able to identify it.

I guessed that made sense. If mortals had been able to see the rifts shadowkind used to travel between their world and ours, their existence wouldn't have been anywhere near as secret. But what were the villainous duo doing that had affected this one enough that I'd caught a glimpse of it?

Hopefully we'd be able to find that out.

Rollick must have been able to sense the rift in some way too, because he veered off onto a side road abruptly but with a clear sense of purpose. He drove up the slope of one of the hills along the coast, the road winding back and forth up the side with signs for a lookout point at the top. But halfway up, he pulled the car as far as he could onto the shoulder and parked. "We'll go the rest of the way on foot."

I gathered my bag and my crossbow, my pulse kicking up a notch. I had no idea what we were going to find out here—whether it might be even more horrifying than what we'd already discovered about these monsters.

The road here was cloaked in almost total darkness. I walked as briskly as I could along the shoulder while placing my feet carefully to avoid falling, thankful again for my past urban explorations tramping around in abandoned buildings and private skyscraper stairwells. Who could have predicted what handy preparation they'd be for this new phase of my life?

"Could it be they're just bringing more shadowkind minions through to the mortal realm?" I asked, keeping my voice low. "They were doing that over by Miami too, right?"

"We never saw any strange energy around the rift there like the one here tonight," Crag said.

Rollick nodded. "For something to be happening that would make the portal visible even to mortal eyes, they're up to more than standard immigration. I'm *very* curious to discover what that is."

We hustled the rest of the way in silence, Crag striding a little ahead to scan the vegetation for lurking beasts, Lance shifting into his dragon form to leap and weave between the shrubs with typical wild grace. Watching him brought a pang into my heart. I glanced at Rollick, who was still marching along beside me.

"Are you sure Lance should have come? If either of the leaders use their sorcery again..."

"I gave him strict orders to retreat immediately if he senses either of those ancients nearby," the demon said. "And I think, given his past experience with them, he'll actually follow my orders for once. We don't have many allies we can count on, sorcerer. We can't afford to coddle those who are willing to stand with us."

I narrowed my eyes at him. "*You* encouraged me to send them away for their protection. What happened to that perspective?"

He shrugged casually as if it didn't matter much to him,

but a twinge of emotion carried into me that tasted like regret. "I didn't know how vast a threat we were up against. We've sorted out the situation now."

"So you're admitting you were wrong," I couldn't help needling.

He cast me a baleful look, his eyes gleaming in the darkness. "It does happen, though only on very rare occasions."

Ahead of us, Crag grunted. He was looking back toward the ocean. "There it is again."

We all spun around. I caught just the faintest waver in the sky beyond the top of the hill before its surface smoothed out again. My pulse stuttered.

Rollick frowned, apparently no surer than before what might have caused the phenomenon. "Our enemies do like to keep busy," he remarked. "Come on."

We left the road and scrambled the rest of the way up the hill more directly. At its peak, I hung back at the far end of the lookout's parking lot with Lance standing guard while the demon and the gargoyle approached the crest overlooking the sea. My fingers tightened around the handle of the crossbow.

After a minute, Rollick motioned us over. He pointed down toward a small peninsula protruding into the ocean, closer to the hill next to ours than to our own. Barely any of the light from the highway lamps reached it, but when I squinted, I made out a few thicker clots of darkness moving through the shadows there.

"That's right beneath the rift," he murmured. "There are a lot of beings around it, but they're mostly in the shadows, hard to pick out at this distance. I suspect if we got closer, we'd be able to sense at least one of the two head honchos in their midst."

"What are they *doing*?" I asked. It was all a vague, dark blur to me.

"I'm not sure. They—"

Lance interrupted with a startled hiss. I stiffened, my gaze flicking over the peninsula and the sky—and snagging on what looked like a wisp of smoke briefly obscuring a patch of stars, there and then swallowed into the brief wobbling of the rift's border.

"What was that?" I demanded. "What happened?"

"Carving up the beasties like they do the sorcerers," the dragon shifter muttered with a twitch of his head.

Rollick's forehead had furrowed. "It looks like they're making some kind of sacrifice out of lesser shadowkind. Killing them and sending their essence into the rift. I have no idea what they expect that act to accomplish, though."

A shiver ran over my skin. "So every time the rift has wavered like that, they've killed something?" I'd seen it three times already just in the short time I'd been within view. How many other creatures had they slaughtered in the hours it'd taken Crag and I to return to the others and then for us all to drive back here?

"Possibly. It could be they're up to other things as well. The being that killed the beast just now didn't even show itself." Rollick glanced at our companions. "You two see if you can get a closer look. Lance, stick to the north—Crag, go south. Don't let yourselves be spotted. They're busy for now, but once the sun rises, I expect they'll disperse."

It occurred to me then that if the behemoth and the leviathan could bring even the powerful warriors sent by the Highest beings under their sway, Crag wasn't necessarily any safer than Lance was. As they vanished into the darkness around us, my mouth went dry.

"What are *we* going to do?" I asked the demon.

"Stay here and keep an eye on the bigger picture." Rollick rubbed his jaw. "I don't like this at all."

I couldn't help thinking that his plan left me pretty useless, since I could barely see any of the picture with my human eyes. I shifted my weight from one foot to the other, restlessness itching at me—but what else could I do? I wouldn't be any more useful trying to scope things out closer to the gathering, and I'd be a lot more likely to get caught than the shadowkind men. I guessed the demon was keeping me in reserve until it seemed like a good idea to bring my powers into play.

We watched until the sky lightened just slightly to a deep blue, the first hints of dawn creeping over the eastern horizon behind us. Rollick stirred, maybe thinking it'd be time to get going soon.

"Stay here," he said. "I want to do a quick search closer by."

Without waiting for a response, he vanished into the night. I grimaced at what I imagined was his retreating back and then peered down the hillside again.

It couldn't have been more than a minute later when my gaze caught on a shape moving through the shadows far down the slope below me.

It was a humanoid form, bald and gangly, its pale skin showing against the darkened landscape as it raised the small animal it'd leapt out of the shadows to pounce on to its jagged teeth. My heart skipped a beat.

Could that be one of the duo's minions on patrol? It looked human-like enough to be able to speak. If I could use my sorcery on it, maybe we could find out what the hell was going on out here.

There was no sign of Rollick's return. I didn't know how long the creature would enjoy its meal before it slipped back into the shadows where I'd never find it. I wavered for only a few seconds, and then I readied my crossbow and hopped over the low crest of the hill.

The slope gave me the momentum for my strides to stretch wide. The creature's head jerked up at my approach, but its eyes only narrowed, probably seeing me as mortal prey just as much as the animal it was snacking on. I propelled myself faster, adrenaline thrumming through my limbs, and raised the crossbow.

Panic flashed across the thing's face. It dropped the furry body in its grasp, but before it could disappear, I fired a bolt into its knobby thigh.

Magic reverberated up my throat. "Stay where I can see you," I said, or at least something like that in the unfamiliar syllables of the sorcery language. My tongue sizzled with the energy my voice expelled. "No ducking into your shadow form."

The creature's body stiffened. My magic had taken hold. I hadn't felt any obstacle to the spell, so this must be a being that was helping the monsters of its own accord.

I was ten feet away and slowing when Rollick materialized, looming over the creature, which only came up to his waist in its hunched pose. He clamped a hand around the back of its neck as if to ensure it didn't go anywhere and then leveled a pointed look at me. "What in the realms do you think you're doing?"

"I saw it—I had to try," I said, drawing up short. "We can question it."

"You shouldn't go running at shadowkind creatures—especially ones probably allied with our enemies—on your own. What if it'd lunged at you before you could work your sorcery? What if you'd missed with your fancy weaponry?"

I glowered at him, my annoyance only slightly tempered by the concern that was wafting off him despite his snarky tone. "You brought me along. Do you trust me to handle myself or not? We need to know what they're doing here. If it's worth risking Lance and Crag to find out, then it's worth risking me too."

To my surprise, the demon looked momentarily chagrined. "Fine," he said. "Let's see what this lackey has to say for herself."

Apparently the thing was female. I wouldn't have been able to tell. I lowered the crossbow and fixed my attention on her. When I opened my mouth, more of that strange language coursed out of me like an electrical current, carrying my will that she should answer our questions truthfully. My skin tingled with the effort, as if it'd only exhilarated me rather than tiring me out.

Rollick's essence had definitely enhanced my abilities in ways I wasn't sure I'd totally discovered yet.

The creature twitched and bared its teeth at me, but it didn't—couldn't?—argue. I met Rollick's gaze again. "It should tell you whatever you want to know now."

He stepped to the side of the creature and jerked her around so she was facing him. "Are you working with the shadowkind who've been killing sorcerers and harassing humans in Los Angeles?"

She let out a little snarl, but she answered in a gravelly voice. "Yes."

The simplest, briefest possible answer. But the demon's lips curled with a smirk. No doubt he was perfectly fine with playing the game of how to squeeze the right information out of it. "And your masters are a behemoth and a leviathan, aren't they?"

The creature made a face at him. "Yes."

"Very good. Now, what are they doing over there with that rift?"

"Offering up dead shadowkind," she rasped, as brusquely as before.

Rollick tsked his tongue. "Yes, but *why*? What are they hoping to accomplish by doing that?"

Her jaw tightened, but she couldn't hold back the words. "The essence is making the rift bigger."

They wanted the portal between the realms to grow? I frowned at the sky and then at her.

Rollick appeared to be equally puzzled. "And why do they want it to be bigger?"

"I don't know," the creature growled. "We do what they say. They know what they're doing. Please stop. If they find out I've told you anything, they'll kill *me*."

The blood stains on her teeth made it hard for me to feel much mercy. So many other lives were at stake if we didn't find out all she knew.

"Why are you helping them?" I asked, stepping closer. "Why are you doing what they say?"

Her round, dark eyes fixed on me. "Why not? They're

going to bring us out of the shadows. We can have everything—this world can be ours. Let me go!"

Her words sent a chill down my back. Bring them out of the shadows? The world would be theirs? What was that even supposed to mean? Nothing good—that much I could tell.

"And how exactly—" Rollick began, shifting his grip on her neck, and the creature must have felt the tiniest loosening of his grasp. She jerked from his hold and sprang straight at me, needle-sharp claws protruding from her fingers, bloody jaws yawning wide.

My chest shuddered with a flash of fear that was both mine and Rollick's. I stumbled backward, jerking my crossbow up—and the demon was already on her.

Rollick punched his fist straight into the creature's chest when she was only inches from me. She sagged with a few spastic twitches, hanging off his arm. He shook her off, looked down at his smoking, gore-smeared hand with an expression of distaste, and flickered in and out of the shadows just long enough to leave the mess behind.

He met my gaze. "We probably got everything useful we could out of her anyway."

He'd acted so fast, without thinking—and if he hadn't, I might be dead right now. I swallowed thickly, my pulse still hammering from the shock of the moment, grappling with the unexpected urge to hug him. "Thank you."

A strange emotion I couldn't identify wisped from him into me, warm but somehow melancholy at the same time. "Just because you want to take risks doesn't mean I'm going to let you succumb to them if I have any say in the matter." He glanced down at the smoking corpse. "It wasn't a bad gambit. We do know a little more than we did before."

"We do." I had no idea what to say next, but then it didn't matter, because a jaunty voice called down from the crest of the hill.

"What are you two playing around with down there?"

As we turned toward Lance, Crag appeared beside him. The expanding dawn shimmered in the sky behind them. At Rollick's gesture, I clambered up the slope beside him.

"We got to have a little fun of our own," Rollick said. "Now I think we'd better get out of here."

On the drive back to the city, Lance and Crag reported their observations, but they hadn't seen much more than we'd already observed, just closer up. "There were a couple dozen beings gathered around," Crag said. "And the one making the sacrifices was moving up and down to the rift through the darkness. I couldn't get close enough to get a strong feel for him, but he was powerful. He felt at home with the ocean."

"The sea serpent," Lance put in. "I could take him, dragon to dragon. If he didn't have his cheating magic."

"But he does, so you'll stay put," Rollick said dryly. "They're expanding the rift for some purpose, and it sounds like they want to establish more of a shadowkind presence in the mortal world. But they wouldn't need a *bigger* rift just for that. There are hundreds across this country already."

"Next time we'll have to catch a minion who knows a little more," I suggested, and he aimed a wry smile my way. But his uneasiness kept reaching me in flickers and flashes. He wasn't happy about what we'd learned at all.

We marched up to the apartment in the brightening morning light. As we strode in through the door, Torrent wavered into view in the middle of the living room, his expression grim.

My heart leapt with relief. "You're back!"

"I am," he said. "But I don't think any of you are going to like what I have to report."

CHAPTER TWENTY-TWO

Quinn

Before Torrent could get into his report, my morning alarm pealed from my phone. The shadowkind men fell silent while I popped my pills and grabbed a glass of water to chase them. Crag followed me into the kitchen and insisted on heaping a plate with slices of fruit and the premade sandwiches he'd obtained for me.

I hadn't eaten all night other than a couple of hasty snacks, so I guessed he had a point. But as soon as the plate was in my hands, I sat down on the linen sofa and focused on Torrent, who'd propped himself against the wall next to the window. "You found out something about the leviathan."

"Yes." His supporting tentacles flexed uneasily. "It took a lot of searching. I got the impression that a lot of the shadowkind who enjoy the mortal oceans have had some kind of encounter with him but were too nervous to admit to it."

Rollick sat down on the arm of the sofa. "And what did you learn from the ones who were willing to talk?"

Torrent's mouth twisted. "Apparently he's been hanging out in the area of the Bermuda Triangle quite a bit for more than a century. Wrecking boats and even managing to take down the occasional plane and hide them away to unnerve the mortals. But he hasn't stuck to that area all of the time. One merman speculated that he might have had something to do with a couple of tsunamis that've caused a lot of destruction on the other side of the globe."

Rollick's expression had darkened. "He's pushing the boundaries of what he can get away with without drawing too much attention to the supernatural source of the disasters. Sounds a lot like the approach I gather the behemoth was taking before they joined up."

As I forced down the last bite of the sandwich segment I'd been eating, my skin crept with apprehension. "And it's all directed against human beings. Is that their end goal? Is that how they figure shadowkind will have this world for themselves—they're going to kill *all* of us?"

Torrent blinked. "They're doing what now?"

I stewed in my horror as the other men filled him in on what we'd found out near the rift. Then Rollick turned to me. "That can't be it. They wouldn't get away with it."

"Even if they bring hordes of shadowkind through that enlarged rift to help them?"

"Even then. For one thing, they wouldn't need a *bigger*

rift for that. They'd just need to call them through all over the world, and there are more than enough rifts to summon a massive army in minutes if they could convince enough to come over."

"You're not being very reassuring," I muttered.

The demon gave my shoulder a teasing prod. "Even the biggest army of shadowkind they could raise wouldn't be a match for humans eventually. There are already hunters scattered across the globe who know what our weaknesses are. If they saw that shadowkind were making themselves an open threat to humanity, they'd share that knowledge widely. Walmart would start carrying copies of that crossbow of yours. We might be powerful, but we do have a few very basic weaknesses. You could kill me right now with that contraption no matter how old I am or how much magic I have."

"They'd lose eventually," Crag put in. "It wouldn't be a good plan. It wouldn't make anyone happy for very long. But a lot of mortals and shadowkind would die if they decided to attempt it anyway."

"Then they're idiotic as well as tricksy," Lance declared. "Why would they want to get rid of mortals anyway? Humans are part of what makes this realm so much fun." He flopped down on the sofa next to me and tucked his arm around my waist.

I set my half-finished plate onto the side table and let myself lean into the dragon shifter a little. "These two don't seem to think so. Or maybe what's fun for them is seeing us suffer."

"I think they've been too strategic to simply be aiming

for temporary chaos," Rollick said, frowning. "And it doesn't explain what they're doing with the rift. I don't think they *are* powerful enough to summon that large an army anyway. They only managed to take control of a couple of the Highest's warriors—they had to kill the others. They have enough of a force right now to put our small group in danger and menace a single city, but the entire world?"

"It does sound like there's a piece we're missing," Torrent agreed, his face gone even more somber.

Crag squared his shoulders. "Then we'll keep searching until we understand."

I scooted closer to Lance, tipping my head against the crook of his neck and letting his nuzzle of my hair comfort me as much as any gesture could. "Whatever it is, it's obviously going to be *bad* for humankind. And any shadowkind who don't want to see us tormented."

Rollick took on his usual confidently authoritative air. "I have contacts looking into all sorts of things around the city. Our opponents seem to mostly be active at night. We'll see what my people turn up in the meantime, and then we'll track down a minion who has a better idea of their masters' plans."

"What if none of the minions know?" I had to ask. "What if the two head honchos are keeping it to themselves?"

A gloom fell over the room. We all knew that wasn't just possible but actually fairly likely.

"Then we'll wait and see their next moves, and learn what we can from those," Torrent said evenly.

While more people would probably die in the meantime. There'd been at least a dozen more attacks across this city tonight. And more shadowkind would die too— the ones being sacrificed, and the ones who dared to go up against these monsters... which might end up including the men around me.

I closed my eyes, wishing I could sink right into Lance and never let him go. Wishing the catastrophe I'd gotten wrapped up in didn't seem to be growing with every passing day.

The dragon shifter pressed a gentle kiss to my temple and let his lips linger there, his claws stroking along the curve of my torso. "We're here with you, baby girl," he crooned. "We're not going anywhere."

He couldn't really promise that, though—not when we were up against enemies this powerful and brutal. But I wanted to believe it.

His head lowered, trailing kisses down the side of my face and nipping my earlobe. His claws skimmed my thigh with just enough force to send a giddy prickling sensation over my skin, and a wash of heat spread from where he'd touched to pool between my legs. Suddenly I wanted a whole lot more than just to believe him.

Lance picked up on the shift in my mood as quickly as he usually did. He dipped his mouth to my neck and tested the fangs he'd brought out against the tender flesh there, bringing a gasp to my throat. "Maybe our woman needs a more concrete reminder of just how much we're here with her."

Yes. If there wasn't any way we could fight these villains right now regardless, I wanted to lose myself in the pleasure my three lovers could conjure in my body. I wanted to hold them close enough to convince myself that they'd never slip from my grasp, no matter what we faced.

I cupped his jaw and tugged his mouth to mine. He threw himself into the kiss, letting his tongue shift from human-like to its ridged dragon form, and yanked me right onto his lap. The bulge of his already rigid cock pressed against my ass through my shorts.

As he caressed my breasts with a growl that seemed directed at the metal beads that made it difficult for him to properly fondle me, Crag sank down next to us. The gargoyle kissed my shoulder with absolute tenderness.

There was a soft rustling sound as Torrent used his tentacles to help him cross the room. He looped one of those tentacles around my bare calf and paused. I drew back from Lance's kiss to see he'd cast his gaze toward the fourth man in the room—the one who'd never been a part of an interlude like this with us before, other than watching unknown from a distance.

My gaze locked with Rollick's. Desire had flared in his eyes, echoed in the pulse of emotion that flowed from him into me. But his posture had stiffened where he was perched on the sofa arm.

So many memories rushed through me: the horror of discovering how he'd violated our privacy back at his hotel, the pained apology he'd offered after he'd saved me from what would have been a deathly fall. The way he'd rushed to my aid at the sorcerers' enclave, the moment in the park near my parents' house when he'd offered me my life back. He'd always intrigued me as much as he'd unnerved me, and I no longer saw *him* as a villain. He'd maybe even become kind of heroic in the past several days.

Of course, he was also a high-level demon used to commanding authority and getting his way. He'd wanted to claim me, but I had a feeling he'd intended that to be only for himself, shunting my other men aside.

Now... now I had no idea what he'd accept. What would win in the potential battle between his desire and his ego.

But I wouldn't get a chance to find out if he didn't realize I wanted him too—fully aware of what I was doing, not the slightest bit intoxicated.

He stood up with an expression of careful composure and gave us a wry bob of his head. "I'll leave you to it."

"Wait," I blurted out before he could disappear. As he paused, watching me with obvious uncertainty, I eased away from my other men. Not even Lance made a noise of protest as I walked over to the demon.

They'd accepted him. They believed he was with us in every way that counted, that he posed no threat to my body or my heart.

I stopped just a foot away from Rollick, starkly aware of the heat wafting off his body and the tangled emotions seeping into me with it. His hunger stirred more of my own.

"We're all together in this mess, aren't we?" I said quietly. "What if you were with us for the good parts as well? Can *you* handle that?"

More passion flared in Rollick's eyes. He glanced at the other men and then back at me. "What do you want from me, Quinn?" he asked, his voice so raw it sent a tremor right down the center of me.

My throat constricted. I stepped even closer, reaching to slip one hand around his neck. "I want you. But only if it doesn't have to be just you and no one else. Only if you can accept that I'm always going to want them too. And until I'm sure of that, they're going to come first."

A husky quality wound through his next words. "I suppose that's reasonable, if you're going to insist on laying down rules, sweet sorcerer."

He inclined his head, and I bobbed up on my toes to meet his kiss. More heat flooded me from the joining of our mouths, searing all through the rest of my body.

The demon did know how to kiss. His lips melded with mine at the perfect angle to set my nerves tingling alongside the surge of heat. I found myself pulling him closer as if I could absorb even more pleasure from the moment that way. He set his hands on my waist, his thumbs arching under my shirt to skim across the bare skin, an encouraging noise resonating from his throat. The quiver I caught of his own delight and something almost like contentment sparked more bliss inside me in turn.

We were really doing this, after weeks of teasing and resisting. But nothing about this moment felt like a mistake. The fire of his kiss burned away any final traces of doubt.

He wanted *me*. Not as a trophy or a tool or to prove a point, but because of the same hunger that was reverberating down to my core right now. He might have been claiming me with his kiss, but I'd claimed a part of him just as much. Somehow in the past several days, our hopes and desires had become intertwined far beyond the point of any scheming or strategy.

With a little growl, Lance came up behind me. He rested his hand on my hip beneath Rollick's fingers and nibbled the curve of my shoulder. "Mine," he murmured against my skin, as if reminding me that he'd been the one who'd started us on this path.

Rollick's grasp on my waist tightened momentarily as I pulled away from our kiss, but he relaxed enough to let me turn and yank the dragon shifter to me next. The demon's hands teased up under my vest and the thin cotton undershirt that kept it off my skin until they cupped my breasts through my bra. My breath caught, and I kissed Lance harder, swaying between the two of them.

Lance had been ready for more since the moment he'd pulled me onto his lap. He hooked his claws over the waist of my shorts and dragged them down my legs, catching my panties along the way. As he kissed me again, his tongue sweeping through my mouth, he tucked his hand between us and grazed the tips of his claws over my pussy. When they glided across my clit, I whimpered into his mouth.

The dragon shifter blinked away so swiftly I barely felt his disappearance other than a current of air before he was standing before me again—buck naked. He grasped my hand and tugged me down with him onto the thick rug, a sly grin stretching across his face. "Everyone can join in with this position. I want to see how you take all of us at once, baby girl. Are you ready for that?"

A thrill shot through me. I looked up, catching the other men's gazes. "Whenever you are."

Lance cocked his head toward Torrent. "I don't think

we should unleash the gargoyle's equipment on places we still need to be careful with, hmm? Do you still have that slick stuff to make her really ready?"

Torrent wet his lips, the hunger in his eyes searing over me. "Just a second."

He wavered away too, and then returned seconds later with the tube from Rollick's guest bedroom clutched in his deformed hand. As the tentacled man knelt behind me, Rollick let out a low chuckle. "So glad you made such excellent use of my hospitality."

I reached one hand toward him and then the other toward Crag, beckoning them down around me on either side. Crag came at once and Rollick more warily, and then I was surrounded in a complete circle of heated desire.

All at once, I felt weirdly shy. I touched Lance's cheek and drew him into a kiss that started out chaste but turned passionate as our mouths lingered together. Torrent stroked his hand up and down my back, not reaching to any more sensitive areas yet. As one of his tentacles looped around my waist to press its suckered kisses against my belly, Crag followed Rollick's example and slipped his broad hand under my shirts to fondle one breast.

For a moment, Rollick just watched. Then I felt the press of his lips against my shoulder. "I look forward to times in the future when I'll hopefully get to see you in all your glory," he said, and eased his hand up my chest to work over my other breast in tandem with Crag.

The rush of pleasure through my body had me arching against the man I was perched on. My sex brushed against Lance's cock, and he let out an eager growl.

"Mine," he murmured again, rubbing his shaft over the

wetness that'd collected between my folds and then sliding right up inside me.

I sighed as he filled me, that fantastic burn searing away any lingering doubts about whether we could make this group collision work. Grasping Crag's shirt, I pulled him into a kiss next, my lips shifting against his as I rocked with Lance's leisurely thrusts. "Clothes off," I ordered him.

Behind me, Torrent's hand dipped to my ass. As he delved lube-slick fingers between my cheeks, the tip of his embracing tentacle dropped to squeeze my clit. I gasped and found myself glancing at Rollick again.

So much passion lit his face now that flames seemed to dance in his eyes. "Fill her up," he murmured with a hint of command in his tone. "Let's see our mortal fully satisfied." He pinched my nipple between his thumb and forefinger, and I tipped my head back with a moan. Then I reached for him to claim another demonic kiss.

His mouth scorched mine as Torrent warmed up my back entrance. When the kiss broke, the tentacled man brushed his lips against the back of my neck and asked, "Are you ready for me?"

The pulsing of his fingers inside me already had me trembling for release. "Yes," I mumbled. "Please."

Lance tipped me forward against him to provide the other man with a better angle, and Torrent lined himself up. The feel of his solid cock sliding into me from behind was totally different from the flexible thrust of his tentacle, but even more giddying in its own way. A ragged moan spilled out of me as I found myself speared by two of my lovers, friction sending its heady bliss through my nerves from both sides.

Torrent matched Lance's relaxed pace as they warmed me up even more together. I kept just enough awareness beyond the surging sensations to motion for Crag to push more upright. The gargoyle had shed his clothes as I'd asked, and even in his human-like form, his cock jutted massively from between his thighs.

I knew I couldn't take it all into my mouth, but I was going to give it my best shot. I stroked my fingers over the silkily firm length and closed my lips around the head.

Crag groaned and swayed to meet my embrace. I sucked hard as my hand worked the rest of his shaft up and down, and his thick fingers tangled in my hair as if he needed to hold on to me through his own careening path toward release.

Lance leaned in to flick his tongue along my jaw. "Not quite all of us yet, baby girl. Can you handle four?"

Hell, yes, I could. With Lance and Torrent holding me balanced between them, I raised my other hand toward Rollick and curled my fingers into his shirt before trailing them down his chest. The demon edged closer, slipping his hand over mine and guiding it lower. When my palm came to rest on the bulge behind his slacks, a rough rumble emanated from his chest.

"Let's stick with one to start," he said in an equally rough voice. For just an instant, the impression of his body vanished. Then he was there again, no layers of fabric between us.

I teased my fingertips over the single taut shaft he sported in human-like form and then gripped it firmly. Rollick kept fondling my breast as I pumped him with a rhythm in time with the other men's movements.

"Let go," he murmured. "Give yourself over to the pleasure, and bring all of us with you."

As if on cue, Lance began to thrust faster, deeper. As Torrent matched his pace, the bliss sweeping through me tossed me even higher. I swirled my tongue around the head of Crag's cock, stroking both him and Rollick faster in turn. We'd all gathered together to form a tidal wave of delight that I couldn't have reined in now even if I'd wanted to.

Torrent seemed determined to make sure I came first. His sucker strummed at my clit as he bucked into me. I moaned onto Crag's shaft with a shudder of ecstasy. Then the pleasure building inside me exploded, crackling through me and whiting out my vision.

It blazed on and on as Torrent followed me with a choked sound and a squeeze of his arm around my torso. Crag grunted with the tightening of my lips, and the salty gush of his release spilled over my tongue. Lance chuckled breathlessly and pounded into me with even more force, and I shattered apart again right on the heels of my first orgasm.

My hand jerked faster around Rollick's cock. He wrapped his fingers around mine to clench them even harder and came with a muttered curse. Then the dragon shifter followed the rest of us, liquid heat spurting inside me.

Lance yanked my face away from Crag's and scraped his fangs over my neck. The pain added one final spark of bliss to my release before he healed it with a waft of fiery breath.

My head bowed forward, my body going slack. Rollick

brushed my sweat-damp hair back from my temple and grinned fiercely. "That's our woman."

As the last quivers of ecstasy seeped out of me, resolve formed in my chest. I *was* theirs, in every possible way, as much as they were mine. And since I hadn't been able to protect them by pushing them away from me, I'd just have to hold them as close as I could—and put up every possible fight to defend the love I'd found with them.

CHAPTER TWENTY-THREE

Quinn

Somehow the darkened coastline looked eerier now that I knew what sorts of plots were being carried out under the cover of night. I rested my hands on my crossbow where it was lying across my lap in the back of the car and willed my pulse not to thunder quite so loudly.

"So, your spy said the leviathan sent some minions off on fishing duty?" I asked.

Rollick nodded from the seat ahead of me, where he was driving as usual. "Something like that. I warned the associates I've been able to call on not to get too close to any unusual activity, because we don't want to tip off the villainous duo that we've noticed. A small group of the minions were messing around on an isolated spot farther down the coast from the rift, pulling something out of the water."

"It would make sense that a being that powerful might send someone else off to catch his favorite food," Crag rumbled from beside me.

Lance huffed in the front passenger seat. "He and his buddy are too busy making their tricksy plans. We can let him starve."

Rollick gave him an amused look. "We're not going out there to put an end to the fishing. If he trusts these lackeys enough to handle his food, it's possible one or more of them has seen or heard things about his larger plans. We catch one, interrogate it, and if that one isn't useful, we move on to the next."

"I'd rather see the *both* of them starve," Lance muttered, propping his legs up on the dashboard.

"At least we shouldn't have to worry about anyone using sorcery on you during this mission," I said. "Since the bosses will be busy with other things." A small comfort.

Rollick veered onto a side road and parked out of view of the highway like he had when we'd observed the rift last night. As we got out of the car, Torrent materialized next to us, having ridden along in the shadows since there wasn't a whole lot of room for five in the car, especially when one of those was Crag. I didn't think the tentacled man minded the excuse not to hold his often painful physical form when he didn't need to.

He'd been listening to all of our conversation, of course. "Any thoughts on what being we should aim to capture first?" he asked. "Are there any that we have reason to believe might be closer to their masters than the others?"

Rollick made a face. "Unfortunately no. The head honchos themselves have managed to stay mostly out of public eye. I say we grab whoever's most easily available and work from there." He glanced at me. "You're staying here—with Lance, so you have a little backup. You'll be too noticeable tramping around over there, and we won't really need your skills until we've caught our first prisoner and need to convince them to talk."

I hadn't really thought that part through. It made sense for me to hang back when I couldn't merge with the shadows like the men, but I couldn't help grimacing at him. "So, I don't get to be anything other than a sorcerer for this mission, then."

Rollick's lips curved into a smirk that was unusually soft around the edges. "I think we all know you're much more than just a sorcerer—sweet, reluctant, or otherwise."

His smile sent a quiver of heat over my skin. I didn't totally know how to react to him after the intimacy we'd shared this morning. It was too fresh, and I wasn't even sure how *he* felt about it now that all was said and done. But this wasn't exactly the time to hash it out.

"Fine," I muttered, and brandished my crossbow. "But if any beings come sneaking around this way like last time, I'm taking them on."

Lance leaned close to nuzzle my hair with a much easier familiarity. "And I'll be here to help you."

Rollick took the two of us in with a twinge of emotion I couldn't quite decipher, though I thought I sensed a little jealousy in it. He didn't say anything, only stepped closer for just long enough to cup my jaw and press a quick kiss to my lips. My heart skipped a beat, and then he was stepping away, motioning to the other two men.

Crag shot me a concerned glance, and I waved him off.

With the dragon shifter watching my back, I didn't think the gargoyle had anything to worry about. Torrent tipped his head to me, and then all three vanished into the darkness.

My human eyes couldn't make out much in the landscape around us, where a narrow road cut through a field with two more rolling hills on either side. We'd parked as far as possible from the sparse lampposts, and even the nearest of those cast small pools of light that barely extended beyond the shoulder of the road. Tonight was more overcast than yesterday, clouds blotting out the stars and all but the faintly glowing edge of the moon.

Lance shifted into dragon form to prowl around me and then sprang back up into his human-like body, flexing his arms. "Let's hope they catch a talkative beastie quickly," he murmured. "We should be part of the fun."

I nudged him with bemused fondness. "I wouldn't call this expedition *fun*."

He grinned at me. "Anything can be fun if you take the right approach. For example, while we're waiting, I could—"

He'd just started to trail his claws down my arm when he froze, his gaze darting away from me to search the darkness. I tensed automatically. "What?"

His tongue flicked over his lips. The lean muscles in his shoulders flexed. "There's something—"

In one massive surge, the darkness around us came alive. A wave of monstrous bodies hurtled down the slopes on either side of the road, rushing straight toward us.

A squeak of startled shock burst from my lips. As Lance

snarled and leapt back into dragon form, I yanked my crossbow up.

My finger squeezed the trigger once, twice, three times, hitting targets because it was almost impossible not to with so many racing toward us all together. Those bodies crumpled, but the dozens of others dashed onward.

Lance whipped along their front lines, slashing through as many as he could reach with his claws and flares of roaring dragon fire. But the ring of protection he was forming around me contracted no matter how swiftly he flung himself onward.

I fumbled with the bolts in my messenger bag, snatching a few up and shoving them into the crossbow with all the speed I could summon. Even as I clicked them into place, my pulse thudded with a rapidly growing sense of futility. I wasn't sure I had enough bolts in my bag to take even half of these creatures down, whether I could load and fire fast enough or not.

We hadn't expected a horde to come down on us. How had they found us here? Why were so many lurking out here by what was supposed to be just a fishing spot?

Did the other men have any clue this was happening, or were they still investigating the supposed fishers on the coastline, totally unaware?

My instinct had been to stay quiet, but that thought jarred a panicked, wordless yell from my throat. I didn't know if we could get out of this if they didn't come back and join the fray on our side.

But I couldn't count on my other men hearing me or being close enough to help. I shot three more bolts into the oncoming horde and gasped for breath. I had to dodge to the side when one creature slashed at my thigh, its claws snagging on the fabric of my shorts in the instant before Lance pounced on it and tore its head off with his jaws. He hurtled onward, but more of the beasts were closing in.

I pushed my back against the side of the car for some minor sort of shelter. It'd be no good getting inside where the creatures could easily leap in after me through the shadows and I'd have no room to maneuver. Adrenaline thrummed through my body—and woke up the other sort of energy lodged in my heart.

I focused on the crackling sense of power with a jolt of hope. Willing it to sizzle up my throat and into my voice, I opened my mouth and shouted out a string of syllables in the language of sorcery.

The idea was to tell them to back off. To stand down and cower before us. But all through the onrushing crowd, I sensed the energy I cast out crashing into barriers like the one I'd felt on the being Rollick had snatched on the mountainside in Oregon.

Most of these creatures weren't here of their own free will. They had their masters' sorcery driving them onward.

I fired a few more bolts into the horde and let my voice ring out again, more forcefully than before. I had to break the hold on them. I had to shatter the sorcery that already gripped them. Even if I couldn't bend their wills with my own magic at the same time, they might not want to take up this battle if they had the choice anyway.

The power of my words rippled through the mass of creatures in a wave. I felt with tingling pricks across my skin as one hold and another snapped. But as even several of the beasts veered away and a spark of triumph lit inside me, one large creature lunged at me just after Lance had whipped by.

I hadn't been able to reload yet. I smacked the panther-like thing in the muzzle with the crossbow, but it was already shoving me to the ground. Its curved talons raked through my abdomen, slicing my shirt, the lower threads of my vest, and right into my flesh with a spike of agony.

I cried out with nothing in my voice but pain now. Lance ripped the thing off me and smacked its head right off its shoulders, but when I pressed my hand to my side, wetness pulsed against it. I was bleeding—gushing blood.

The dragon shifter kicked a few more fiends out of the way and dipped his head toward me. I jerked my hand out of the way just in time for him to send a blast of his fiery breath over my torso.

In his haste, Lance hadn't been able to work as carefully as usual. The heat stung badly enough to force another whimper from my lips. He must have sealed some of the wound, but I could still feel blood trickling over my skin and soaking into the rest of my shirt.

My entire abdomen blared with pain. I could hardly breathe.

Lance snarled in frustration, whirling to savage a few more creatures who'd leapt in at us. A lithe humanoid figure sprang onto the hood of the car, and he swung toward her with a threatening growl.

She held up her hands, the image of her doubling before my wavering vision. "I'm not going to hurt her. I want to help." She looked down at me. "Thank you for severing their spell. The beings that had me under their control want you destroyed by whatever means necessary.

They see you as nothing but a threat now. Stay away from them if you want to live."

With that warning, she fled into the shadows. I clamped my hand to my side, too dizzy with agony to fully process her words, and groaned. Even if I wanted to follow her advice, I had the sinking suspicion it might be too late.

There was a shriek, and a tentacle lashed into view, slamming several creatures head over heels. A huge, stony body landed beside me with a heavy thump. Crag stared down at me, his eyes blazing with fury and horror.

"Get her out of here!" Rollick's voice rasped from somewhere nearby.

The gargoyle didn't hesitate. He swept me up in his bulging arms, his muscles flinching at my hiss of pain, and launched himself into the air. As the ground fell away, the dizziness swelled right through my brain, and my mind fell away into a blackness even deeper than the night.

CHAPTER TWENTY-FOUR

Quinn

Pain blazed all through my mid-section. I sucked in a breath, my eyelids fluttering, and winced at a sensation that felt like several shards of glass poking deeper into my belly.

Crag's rumble of a voice came from somewhere over me. "Quinn? Lie still—you need more time to recover." He raised his voice slightly to call to someone farther away. "She's waking up!"

The gargoyle's broad hand came to rest on my shoulder. As the shock of the pain ebbed, I became more aware of the other sensations outside my body: soft blades of grass covering a lumpy stretch of earth beneath me, hazy morning light seeping into my eyes, a rush of warm breeze carrying the scent of wildflowers and not a trace of salt.

I blinked, focusing my vision. I was lying on my side in

a small clearing sheltered by looming trees. Pale clouds still covered most of the sky; the sun hadn't yet risen above the level of the treetops. Crag was crouched behind me. As I parted my lips, attempting to work sound from my parched mouth, my other three shadowkind men materialized around me.

"Bring her water bottle," Rollick ordered, coolly and briskly but with a waver of worry that passed from him into me. "She needs hydration after the blood she lost."

Torrent snatched the bottle from my bag and brought it to me with a tentacle. His expression was tight, his sea-green eyes stormy. "Don't move," he told me.

Lance leapt in to open the bottle and hold it to my lips. With Crag supporting my head, I raised it a little to sip the water. The liquid had warmed in the few hours since I'd refilled the container, but right then I wasn't feeling picky. It slid down my throat like some kind of elixir. My belly twinged, but the discomforts beyond my wound retreated.

"What happened?" I asked with a rasp. I couldn't feel any blood where my arm was leaning against my belly, although my shirt clung to me here and there with damp splotches. "Am I going to be okay?"

"We'll have to keep a close eye on you," Rollick said grimly. "But I think Lance managed to seal your wound all right once he didn't have those creatures swarming him. It'll take a while before the flesh all knits together properly—a lot of it will be scar tissue right now. I'll get you some painkillers when we're back in the city."

"Okay." Lance had patched me up enough times that I trusted his dragon fire to have seared away any chance of infection. I let my head droop back against the grass. "How did we end up getting attacked? What were all those creatures doing there to begin with?"

Torrent sank down next to me and stroked a careful hand over my hair. "It looks like they set a trap for us. Someone must have spotted Rollick's spies and reported that the site had been compromised. Instead of moving elsewhere, they prepared an ambush assuming we'd come investigate ourselves."

The thought of our enemies following our moves that closely made my pulse stutter. I shifted slightly, feeling the press of the silver and iron beads across my chest—but not as far down as the strands used to fall. "The one that got me broke my vest. If they track me down again—"

"It still seems to be offering enough protection to mostly disguise your sorcerer energy," Rollick cut in. "I can catch a little of it from here, but at the far side of the clearing, I couldn't pick it up at all. That should be enough protection until we can arrange something else. I've already had a few of my contacts working on putting together a few items with silver thread woven in like I talked about before. As soon as one is done, you can try it out instead."

I sighed and slowly rolled onto my back. This movement only set off the impression of a couple of shards of glass digging into me instead of a whole bunch like before.

I touched my belly tentatively and found the skin there was dry but rippled with the scar tissue Rollick had mentioned. Even the swipe of Lance's tongue with its special saliva hadn't been able to smooth this spot out completely.

Oh, well. I wasn't any stranger to scars.

"So, what now?" I asked the group around me. "What else can we do to find out what they're doing—to stop them?"

Lance let out a little growl. "You need to rest and get better. No more fighting. If they'd hurt you any more..." His face darkened with a haunted expression that looked totally wrong there. My dragon shifter was meant to be smiling and laughing.

"They know for sure that we're in the area now," Crag said. "We should leave, go somewhere they won't think to look for Quinn."

"No," I protested. "We can't—that'll give them even more time to prepare whatever it is they're working toward. And we know they're out to hurt people however they can. If we back down now, we might not get another chance."

Torrent's mouth twisted. "I don't know how much of a chance we have even now."

"That being you snapped out of their sorcery, she said they're out to kill you now, not just capture you," Lance reminded me, slinging a possessive arm over my legs.

The memory of her words left me cold, but I couldn't let that shake my resolve. "It doesn't matter. I'll be in danger no matter where we go and what we do. I'll be in *more* danger if these monsters gather more power than they already have. We have to... Maybe we should stop trying to figure out what they're doing and why, and just go straight to shutting them down."

Rollick let out a dark chuckle. "If accomplishing that was as easy as saying it, we'd already have done it."

"There has to be a way..." My mind drifted through the events of the past few weeks. "I'm a sorcerer. Sorcerers have ways of controlling shadowkind. That's *why* they want me dead, isn't it? They don't think there's any chance they could really use me now, but they're afraid I might be able to control them. They can't control me themselves, right? The sorcery they've absorbed only works on other shadowkind."

"We can't count on you being able to overpower them," Torrent said.

"No, but... what if we used more sorcerer strategies in general? They have all kinds of ways of manipulating shadowkind. They kill them to bring out their own powers. They know how to weaken them and threaten them..."

The image swam up from my memory of the cages where the enclave had held the creatures for the rites—and who knew what other purposes. Made out of silver and iron, yes, but also with those blades ready to spear right into the beings if need be.

"We could set a trap for *them*," I said slowly. But how the hell would we get one of those immense beings into any kind of cage? Even making a cage big enough seemed like a monumental task—and neither my men nor Rollick's other shadowkind allies could construct anything made out of the toxic metals.

But mortals—mortals could handle silver and iron without any trouble. I glanced at Rollick. "You have contacts who are human—the ones who're working on my new protective gear. The ones who set up the protections around your properties and inside the hotel. If we gave them a design, they could build whatever you asked, couldn't they?"

Rollick raised an eyebrow. "I suppose I could pull

together the manpower and resources to construct just about anything, given enough time. What are you scheming now?"

All at once, my fingers were itching for a pencil and sketch pad. An image of the trap I wanted to design was unfolding in my mind, a larger and more concealed version of the vicious cages from the enclave.

"I think I could make plans for a structure we could use to... to kill the behemoth and the leviathan," I said. "I might need someone with more advanced engineering knowledge to adjust the mechanical parts, but I'm almost sure it should be doable. We could take a similar approach to something I saw the sorcerers in the enclave using."

Lance shuddered. "Nothing they do is good."

His response sent an ache through my chest that had nothing to do with my injury. I reached out to squeeze his forearm. "I know. They're horrible to the shadowkind. But now we're dealing with shadowkind who are horrible too. The sorcerers have spent their entire existence honing their ability to control beings like that—and destroy them if they feel they need to. We're running out of time. We have to make use of every advantage we can."

"She's right," Crag rumbled. "Whatever it takes. They've done too much damage already."

Torrent nodded. "I'm on board. Our usual tactics haven't gotten us far enough."

Lance grimaced but then dipped down to kiss my hip. "I don't want them or their beasties getting any more claws into our woman. If we need to act like sorcerers to do that, then fine."

Rollick folded his arms over his chest with a

contemplative air. "I think we're forgetting one thing. We can make a trap, sure. But how are we going to get these menaces to stroll on into it?"

"They came to the camp in Oregon when we compelled one of their lackeys to say I'd show up," I said.

"Yes, but they're not likely to fall for the same trick twice. And I'd already used similar tactics to redirect their attention before, so I think using *you* as bait in any way is all tapped out."

I stared up at the drifting clouds, considering the situation. When the idea came to me, my stomach twisted, but I couldn't think of anything better to suggest.

"What if we don't present me as willing bait? What if we make them think I'm an even bigger threat than they already believe, and they've got to hunt me down and ensure I'm destroyed if they want to go through with their plan?"

Lance's growl revealed exactly what he thought of that plan. Crag let out a similar ragged huff. "I'd rather you weren't in their sights at all, Softness."

"But I am anyway," I pointed out. "We might as well use that fact. We can make our trap in a building, and let word get out that I'm gathering an army of my own there. Subtly, so they think we're trying to hide the information from them. I can... I can enslave at least a few shadowkind, make sure other minions of theirs are nearby to witness it. I can break the duo's sorcery. They won't like that."

"I don't know if that will be enough," Rollick said with obvious reluctance. I got the sense he didn't particularly care for this strategy either.

I bit my lip. "What if we also—we could reach out to

whatever sorcerer families you're aware of that they haven't already attacked. Send a message asking them to come ally with me. Make sure at least one of those messages gets intercepted, so our enemies know we're gathering those sorts of forces too."

"Bring the actual sorcerers in?" Lance said with a hiss of breath through his teeth. "They'll try to capture *us*."

"We won't let them. And they probably won't even come. It'll look like a trap to them. We just want to make the big bosses worried that they might come. And if they do show up... then that'll just be extra bait."

My gut knotted just for a second at the thought of luring fellow humans into my scenario. Only for a second, because then I thought of all the ways these humans had manipulated shadowkind over the years.

Did it make *me* a monster that I was willing to risk sacrificing them to take down an even greater evil?

A few weeks ago, I'd have shied away from that thought. Now, it settled inside me next to my resolve, not a blessing or a curse, just the way things were.

I'd do whatever it took to protect the people who deserved it—and there were a heck of a lot more of them than there were innocent sorcerers.

"What if the fiends send a bunch of beasties in again and don't come themselves?" Lance asked. "Like they did at Rollick's hotel."

I'd already pondered that point. "Rollick has made buildings where most shadowkind can't get past the silver-and-iron barriers without a special access point, right? In the hotel, he'd let them in to try to prove his innocence. We could set up this entire building like that—and obviously we wouldn't let the less powerful beings in. It'd make the story that I'm gathering my forces to take down the big baddies more plausible too. We'd make the protections strong enough to ward off all but particularly powerful shadowkind. If they wanted to get at me, they'd *have* to come themselves."

Crag frowned. "That'll make it hard for all of us to protect you in there."

"If the trap works the way it's supposed to, I won't need anyone protecting me. As soon as they come into the building, we can activate it, and it'll kill them all on its own."

Talking so casually about slaughtering another living being—even mostly immortal beings like the shadowkind—sent another jab of nausea through me. But then I thought of the man we'd found dead in the alley, of the toddler slaughtered in that sorcerer house near Boston, of the being last night who'd thanked me for freeing her from them.

These two monsters were threatening all of us. Something had to be done about them. And if we were in the best position to do it, then it was up to us not to let the rest of the world down.

"It sounds like you have your mind made up," Rollick said in a ghost of his usual breezy tone. "And you figure you're going to set all this up while recovering from a near-fatal disembowelling?"

I glowered at him. "Get me back to your apartment, bring me a sketchpad and my laptop—you can keep the wifi password to yourself, I don't need the internet—and I'll have a blueprint worked out within twenty-four hours." I paused. "And then most of the rest will be up to the four of you."

"Until you have to go into the trap to lure them after you," Lance said discontentedly.

I set my jaw. "Yes. Until then."

CHAPTER TWENTY-FIVE

Lance

It was a strange kind of tricksy, pretending to be sneaky while actually trying to catch other beings' attention. I slunk through the shadows as if I intended to avoid getting noticed, weaving to the side here and there, glancing at the houses and sprawling lawns all around me regularly. But I'd purposefully never gotten too far ahead of the being that'd been tracking me since shortly after I'd left Los Angeles. I could sense it at the very edge of my awareness, just distant enough that it was believable I might have missed it.

It needed to think I was on a special secret mission. That my woman, my friends, and I didn't want it knowing what I was up to. Because if it realized our whole plan was for it to overhear the message I was going to deliver, it would know this was part of a trap.

Rollick had shown me the sorcerers' house on a map, although my memory of the paper landscape didn't seem to have much in common with the paved terrain I was crossing over. I knew what direction I had to go in, though. And with each mile I crossed, the apprehension prickling over my skin dug deeper.

I didn't want to be anywhere near the mortals who warped shadowkind minds. I didn't want to tell them anything, even if it wasn't really for their benefit.

But I wanted the brutes who'd been threatening Quinn and so much else in this world gone even more. So I kept going, keeping up my ruse of caution.

Thankfully, I didn't have to get too close to the actual sorcerers. Like most, they had their own minions lurking around in a wide radius around their home, watching for threats. This family was less isolated than others we'd dealt with, living in a quiet stretch of widely-spaced homes that Quinn had called a "suburb." Rollick said they were hiding in plain sight, which didn't make a whole lot of sense to me. How was it hiding if people could see you?

In any case, they had creatures staked out in the shadows well before I could catch so much as a glimpse of their actual house. I could tell the one under a mailbox was a fierce but lesser being, unable to convey my message for me. I veered away from her until I came across the next sentry, this one a young-feeling nymph in the shade of a vast tree.

I paused several feet away from it and postured a bit both to get its attention and to give my follower time to catch up. The nymph shivered when it noticed me, but it slunk a little closer to the edge of the tree's shadow.

"Go away," it told me. "No shadowkind should come this way."

"You're here," I couldn't help pointing out. "I have a message to give to some people who live nearby."

"I'm not supposed to let anyone pass," the nymph insisted, but I could taste the tension in the air with its movements. It was struggling against the hold of their magic, the power propelling the words from its mouth, and failing to free itself. If I pushed the issue, its orders might compel it to try to fight me—a battle it wouldn't win. Or maybe it'd just run to warn its masters.

My skin itched even more at the thought. This being should be roaming around as freely as I could now, but instead the sorcerers had forced it into their service. Did it get any enjoyment at all out of its life? A memory flickered up of how it'd felt when that kind of power had locked around my mind, caging me from the inside out, and I held back a shudder.

And here I was using its state for my own benefit.

For good reasons, I reminded myself, and forced out the words. "I think the people I need to give the message to might be the ones you work with. You protect some sorcerers, don't you?"

The nymph gave me a narrow look. "I won't speak of that."

"Fine. You can speak to them about what I'm going to tell you. There's a new sorcerer in Los Angeles, one who's gathering enough power to challenge two very powerful shadowkind beings who've been killing other sorcerers and bending our kind to their will. She's building up her strength to enslave them herself, but that'll take a lot of her power, so she's hoping to get help from other sorcerers to deal with their minions."

"Why should anyone help *your* sorcerer?" the nymph muttered.

"Because otherwise these beings will probably kill all the sorcerers out there. Quinn is going to stop them. It'll just be faster with your masters' help. Tell them, and let them decide. They can find her in the building where she's preparing for the battle and stockpiling her resources."

I rattled off the address I'd memorized, slow and clear the way Torrent had reminded me to. It was very important that not just the being in front of me but the lackey who'd trailed me this far heard exactly where Quinn would be— exactly where we wanted those massive beasts to come looking for her.

Not yet. It wasn't quite ready yet. But Rollick's people were already hard at work following the design Quinn had worked out. He thought it would only take a few more days. It wouldn't be until it was ready that she'd walk in there, and by then we hoped that our enemies would be watching, waiting for the chance to strike.

But we'd be the ones who'd strike out at them.

My claws flexed at the thought, bolstering my determination despite my discomfort seeing this enslaved being. I dipped my head to him, hoping he understood that I wished for his freedom too. "Please let them know. Whether they come or not is up to them."

Then I hurried back the way I'd come, still acting like I wanted to dart away before anyone else realized what I was up to.

The images of the nymph's shiver and the tension

wound through its presence dogged me as I rushed through the streets and across the countryside beyond as fast as I could. On the highway, I leapt into the shadows on a passing bus and sped off before my follower would have any hope of tracing me back to the apartment where Quinn was currently staying. I didn't need him watching me any longer.

When I made it back to the apartment, still slinking through the patches of darkness throughout the building, I passed Crag in the stairwell. He nodded to me without emerging from his own shadowy state. He was standing guard while Rollick oversaw the construction of the trap and Torrent reached out to a couple of other sorcerer families.

I found Quinn in the living room, curled up on the sofa, frowning at the blueprints on her computer. I dropped onto the cushion next to her and lifted her feet onto my lap where I could stroke my claws over them. "Is there something wrong?"

"No." She sighed and set the device aside. "I'm just triple-checking that I've thought of everything. The engineer Rollick talked to made some tweaks. I think it's really going to work. As long as we can get the big bads in there to begin with."

She pushed herself a little more upright with just a hint of a wince. My claws curled toward my palms, away from her skin, even though I knew I hadn't provoked that response.

I wanted to find the being that'd dug his own claws into her and eviscerate him all over again. Shred him into itty bitty pieces. The sight of the blood gushing from her side in the dimness of the night flashed through my mind, and my fangs sprang from my gums of their own accord.

She was much better now, able to walk around the apartment on her own and only showing a little pain now and then, partly with the help of the pills Rollick had gotten for her. But I knew how close she'd come to dying. I knew she would have died if the others hadn't leapt into the fray as soon as they did. I hadn't been able to protect her from that onslaught all on my own.

It wasn't my fault. No being could have fended off a whole army alone. But thinking about it still chilled all the fire that normally coursed through my body.

How long would it take before she could move around as swiftly and gracefully as before her injury? Would the scar on her side ever completely heal? Last night I'd given it another several swipes with my tongue, bathing it in dragon saliva, but the skin had remained a bumpy peach shade against the rest of her pale abdomen.

There was one other thing I could offer her that might at least improve her spirits. "I delivered the message I was supposed to—and one of the sorcerer-killers' minions was definitely spying on me. *They'll* get the message too."

"Oh, good," Quinn said, and then studied me more carefully. I smiled at her, but my insides still felt wobbly after the mission I'd just carried out.

Our woman didn't miss very much. She knew us so well.

Her brow knit. "I'm sorry. I'm sure it wasn't easy for you going that close to where you know sorcerers are living —or talking with a being they've captured."

I shrugged. "It needed to be done, so I did it. Now it's

over." But her sympathy struck a chord in me, bringing out a peal of longing. I leaned closer and eased all of her onto my lap. Tucking her close against my chest, I buried my face in her soft hair and drank in her fresh, tangy-sweet scent.

Quinn slipped her arm around me and hugged me in return. "I'm sorry that I put you through that kind of magic again too. I know I said it before, but I want you to know how much I mean it. I was just so worried about you—but it was a mistake. A horrible mistake."

"I know you were trying to stop me from being hurt, not to hurt me," I told her, but a tremor ran through my body even as I spoke. Having *her* strange energy rippling through me, stealing my will and compelling my limbs, had been its own kind of horror. I wished I didn't have to connect that experience to her, but there was no getting away from the fact that she was the one who'd caused it.

"It'll never happen again," she said, so firmly her voice reverberated into me from where her face was tipped against my shoulder. "I promise you I'll never use my power on you for any reason. And when this is over, when that monstrous duo is dealt with, I won't use it again on anyone at all."

I wouldn't have asked her to go that far, to completely shun the power she'd found in herself, but the words sent a rush of relief through me. I hugged her tighter. "I know you wouldn't do bad things with it."

"It's a bad power," she said. "It comes out of hurting beings that don't deserve it. I'm going to try to force whatever other sorcerers have survived the battle to stop too. No one deserves to go through what you did."

And this was why I could still hold her now despite

what she'd done, still take comfort in the feel of her against me, still want more than anything to absorb every smile and laugh she could offer. Her love for *me* rang through her voice and into me, right down to my bones. I meant that much to her, when I'd never meant much of anything to anyone before.

So I needed to do whatever I could to preserve the most special being who'd ever entered my life.

I glanced toward the kitchen and scooped Quinn up. I couldn't carry her quite as deftly as the gargoyle managed to with his vast arms, but it wasn't much strain bringing her over to the stools by the kitchen island. As I set her down on one, she raised her eyebrows at me. "What are you up to?"

I grinned at her, more freely this time. "You need to keep your strength up, baby girl, and I'm going to make sure you do. It's just about lunch time, isn't it? Let me know what you'd like me to slice and dice or charbroil, and I'll make it happen."

And I wouldn't let myself think about what might happen if this plan went wrong and none of us could save her after all.

CHAPTER TWENTY-SIX

Quinn

I adjusted the leather belt around my waist, making sure it didn't dig into the still slightly tender spot above my hip where my wound had mostly healed. I wanted to balance the pouches that held my crossbow ammo on either side so they didn't throw off my equilibrium if I needed to move quickly.

Never had I been more grateful for the reflexes I'd honed wandering around abandoned and supposedly inaccessible urban terrain for the past several years.

And hurray for shadowkind healing powers too. I doubted I'd have been feeling anywhere near as limber as I did with regular human medical treatment rather than Lance's supernatural breath and tongue. Other than when I got the occasional twinges of pain, I could mostly forget I'd been sliced wide open a week ago.

I took a stroll around the apartment's bedroom, getting comfortable with the belt on. In just a few hours, I was supposed to make my debut at the old factory-building-turned-monster-trap that Rollick's people had just put the finishing touches on.

We didn't know if the villainous duo would turn up right away. It could be a while before they came hunting me. But my men had noticed other beings spying on the area from the shadows. Rollick had been careful to ensure they'd get no glimpse of what was going on inside the building, but they knew we were up to something big there. The two sorcerer-killers would hear the moment I was seen entering.

Hopefully I wouldn't need to shoot them or any other beings anyway. Hopefully I'd be able to dash out via the trap's human escape route before I was in any significant danger. But I intended to go in prepared for worst case scenarios, and my men definitely hadn't been arguing about that. Although they'd have preferred if I hadn't needed to be there at all.

It'd been hard enough staying hidden and recovering when I knew the duo's minions were still out there attacking more humans across the city every night, when they were conducting more sacrifices at the rift for who knew what awful purpose. But getting spotted and cut down before the plan was ready might have doomed so many more people.

My men had been intervening and preventing the attacks as much as they could, both to reduce the carnage and to put the pressure on our enemies. The behemoth and the leviathan needed to believe that me and my "army" of shadowkind posed a real threat to their plans.

I undid the belt bucket and set it on the armchair in the corner, thinking I might lie down for a bit to settle my nerves before it was time to go. But before I'd made it to the bed, a jolt of intense emotion that wasn't mine socked me in the chest.

It was a sharp, ragged burst of anger. My head jerked toward the door, knowing that if I was picking up on Rollick's inner state, especially this intensely, he had to be nearby. I hadn't realized he'd gotten back to the apartment, but shadowkind didn't typically make a whole lot of noise with their comings and goings.

Had our plan been ruined somehow? Had something happened to one of the other men? I pushed past the door and hurried into the living room.

"What's going on?" I demanded the moment I spotted Rollick standing by the sofa, his back to me. "What's wrong?"

Rollick turned slowly, revealing his phone clutched in his hand. His grip was loosening, but his knuckles were pale as if he'd been gripping it tightly a second ago. He'd composed his expression into casual bemusement, his eyebrows arching with a quizzical look. "What makes you so sure that something's wrong?"

"I—I just had a feeling." I tipped my head toward his phone. "Did you get some bad news? Is everyone okay?"

"The three mutinists you're so enamored with are just fine," Rollick said, still studying me. "And 'just having a feeling' doesn't explain why you burst into the room like the place was on fire. You're not the type to jump at, well, shadows. *Something* set you off. I think you'd better tell me what."

I swallowed thickly. If I'd realized that revealing my concern would take us down this path, I would have reined myself in, pretended to only notice something might be bothering the demon after I'd greeted him.

But then, maybe he deserved to know. A flicker of guilt rippled through my gut at the thought of how long I'd been hiding our connection from him. Of course, he'd forced it on me in the first place. But I understood why. And I no longer saw him as someone I'd need a secret advantage against.

We were on the same side in every possible way now.

I couldn't help folding my arms over my chest in a defensive stance as if to ward off any criticism. "I—When you fed me your essence, I started sensing how you were feeling. It faded afterward, but with any strong emotions, if you're nearby, I still get a taste of them. And just now you were feeling very angry about something."

Rollick blinked at me. He kept his expression nonchalant, but he couldn't obscure the tremor of uneasiness my revelation had stirred up. It wasn't surprising he'd react like that—I'd known him for long enough to realize how much he prized his ability to hold his cards close. It couldn't sit well with him that I had a direct inside line to his deepest feelings.

"Well," he said. "I thought the sharing of energies might encourage some sort of bond of trust, but I'll admit that wasn't exactly what I had in mind. I guess I should be glad that you haven't picked up on anything that's sent you running for the hills all over again."

He didn't even ask why I hadn't told him right away. Maybe that was as obvious as his own preference for discretion. I wet my lips and dared to press the point. "So what were you angry about? What's the matter?"

For a few seconds, I thought he might not answer. Then he sighed and glanced at his phone before stuffing it into his pocket. "The bastards know that I'm still helping you. They're clearly peeved about that fact. I just got word that they've completely destroyed the Sunshine Sin Hotel."

His hotel here in LA—the one where I'd stayed for ten days while we started to figure out where we stood with one another. The business he'd set up to help shadowkind enjoy the mortal realm while protecting the mortals they mingled with, the current addition to his millennia-long legacy.

My stomach twisted. Even when I hadn't trusted Rollick at all, I'd been able to see how much the hotel meant to him. "Destroyed as in...?"

He kept a flippant tone. I didn't know whether he was trying to convince himself or me—or possibly both of us— that he didn't really care. "As in reduced to rubble. It was a little damaged after the fight there, but nothing I couldn't have patched up within a few days. Now I'd have to rebuild it from the ground up."

My heart sank. "I'm sorry. That was a low blow."

"They haven't been the most sportsmanlike of opponents in general. I'm not even really surprised." Rollick gave a dismissive wave of his hand. "The news disturbed me on first hearing it, but I've rebuilt hundreds of times over. I'll take this as a sign that it was time to set down new roots."

"You don't have to pretend to be okay with it," I said.

"I'm not pretending. When you've been alive for thousands of years, it takes a lot to really get under your skin." He stepped closer, still studying my face. "I'm more interested in the fact that you noticed that a very powerful demon in your presence was enraged, and your first instinct was to come running *toward* me."

I rolled my eyes at him. "I knew you wouldn't hurt *me*."

The words spilled out into the air, and it was only as I heard myself saying them that I registered just how momentous they were.

Rollick's eyes sparked with a rush of pure delight. "Is that so?" he purred, stalking closer, his mouth curving into a sly grin. "Not a single shred of fear left for the mighty demon?"

I gazed back at him with my chin high as he paused just inches away from me, standing nearly a foot taller than my average height. But there was nothing menacing about his loom. The force of his nearness sent a heady tingle all through my veins.

I held myself back from reaching for him to pull him the last short distance to me. "Nope," I said. "I've seen who you are. I know why you do what you do. I know you'd sooner take on the kind of fiends who could challenge the strongest warriors from the shadow realm alone than put me in harm's way, if you have the choice. What's there to be afraid of?"

Rollick let out a low chuckle. He brushed his fingertips over my cheeks with the faintest scrape of the claws he'd let loose. "You make me sound so tamed. I do have a reputation to uphold."

The corner of my own lips quirked upward as my whole

body thrummed with anticipation. "I'm not saying you're not a monster. Only that I know you'll be one for me, not to me." Just as I would be for the ones I cared about.

I paused, desire coursing deeper inside me. I could have this now—I could have *him*. And depending on what happened tonight, I might never get another chance.

I wet my lips and added, "Maybe unless I ask nicely?"

The new light that glinted in the demon's eyes was all heat. He bowed his head toward mine. "And what are you asking for right now, sweet sorcerer?"

There seemed to be no possible answer other than the words that bubbled up my throat. "Show me what it's like to be taken by a demon."

A soft growl escaped Rollick's throat, and then he was surging forward, his form shifting as he did. He caught me up in arms already bulging with more muscle as his dress shirt fell away, lifting me both with his grasp and the spurt of height that shot him at least another foot taller. His dark eyes glittered at me like embers amid the sharp angles of his ruddy, monstrous face.

He strode into the bedroom so fast the door hinges squealed at the shove and set me down in the middle of the bed. Then he braced himself over me in all his demonic glory, his lips pulling back in a smile that showed off his pointed teeth.

I couldn't resist the sight of his horns, sprouting in their graceful curves from his temples. As he opened his mouth to speak, I reached up to trace one hand along the smoothly spiraled surface, and Rollick's breath caught around whatever he'd been going to say. Instead, he leaned in and captured my mouth with a searing kiss.

He had a smoky taste I hadn't been able to savor quite so intently when he'd joined me with my other men before. I'd been too focused on his outward reactions then. Now, I drank in the flavor of him with every movement of my lips, wanting to get as high on him as I had when he'd fed me his essence. Except this time, I'd have thrown myself into that wild delirium willingly.

I might die a few hours from now or be injured beyond even Lance's ability to repair. I'd found something strange but wonderful with all of my monstrous men, and I hadn't really gotten to appreciate everything the demon could offer yet. If there was one thing I'd believed in since I'd needed my transplant, it was squeezing every bit of joy out of life that I could while I had the chance.

Rollick deepened the kiss with a flick of his tongue around mine. He dipped his body closer so the heat of his massive demon body wrapped around me, but I could tell he was being careful not to press too firmly in case he aggravated my mostly-healed wound. A weird thread of tenderness wove through my hunger. The emotion flooding me from him was all eager desire.

"And what can you sense from me now, my sorcerer?" he murmured as he kissed the edge of my jaw and then my neck.

I shivered with my own eagerness. My voice came out husky. "I sense that you want me just as much as I want you."

He made a rough sound in his throat even as he smiled against my skin, and teased the sharp tips of his teeth down to the crook of my shoulder, drawing giddying lines across my skin. At my whimper, he nibbled my shoulder a little more forcefully while his hands slid my shirt—and the silver-threaded undershirt he'd had made for me, as promised—partway up my ribcage.

He licked my collarbone and gave my shirt a momentary glower. "I'm looking forward to a time when I can spread you naked and enjoy all of you like the delicacy you are. For now, I'll just have to work with the territory I have access to."

Easing to one side, Rollick lifted my arm and pressed a kiss to my palm. He nibbled his way over the heel of my hand, across my wrist, and down the inside of my arm, until the movement of his lips against the sensitive skin had me quivering. When he reached the short sleeve of my shirt, he reached for my other hand.

By the time he'd worshipped both of my arms, my panties were drenched and I was swallowing whimpers. Then in one swift movement, he dropped to the skin he'd cleared on my belly.

The demon kissed and licked and sucked at every inch of my lower abdomen, grazing me with his teeth here and there, trailing his claws up and down my sides. When a gasp burst from my throat, he smirked up at me.

"I've barely even gotten started on the good parts."

Having seen his reaction the first time I'd touched one of his horns, I curled my fingers around both of them now. As I stroked them up and down from the base to the tips and back again, Rollick gave a little shudder with a waft of his own giddy enjoyment.

He yanked my shorts and panties down and dappled kisses across my hips, leaning into my caresses here and there. Then, with a faint noise of consternation, he pulled lower, tugging my clothes completely off.

This time, he started at my feet. He kissed the soles and my ankles, charted every curve of my calves and thighs with his short claws, nipped the undersides of my knees, and breathed close enough to the apex of my thighs that I moaned in frustration.

"Have I not quite satisfied you yet?" he teased.

"Rollick," I growled, grasping his horns again.

He hummed with a mix of amusement and pleasure and lowered his head between my legs.

The first swipe of his tongue over my cunt had me shuddering. He knew exactly the right pressure and pace to have my clit pulsing in a matter of seconds, my pussy gushing with arousal to the point that it would have been embarrassing if he hadn't lapped up the reaction to his attentions so enthusiastically.

Retracting his claws, he slid a finger between my folds to swirl inside me in a slow circle, stretching my inner walls. When I rocked into his touch, he chuckled before sucking on my clit again. Bliss swelled all through my core.

"I need to get you ready for all of me," he said. "If you want to be taken by the demon, you're going to need to be ready for both of my dicks."

The moan that spilled out of me at the next swivel of his tongue was nothing but approval. He spread the slickness seeping from my slit down to my other opening and then tucked a finger into that entrance as well.

More pleasure quivered through me. With a strangled sound, I pushed into his touch.

"So impatient, lovely mortal. But you're right—I don't want to hurt you. I want you to get nothing out of this encounter but the highest of pleasures. So we'll do this right."

He pumped his fingers in and out of me, rotating them in expanding circles as he did. His lips closed around my clit, and then he brushed the edges of his teeth over it, and all at once I careened over my peak. Bliss rushed through my body in a wave. I rocked with it, letting out a sob that was nothing but joyful.

"Hmm. A very good start." Rollick crawled up over me again, tucking my legs around his hips. I trailed my hands down his sculpted chest to the two cocks jutting down below, one right above the other.

The first twitched at my grip. I slid my fingers up and down it a few times experimentally, and the demon let out a muted snarl. But he didn't stop me from reaching lower and stroking the other one too. That one had already beaded with a thick precum that glided over both his shafts under my exploring fingers with a consistency not much different from the lube Torrent had confiscated. He was obviously built for penetrating multiple holes at once.

The discovery sent a quiver of delight through me. I spread my legs wider and teased my hands back up Rollick's body to grasp his shoulders. "I need you."

The words set off a flare of contentment in the demon that I didn't have time to consider too closely, because the next moment, he was sliding into me, both dicks in their separate openings simultaneously.

At the heady rush of being penetrated both ways in tandem, my head tipped back into the pillow with a cry. As

Rollick pushed deeper, the blissful burn spread all through my body. My breath broke into panting.

Even in the haze of pleasure, I couldn't help remembering how the demon had promised he'd have me like this—willingly—one day, back when I'd recoiled from the thought. My hand tightened around his shoulder, the other rising to caress one of his horns again. "Is this... how you thought it would happen?"

Rollick plunged the rest of the way into me with a groan. He held there, claiming a kiss and then bowing his head next to mine.

"No," he said quietly. "This is much better. This is something I didn't know I could even aim for."

Then he began to move again, thrusting in and out with quickly increasing speed. His renewed claws curled against my side, my hip, and my thigh in time with his rhythm. His tail swooped around his own hips so the tufted tip could trace its own delightful trails across my skin.

"Oh, God," I mumbled. My second orgasm was building so swiftly I couldn't do anything but clutch onto Rollick. He thrust into me deeper, angling himself so the base of his upper cock brushed my clit. His shafts pounded in and out of me, filling me with bliss again and again, sending me spiraling higher and higher until everything around me was a searing mist of pleasure—

And then ecstasy crackled through me twice as hard, my pussy clamping around one of his cocks, my body arching. Rollick slipped his hand under my back to press me to him and stole one last kiss with a groan as he came with me. His release sent a fresh flood of delight through me that had me shuddering and gasping all over again.

He lowered his head so his forehead rested against mine, his breath only slightly broken. A glow of satisfaction radiated from him into me. I slung my arms around his neck in a loose embrace that was the best I could offer in my current bonelessly sated state.

"Well," I said, "I really hope I don't die tonight, because I'd like to do that again sometime."

I'd meant to make Rollick laugh, but he tensed, his happiness vanishing with a surge of fiery protectiveness. "If they get to you, it'll only be over *my* dead body."

I gazed up at him, somehow still startled by the proclamation—and horrified by the thought of him losing his life over me, no matter how willing he might be to give it.

"Let's hope it doesn't come to that, then."

His lips curled into a tight but affectionate smile. "Yes, let's."

As if we'd have a whole lot of choice in the matter.

CHAPTER TWENTY-SEVEN

Rollick

Quinn didn't show an inclination to leave the bed, and we didn't need to head out of the apartment for a couple more hours anyway. So I lay there next to her, absorbing the sensation of her body unwinding in my arms.

After those couple of hours, she'd have to tense up again to meet the threat we'd called down on us. But for now, she deserved all the peace I could offer her.

It was a strange thought—that I might be bringing *peace*. The momentary contentment that had settled over me was equally unfamiliar. I provoked passion and pleasure, excitement as well as horror when I needed to, but quieter emotions weren't generally my domain.

How much could she sense of my inner state right

now? She'd said it was only strong emotions that she picked up on, but I had no idea where the threshold might be.

She had a direct line to my soul, whatever I had of one. It'd be a trial trying to hide anything from her from now on. But even though I'd recoiled from the idea of her reading my inner state when she'd first told me, my instinctive discomfort had faded.

I didn't want to hide anything else from her. After everything she'd been through—everything I'd had a hand in putting her through—the least she deserved from me was honesty. I couldn't promise the truth would always or even usually be pleasant, but I could give it to her.

The connection I hadn't known I'd forged might even have worked in my favor. Would she have trusted me as much as she appeared to now without it? Would she have believed that my attempt to give her life back was genuine and not a ploy?

Somehow she had come to me, on her terms rather than mine, and I couldn't have said I'd have preferred it any other way.

I didn't like how small she felt next to my demonic body—how breakable. I stroked my fingers down her side, skimming the edge of scar tissue where the dragon shifter had done his best to heal her. My dignity insisted that I keep my tone wry rather than revealing the full extent of my concern. "I hope you didn't strain anything during that workout."

Quinn laughed and snuggled closer to me, which I liked far too much for my dignity to have any hope at all. "I have no complaints."

"Good. Because I have a reputation to keep up there too."

She tipped her head to look up at me, her sky-blue eyes thoughtful but not worried. "You have gotten around quite a bit, haven't you? You've kind of mentioned it a lot. Is that —are you going to be hooking up with other people too? I mean, when there's much of a chance once we've dealt with all the problems we're facing right now. I obviously can't complain about it when I'm with three other men, but... it would be good to know."

So she could decide how invested or not to get in me? I had no doubt that my three former employees had completely devoted themselves to her. Picturing them with her, even after having joined in that group love-fest once, set off a brief flare of jealousy in my chest.

But I couldn't have her all to myself. She'd made that abundantly clear... and when I thought with my head instead of my dicks and my monstrous impulses, which was part of what had kept me alive this long, I couldn't see it as a bad thing. Possessing her for myself but in the faded, melancholy state she'd fallen into with their absence wouldn't be any kind of victory.

A different instinct gripped me: to be noncommittal, to leave a touch of uncertainty to keep her on her toes. But I didn't really want her on her toes either. I wanted her sure. If I was going to share her with three other beings, I didn't want any chance of her thinking I was the spare she could cast aside.

"I've had millennia to experiment and spread my talents around," I informed her. "A little monogamy might be a nice change of pace." I paused, grappling with how to express the rest of it without rubbing her mortality too much in her face. "I don't know how long I'll get to enjoy your company, so I intend to savor as much of it as possible as long as you'll bestow it on me."

My formal phrasing brought out another light laugh, but her expression had softened. No doubt she was aware enough of her uncertain lifespan without any reminders to fill in the blanks.

I'd already lived more than a hundred times longer than she might survive in this world. What could I possibly lose by focusing on her for such a short part of *my* life when that was all I'd get of her?

The thought of losing her made me want to bare my teeth with a snarl. But the greatest threat to her survival might not even be the menaces we'd go up against soon but that borrowed heart beating in her chest. I couldn't fight it into doing right by her.

If there was some way I could ensure she got as full a life as any mortal should, I'd see it happen.

A glint of mischief lit in Quinn's eyes. She cocked her head. "I suppose we're all one happy family now. You mentioned that you've been involved with men before. Have you ever thought about propositioning my other three?"

I should have seen that question coming. I chuckled and tucked one claw under her chin. "None of them is really my type. And I doubt any of them would want to be diverted from you anyway. But you don't need to worry. Somehow I doubt that I'll ever get bored while I'm with you."

Quinn huffed. "I never thought I'd say this, but I

wouldn't mind a little less excitement following me around. Or at least if it was of the less deadly variety."

"We'll see if we can't set you on that path tonight."

I kissed her, hard and long enough to draw one of those lovely, eager sounds from her throat, but my heart wasn't totally in it. The conversation had stirred up too much apprehension about the job ahead of us. When I released her, I sat up, contracting my demon body into my typical human form.

"I should call in the others so we can hash out the final details. We don't want to leave any possibility unconsidered."

"Of course." Quinn pushed herself upright with a stretch and scrambled out of bed. As she pulled her clothes back on, I stalked into the living room with my phone in my hand.

Torrent had agreed to check for messages from me regularly, and while he might have played the traitor before, he was generally good to his word. He answered my beckons right away, and within half an hour had rounded up the gargoyle and the dragon shifter and returned with them to the apartment.

We gathered in the living room, Quinn with her crossbow already in hand and the custom belt I'd commissioned slung around her waist. She didn't look small or breakable now. No mortal would have stood a chance against the resolve she possessed. If the contraption she'd designed worked as intended, no shadowkind would either.

"Have you seen any new activity monitoring the streets around the building?" I asked the others.

"The minions are still watching it," Lance said with a click of his claws. "Waiting for us to put on our show." He grinned. "I think we're going to like it a lot more than they will, though."

"I haven't sensed either of the bosses nearby," Crag put in. "I think they must be keeping their distance until they hear more from their followers."

Torrent nodded. "After the moves we've already made against them, it's unsurprising that they're being cautious. But they've also seen how far we'll go to interfere with their plans. I can't imagine that they're *not* concerned about what else Quinn might have up her sleeve."

"They wouldn't have their lackeys watching the building so closely otherwise." I rubbed my chin, contemplating the best opening strategy, but Quinn spoke first.

"Has there been any sign of the sorcerers we reached out to?" she asked quietly. "Have any of them turned up looking for me?"

The three exchanged a look I could instantly read. But they appeared to be as dedicated to honesty as I'd newly become, at least when it involved our shared lover.

"A woman who we believe was from one of those families was found dead in an attack near the city limits a couple of nights ago," Torrent said, his tone as even as usual but with a gentle note to it. "If we'd known she was on her way, we'd have done our best to guard her..."

Quinn's face tightened. Then she let out a sigh. "I guess she was in almost as much danger staying where she was. Only one of them was willing to risk coming out here to help? This plan might have been easier to pull off if they'd work with us on this one thing."

I grimaced. "It's possible that the enclave in Norway has spread out a warning about you through the wider community. A not very accurate one, of course, but sorcerers aren't much for socializing outside their trusted allies anyway."

Quinn squared her shoulders. "That's fine. We weren't counting on them helping. Is there anything else we need to go over before I make my grand entrance?"

I glanced at the other men. "I think it's best if the three of you stay outside the building. The amount of silver and iron in that place will weaken even you quickly. We need you at your best. My suggestion would be that Lance and Torrent monitor opposite sides of the place and take down any minions these fiends send into the building—as many as you can. If we can avoid anyone getting in other than the main duo, that would be best."

I turned to the gargoyle. "Crag, since you're the most able to identify other beings at a distance, you could patrol a little farther abroad to sense when the villains are approaching and give the rest of us a warning." My lips slanted into a crooked smile. "That's how I'd handle it, at least. I'm well aware that none of you are obliged to follow my orders at this point."

Lance let out a little hiss, clearly unsettled by having to protect our woman from a distance rather than right beside her, but he didn't argue. Torrent inclined his head. "That all sounds reasonable to me. And you'll be Quinn's last line of defense against whatever does breach the walls?"

"Yes. I've been inside the building multiple times. I

won't *enjoy* it, but it shouldn't hamper my abilities too much." I cast my gaze toward Quinn. "Assuming you're fine with all of that too."

She nodded immediately. "I don't think we should weaken ourselves any more than we absolutely have to. But—the secret exit has the chime we talked about built into it, right? Everyone else will know when I've left so they can meet me there?"

"I've tested it myself," I assured her. The last thing I'd want was for her to dart out into the street and fall prey to a horde of other minions right outside.

"I'll have returned to the building by then," Crag said. "I'll stay close to the back door so that I can grab you as soon as you're out."

"Perfect." I clapped my hands. "I think we're all set. Why don't the three of you get into position, and I'll escort Quinn over once you've had time to prepare yourselves?"

Torrent and then Crag and then Lance each stepped toward Quinn to offer her a tight embrace and a kiss. More jealousy flickered in my chest, but it passed in a moment as I saw how she beamed back at them, bolstered by their affection.

The dragon shifter held her for the longest, as if he thought if he kept hugging her he might just not have to stop. He finally dragged himself away, started to turn to follow the others, and jerked back toward her with a flash of determination crossing his golden face.

"Wait," he said. "Before we go out there, I think there's something Quinn should do first."

CHAPTER TWENTY-EIGHT

Quinn

Lance looked so resolute, his violet eyes both bright and hard, that my stomach flipped over. His words reverberated through my head. *There's something Quinn should do first.*

"What?" I asked. "Anything you need, just ask." It was bad enough having to watch them go out there ready to do battle on my behalf where I'd have no way of helping them or even knowing what they were going through. If I could make their fight easier, I'd do it in an instant. But the dragon shifter didn't look exactly *happy* about whatever he was going to say.

A little twitch ran through his stance, making me even more sure that he was uneasy about his suggestion. But he flicked his tongue over his lips and put on a smile that was only a little forced.

"We know the big baddies are supposed to be coming to get you. We know how much sorcery they have that they could use on us. When their beasties are compelled by them, it's harder for you to hook them with your own magic. So... I think you should give us some kind of command. With sorcery. That'll go against anything they might want us to do."

I stared at him, losing my breath in shock. "You *want* me to use my sorcery on you?"

He held my gaze, still tense but not backing down. "It wouldn't be to control us. You could tell us to do something we'd have been doing anyway. It'd just be like a shield to stop their magic from getting in. Or at least make it harder."

Torrent sucked in a breath. "Lance does have a point. It wouldn't be perfect protection against them affecting us, but it could buy us enough time to get out of the way or take other precautions before their magic took hold."

Crag glanced at the others and then at me, his expression somber but unworried. "That makes sense to me."

Sure, it made sense the way the dragon shifter had put it. But nausea had coiled in my gut at the thought of aiming any of my power at these men again. Even if it was technically for their own good, what if the gambit misfired? What if I gave them an order that they'd end up needing to go against to protect themselves—or me?

"I don't know," I said slowly. "It seems pretty risky. I'm still getting the hang of how the magic works at all. We don't know exactly what you'll encounter out there or what tactics you might need to use. I don't want to force you into a situation where you can't defend yourself because of what *I* told you."

Rollick set his hand on my shoulder, tentative despite the intimacy we'd shared just an hour ago. "I'm sure we could come up with wording that allowed a lot of flexibility while still being a command in essence. If you want to be extra careful, you could skip me. I'll be inside the building with you beyond their reach anyway, but if something goes wrong, I'd be able to act quickly enough."

Even with that compromise, my stomach kept roiling. But a lot of that was my own guilt over using my power on these men against their will before. They were asking me now—they could use my protection. How could I say no?

I dragged in a breath. "All right. But we have to be *really* careful about what exactly I order you to do. Let's not rush this."

We spent the next half hour hashing out various wordings, debating some and discarding others immediately, tweaking the ones that seemed like the best bet, until I was finally satisfied. I'd been doing most of the vetoing, but my men hadn't shown any impatience. If anything, Lance still looked like he kind of wished he'd never suggested this strategy in the first place.

Still, he stepped in front of me first, his jaw tight. "You should put all the power you can into it. Each of us, one at a time. That'll give us the most possible defense."

He was probably right. I readied myself, reaching toward the now-familiar sizzle of energy rippling through my chest. It didn't take much coaxing to expand it and urge it up my throat. I fixed all my attention on Lance and the precise phrase we'd chosen.

Several syllables in the sorcery language tumbled out first as I focused on my intent, but with the men I was so close to, I was able to channel the energy into English words as well, just like in my earlier orders. "While I'm inside the building where we've laid our trap, you will prevent shadowkind beings from entering that building using tactics based on your best judgment, and refuse any orders given to you by the behemoth or the leviathan."

The command was open-ended enough that only a twinge of worry remained in my chest. I repeated it with Torrent and then turned to Crag, who needed a slightly different version with his separate duties. "You will keep watch for the behemoth and the leviathan approaching the building where we've laid our trap as long as you feel it's wise to do so, and you will refuse any orders given to you by those two beings."

"There," Rollick said, brushing his hands together. "That's settled. If it comes to sorcery against sorcery, I know who I'd place my bets on. Now get going without any more dawdling, the three of you."

Each of my men offered me one last swift embrace and then faded into the shadows. I paced the room, knowing they were racing across the city toward the factory while we waited. It wouldn't do us any good if I arrived before they were ready and faced an attack before we had all the pieces in place.

It felt like I'd been waiting forever when Rollick said, "That's enough time. Come on—let's get the car."

Nothing stirred in the underground garage as we walked to his sedan. I sank into the passenger seat with my crossbow on my lap and the ammo pouches on my belt clinking faintly. Dread wound all through my body.

"What if it doesn't work? What if we haven't done enough?" I really didn't know how much else we *could* have done, but that didn't guarantee success.

"Then we'll lick our wounds and come back stronger," Rollick said with his usual confident air. I didn't sense any deep concern or fear from him, so maybe he really was that sure of us. As he started the engine, he glanced over at me. "You've come a long way, and you already had one of the strongest wills I've ever encountered when I first met you. You're going to get through this."

His words from our bedroom interlude rose up like a ghost. If I didn't get through it, it'd only be because he'd fallen too.

Oh God, please let it not come to that.

The demon had carefully planned our route ahead of time. We wanted to be sure the villainous duo's spies saw me arriving, but we knew they most likely had orders to try to slaughter me before I could make it to the building when they did. He'd picked a car with tinted windows so I couldn't be identified from outside, and he parked right outside the door.

There, Rollick flicked through the shadows to emerge next to me the instant I stepped out of the car. In the few seconds it took for him to usher me across the sidewalk to the factory door like a bodyguard, I ran my fingers through my hair to toss it so it caught the late-afternoon sunlight to make sure my arrival was marked in the brief time I was visible.

My other men had noticed multiple minions keeping

watch over the front door. They'd clearly spotted me as I'd hoped—and sprung into action even faster than expected. Just as I pushed open the door, a barrage of shadowy forms blinked into being in mid-pounce.

Rollick shoved me into the front hall and whipped around with a growl. Bodies thumped and whimpers of pain sounded behind me. As I spun toward the doorway, he slammed the door shut, only a few wisps of smoky essence wavering through the air before dissipating. He swiped his hands together. "Those beasties won't be making it past the barriers. The few that survived can go off to notify their masters now."

I exhaled shakily. So far so good.

Rollick locked the door for good measure, and we hurried past the factory's old office rooms to the big space farther back where we'd constructed our trap.

The room had once been forty feet long by thirty feet across with a ceiling some fifteen feet high. It'd shrunk quite a bit since Rollick's workers had built the additions called for in my designs.

Stark white lights blazed over us from various small but bright fixtures on the lowered ceiling, ensuring that any beings that made it this far inside wouldn't have shadows to hide in. The floor was the same scuffed linoleum it'd been before, marks showing where tables and conveyer belts had once been set up, but smooth gray walls surrounded us. You could barely make out the outlines of the slots that would pop out when the blades hidden behind them and the ceiling shot forward.

When the trap went off, any shadowkind within this space would find itself speared by a barrage of mechanized blades, each of them constructed out of melded silver and iron. Rollick had confirmed that they would do enough damage for even the most powerful being to quickly bleed out, if not die on impact.

Now we just needed to get at least one of our foes, ideally both, in here.

The place had the lingering new construction smell of sawdust and mechanical grease. It tickled my nose as I walked all the way to the back of the trap room with Rollick still trailing behind me.

Under more searing lights, there was a little booth built into the new walls there with a window where I could watch over the space like a foreman might have decades ago when the factory was still in regular use. A control panel with a large, red button was mounted right beside the door where I could smack it easily the second I needed to.

At the other end of the booth, a narrow passage led to the factory's original back door. The door was locked with a deadbolt and reinforced with so much silver and iron even Rollick wouldn't be able to exit that way unless I opened it for him.

I sank into the office chair set up in the booth and rested my crossbow on my lap. Rollick scanned our surroundings with a satisfied air. "Everything appears to be in order. Now it's time for the great camp-out. Aren't you lucky you have me for company to stop you from getting bored?"

He shot me a smirk, but I knew he was only teasing. I stretched out my legs. "I don't think we should get *too* distracted. Let's hope the creeps don't leave us waiting too long." If need be, there was a sleeping bag and some nonperishable food stashed in the booth's built-in cupboard, but I'd rather not have to resort to using them. Especially for multiple nights.

But who knew how cautious the villainous duo would be?

It'd only been about twenty minutes when the ping of Rollick's phone had me jerking upright with a jolt of adrenaline. He glanced at the screen, and his smile flattened. "More minions incoming. The poor bastards. Well, any of them who wanted to be in this fight of their own accord will get what they deserve."

The men outside were supposed to be dealing with the lackeys, and any lesser creatures wouldn't be able to make their way into the building to begin with. But we had no idea how many higher shadowkind would come. I stood up, rechecking the bolts in my crossbow, and moved to the main room where the lights were brightest. My heart thumped erratically in my chest, and suddenly I regretted my wish for the battle to come to us sooner rather than later.

The duo had obviously sent more powerful minions to try to drag me out of my protected space than my other men could handle all at once. But not many of even the higher shadowkind could handle the protections easily, even if they managed to slip inside through the shadows we couldn't totally eliminate beyond the main room. The first being that wavered into sight by the wall lurched at me with a clumsiness that showed how the metals embedded in the building had drained its strength.

A startled squeak broke from my throat, but I whipped up my crossbow and squeezed the trigger before its knobby fingers closed around me. The bolt hit the thing square in the throat. It flinched backward, and I shot it again in the middle of the forehead. That was enough for it to crumple, gushing essence.

There was a thump behind me at the same moment. I jerked around to see Rollick punching the head right off another two-legged being that'd leapt at my back. He crushed its ribs under his heel for good measure and then stalked over to pummel the other creature's skull into the floor.

"Can't risk them getting up again," he said, his voice cool but taut.

He'd barely finished speaking when two more beings materialized, leaping from the slots on the walls on either side of us. We each spun toward one, backs to each other in an instinctive protective pose.

The harpy-like woman who charged at me looked steadier on her feet than the first beings to make it through —a little stronger, a little less affected by the building's protections. But I was ready now, my nerves humming with determination and adrenaline, my reflexes honed. I shot her in the head and kicked her away from me as she stumbled.

As I yanked more bolts from the pouch at my hip to reload, Rollick gave the being he'd faced one last slash and sprang past me to ensure the harpy was gone from this world. He glanced over his shoulder at me, a gleam lighting in his eyes. "Not so hard. But it's a good thing you kept me with you to have your back."

The corner of my mouth twitched upward. Sometimes it was fun to take his ego down a peg, but not when I agreed with him so much. "Yeah, it is."

He smiled back at me, and for that moment, everything seemed okay.

Three more beings came at us, streaks of shadowy bodies racing across the floor and rising into physical form for their final lunge, and we tackled them with the same efficient teamwork. The swift pounding of my pulse steadied me rather than unnerving me now.

When we had a lull, I grabbed a drink of water from the bottle in the booth and then returned to wander carefully through the main space. I was on high alert now, my gaze twitching toward the slightest sound or movement, my finger hooked around the trigger. Rollick left his phone on the floor by the wall and prowled around the edge of the room in his demon form, his hooves rapping against the linoleum and his tail lashing.

My flow of adrenaline had ebbed when five monstrous forms rushed at us from different ends of the room.

I whirled around, shooting at one being and then another. In motion, it was hard for me to aim as well. I caught one in the shoulder, another in the side of the chest, the third in the gut. They staggered, one slumping to its knees, but the other two kept hurtling toward me.

Rollick's phone started to ping. He couldn't do anything about that or my oncoming attackers while he tore through one and then another of the beings at his end of the room.

I fumbled for more bolts while sorcerous energy crackled through me. Words I didn't know burst from my throat and smacked into the barrier of existing magic in the beings' heads. My power didn't quite crack it on the first try

—and I didn't have time for a second before they were on me.

The one that looked like a skinny, patchy polar bear swung a massive paw at me, and I managed to dodge. I scrambled away, shoving one and another bolt into the crossbow. The third being I'd shot was heaving back onto its feet. Were they slowing down a little with the continued exposure to the silver and iron?

When I opened my mouth to attempt another sorcerous shout, the bear-ish one flung itself at me. I shot it in the underside of its jaw just as its claws raked across my arm. It collapsed on top of me, which might actually have worked in my favor, since it shielded me from its companions.

As I squirmed out from under it, the sounds of ripping flesh reached my ears. Rollick was carving his way through the rest of them, having an easier time of it with those I'd already wounded. I looked at the smoking remains scattered across the floor, shuddered, and clapped my hand to the talon marks on my upper arm.

Rollick was at my side in an instant. He couldn't seal the wounds with his breath like Lance, but he'd come otherwise prepared. He snapped back into human form for long enough to pull a roll of gauze from his pocket and wrap it tightly around my arm.

"Can you still handle the bow all right?" he asked.

"Yes," I said, the pain a distant throbbing compared to the renewed roar of tension and anticipation filling my head. "What was the text you got?"

Rollick swore and dashed to the device. He flicked through to the messages. "At least one of the head honchos on the move this way. Crag felt he'd better pull in to the entrance now."

"Okay." One was enough. Even taking down one half of the duo would diminish their power significantly. Then tackling the other wouldn't be so bad.

The thought had barely crossed my mind when the floor shook beneath my feet. There was a creaking sound followed by a drawn-out screech as if the building itself were being wrenched apart.

My pulse stuttered. My gaze shot to Rollick, who stepped closer to me, looming into his demon form again. He flexed his clawed fingers.

I felt it. The immense, ponderous presence that'd intruded on the sorcerer village in Utah and ravaged their bodies. Every nerve in my body twanged with alarm. But before I'd even seen it, a low groan of a voice reverberated across the walls.

It spoke in words I knew and yet didn't—and Rollick clapped one hand to his head. He reeled, his face contorting as if he were in pain.

"What's the matter?" I blurted out, but then understanding hit me like a smack of frigid water.

The being that'd come was using its sorcery on him, and the magic was starting to work.

If Rollick couldn't fight it off, I was as good as dead.

CHAPTER TWENTY-NINE

Quinn

My voice tore up my throat as I backed away from Rollick, my hand clutched unwillingly around my crossbow. "Listen to me, not him. You belong to *me*." At least, that's what I thought I was saying in the eerie syllables that spilled from my mouth with a rush of power.

But it didn't matter. The villain's magic was already fighting its way into the demon's brain, and my own power bounced off him like it had their minions.

Rollick clamped his other hand to his ruddy temple, his claws digging into his own skin to set off tiny plumes of smoky essence.

"No," he snarled under his breath. "You're not having me. *No.*"

I hurled another command with my sorcery at him, but

it didn't connect. At the same time, the thing at the front of the building gave another bellow that seemed to rock the demon on his feet. It must have been driving its influence in even farther.

Rollick's body swayed on his cloven hooves. A tremor ran through his body. He squeezed his eyes shut, his jaw flexing, the turmoil inside him as he struggled wafting from him into me.

I stood rigid, my crossbow half raised, my hand moving automatically to reload it again, although I found it hard to imagine shooting *him*.

This couldn't come to that, right? He was a millennia-old demon. Even if our opponent was a little more ancient, a little more powerful, sorcery wasn't its natural talent, only something it'd borrowed.

But then, you could say the exact same thing about me.

Rollick swung his head toward me. His penetrating eyes smoldered with rage... and what I knew was a flicker of fear. The most assured being I'd ever known wasn't totally sure he could fight this off.

"Go back to the booth," he rasped at me. "Get ready to do what you have to do once he's here. You shouldn't be near me like this. I—"

Another roared phrase echoed through the room, and Rollick snapped his mouth shut. I backed up toward the short hall with the booth, but my stomach twisted with queasiness.

Did he expect me to set off the trap with him still in the room? Why hadn't I cast my own sorcery on him ahead of time?

I would have if we'd known early enough that this fiend

was on its way, but we'd been too caught up in the fighting —and I'd been too afraid of my powers to insist on that protection up front.

And my refusal to fully accept what I was and what I could do might mean the death of one of the men I'd come to care for in ways I'd once doubted were even possible.

I stopped by the entrance to the hallway, ready to bolt for the booth if Rollick turned on me, willing more of my sorcerer energy to swell up inside me with a surge of the newfound exhilaration it could bring. I'd broken the villainous duo's hold on other shadowkind—but this monster was pummeling Rollick with his influence right in front of me, far fresher than anything I'd shattered before.

It wasn't coming into the trap either, I realized. My sense of it still quivered over my skin with an unsettling tingle, but it hadn't pushed closer since I'd first felt it shoving into the building. The floor had stopped trembling, the walls stopped groaning.

It must suspect that I had something else up my sleeve. It was hoping to use my companion to finish me off where its own minions had failed.

Maybe I was focusing on the wrong monster here. The thing that was assaulting Rollick with its magic didn't have any sorcery on it for me to break. I didn't know it the way I did my men, but I'd compelled less powerful higher shadowkind.

I had to try.

I dragged in a breath and shouted toward the entrance of the building as forcefully as I could. The sorcerous words hurtled up my throat with a crackle of electricity. I focused all my attention on the vast, ominous presence at the front of the building.

Do as I say. Come toward me. Leave my companions alone.

For just a second, I thought I had it. I had the impression of my influence catching on the massive being like the tug of a fishing line when a fish has just taken the bait. But however much I'd hooked it, the next second, it slipped free, shaking off my energy.

My shoulders slumped, my chest heaving as I recovered from the effort I'd put into that spell. I'd thrown enough of myself into that command and the ones I'd aimed at Rollick that even the exhilaration of my enhanced magic was dwindling into exhaustion.

Rollick spun and staggered toward the side wall. He smacked his head into it, his horns digging into the drywall, as if he thought he could propel the fiend's influence out of his skull through physical force.

It didn't seem to be working. He shook himself with a furious growl, and the flare of emotion that hit me was laced with hopelessness.

My sense of his inner state was fading. The sorcery was dulling his resistance and the emotions that came with it. How much longer did we have before he succumbed completely?

I'd given everything I had to my attempt to control the monster that still hadn't entered the trap room. If even that hadn't worked—

My gaze stalled on the trickles of smoke trickling from the scratches Rollick had carved into his face. A memory hit me of being pinned beneath him in the back of his car, that cloudy essence coursing down my throat—and waking up all kinds of unearthly energies in me.

There was more smoke pouring up all throughout the room from the bodies of the minions we'd killed. Minions the creature that threatened us had compelled and forced to carry out his orders.

They were the closest things to a connection to the beast itself that I could get.

A wave of horror washed over me at the thought that'd just unfurled in my head, but I shoved it away as I dashed across the floor toward the nearest fallen creature—the torso of the polar-bear-ish thing.

It didn't matter if the idea sickened me. It didn't matter if this act took me farther down a path I'd never wanted to be on in the first place. My men were willing to be total monsters for me, so I shouldn't shy away from any bit of monstrousness if it meant saving one of them—maybe all of them. Maybe the whole city around me as well, and who knew what else.

When I looked at it that way, it was a minor sacrifice. I wouldn't be around all that long to regret whatever the act did to me anyway.

I threw myself to my knees beside the smoking torso and dropped my head to its ragged ends. Opening my mouth wide, just an inch from the disintegrating flesh, I inhaled the deepest breath of the stuff that I could.

The essence flowed into my lungs and sizzled through the rest of my body, waking up the chaotic sensations I'd felt with Rollick's. But they were familiar now, less stupefying now that I recognized them.

I was in control. I was *deciding* to take this step. I was a sorcerer, and I'd take in all the power I could.

I gulped mouthful after mouthful of the acrid essence as quickly as I could. A thump and a dwindling snarl from behind me told me that Rollick was still fighting, but continuing to weaken with every passing moment. I drank in another waft and another, every nerve lighting up with the wildness of the shadowkind—and then I yanked myself upright.

Electricity seemed to sizzle over every inch of me. I wouldn't have been surprised to catch a glimpse in a mirror and see my body lit up with a vicious glow.

"Go to the back door," I yelled at Rollick, hoping he had enough will left to manage that much even without my magical compulsion, hoping he'd listen if he did. I sucked in one more lungful of the essence and focused on all the energy zinging through my veins.

I was powerful. I was invincible. I was a monster, and nothing could stop me.

Then I flung the full force of my renewed power at the monster lurking beyond the room.

The words tore my vocal cords as they burst out of me, leaving my throat raw. *Do as I say. Come toward me and show yourself. Leave my friends alone.* I battered the presence in front of me with every shred of strength I had in me.

My legs wobbled, but with a burst of joy, I felt the hook snag deep. The fiend moved, finally. My awareness of its immensity expanded as it trudged toward me, its steps thundering over the floor.

"Keep coming!" I shouted at it, every particle of my body quivering. "All the way in."

The doorway at the far end of the room shuddered and split—but we'd been prepared that these massive beings might not fit. The beast that shouldered into the room past the chunks of wood that fell around it was nearly as tall as the ceiling and half as wide as the entire space.

It looked like a cross between a hippo and an ox—if ten times more immense than either of those animals would have been. Its rounded snout opened to reveal a gaping maw of crooked teeth. Curved horns protruded forward at an aggressive angle from its forehead. Each of its hooves on its thick legs, solid rather than cloven like Rollick's, was wide enough around to stamp me flat.

Bristly hair sprung from all across the thick, wrinkled hide that covered its broad body. A smell like the darkest, deepest cavern wafted off of it, sending a chill through me.

This must be the behemoth.

He was still coming, step after heavy step. I whirled around and saw Rollick stumbling by the back hallway, still clutching his head and shaking it. Throwing caution to the wind, I ran at him and shoved him forward.

"Go, go, *go!*" I screamed, and more of my amped up magic seared through my voice with the command. I didn't manage to break the behemoth's hold on him, but I felt it crack. With a ragged breath, Rollick lurched on down the hall.

He stopped by the door, waiting for me. I glanced back at the beast heaving himself into the room, my pulse racing.

I could only be sure of our victory if it made it all the way inside so the trap would fully spear it. Come on.

The behemoth pawed the linoleum, and a spark of fear jittered through me. Was he throwing off my influence?

"Get in here," I screeched at him, not caring what I sounded like as long as the sorcery reverberated through my voice. My body outright shook with the energy jittering out of me. "Come all the way in *now*."

My fingernails dug into my palms, but the behemoth pushed farther forward. I spotted the flick of his tail behind its haunches as its rear end finally passed the larger entrance he'd smashed into the far wall.

He was in. We could do this.

My triumph was muted by the panic still blaring through me. Every part of me was aware that the thing just ten feet away from me was powerful enough to squash me like a flea.

I ducked into the booth and slammed my hand on the red button. Then I bolted for the back door.

Gears squealed. A vicious light flared in Rollick's eyes, and he swung one clawed hand toward me. Moving only on instinct, I threw myself forward, ducking down at the same time, and rammed my side into his legs to propel him into the door.

We hadn't bothered to lock it, since no being should have been able to touch it anyway. As it popped open with the force of the impact, we both tumbled onto the sidewalk outside. Crag grabbed my shoulders an instant later, but my gaze was glued to the scene at the other end of the short hall.

The silver and iron blades slammed forward simultaneously. They lanced into the behemoth's body from all sides, slicing into his abdomen, his neck, his skull.

A groan loud enough to shake the pavement in the alleyway where I stood resonated from his throat. A vast cloud of smoke exploded from his form. He twisted once, twice...

And then he sagged between the weapons that'd skewered him, the presence I'd felt snuffing out like a forest fire doused by a downpour.

CHAPTER THIRTY

Quinn

A gasp caught in the back of my mouth. Then a laugh of relief jolted out of me.

The beast was down—one of them anyway. I didn't know what the continuing effects of my gamble might be, but I had no regrets about making it right now. Even if I felt so drained I needed to lean into Crag's grip to keep myself upright.

Rollick shook himself with a ragged exhale and contracted into his human-like form. Of course—out here in the relative open, who knew what mortals might see him? He stepped over beside Crag to grasp my arm as he stared past me at the immense smoking corpse. Tendrils of his own essence seeped from the smaller scratches he'd carved into his face, but they were already shrinking.

"Nice work, reluctant sorcerer," he said with a bit of a rasp in his voice that provoked a flutter of concern. The behemoth's influence over him had ended with the beast's death, but he didn't sound totally recovered yet mentally either. The hint of emotion I caught from him was full of turmoil.

Lance appeared beside us. "The beasties are going haywire. Most of them are running away—or around in circles like they don't know where to go." He chuckled.

"They were probably all under the behemoth's sway," Rollick said. "Since he was the one who came. I'd imagine that he bolstered his control over them before sending them at Quinn to make it harder for her to shake his hold." His smile down at me might have been a bit tight, but I felt the warmth in it all the same.

"Halfway there," I said, smiling back at him. "Should we go to the apartment? I'm sure you'd say we deserve to celebrate." My gaze flicked back to the sagging beast. "Or do we have to do something about the corpse?"

The demon shook his head. "I can keep any unwanted intruders off the property until the essence totally dissipates. I definitely think this warrants breaking out the—"

He froze, his gaze darting to a spot in the near distance. I tried to follow it, but I couldn't see anything there except the dusk-shadowed side of a nearby building.

Rollick swore under his breath. He motioned to Crag. "Get her out of here."

My pulse skittered. "Why? What's happening?"

Crag didn't wait around for the demon to answer. He hauled me up toward the sky despite the dim evening light still wavering over us. But from that height, I got my answer.

A serpentine form as tall as the factory wavered into being as it smashed through the outer wall. Bricks crumbled and beams toppled. The monstrous, finned snake I knew had to be the leviathan reared back and plunged its head into the depths of the building, heedless of the shrieks that rang out from nearby bystanders who couldn't miss that terrifying form.

"What is it *doing*?" I cried out as Crag hefted me higher.

"Whatever it's doing, we don't want you anywhere near it," the gargoyle growled.

He was right. I couldn't summon more than a faint crackle of magical energy at the base of my throat. I'd hurled everything I had at the other half of the villainous duo just minutes ago.

It shouldn't have mattered. I'd already known we still had the second ancient monster to tackle. But as the roof collapsed around the huge serpent, I abruptly understood.

The leviathan had lowered his head right to the behemoth's body—and was tearing it apart. Swallowing down every shred of its smoking corpse.

My heart plummeted, my blood turning to ice. He'd been waiting nearby, not helping his partner while I got control over the behemoth, while the beast had died, and then he'd leapt in to reap his own benefits.

He didn't care that his ally was dead. Maybe he'd always wanted to rule whatever world he meant to create on his own.

And now he was absorbing every bit of sorcery the

other monster had possessed, the sorcery that I'd already struggled to deflect, to make himself twice as strong.

I blinked hard as Crag whirled me away, but I couldn't stop the rush of hopelessness from flooding me.

Oh, fuck. There was nothing to celebrate now.

We were so, so screwed.